An Outcast Among Wolves

CATHERINE BANKS

TURBO KITTEN INDUSTRIES

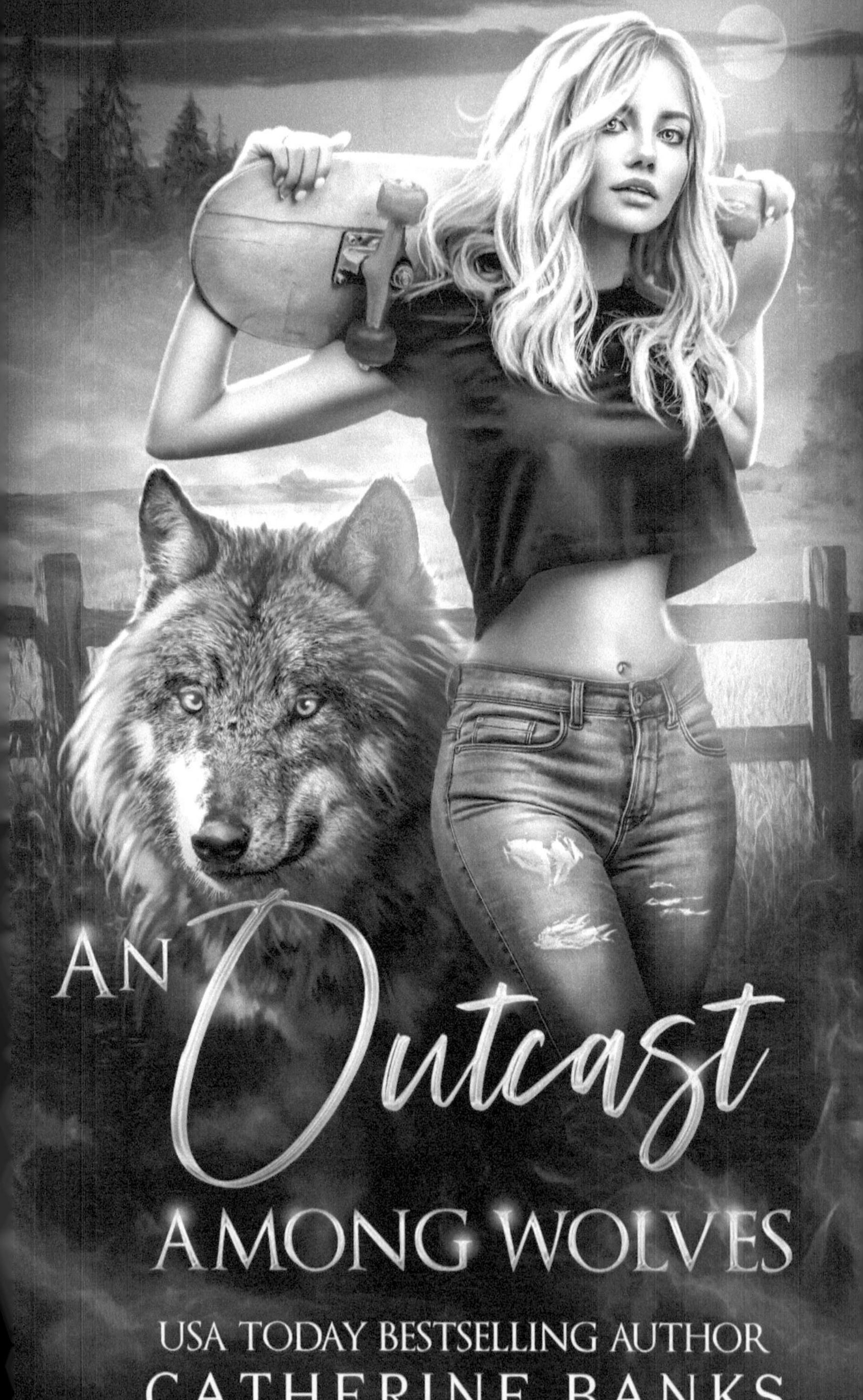
An
Outcast
AMONG WOLVES
USA TODAY BESTSELLING AUTHOR
CATHERINE BANKS

TURBO KITTEN™
INDUSTRIES

Thank you, Avery for being my biggest supporter, my best friend, and husband. I love you.

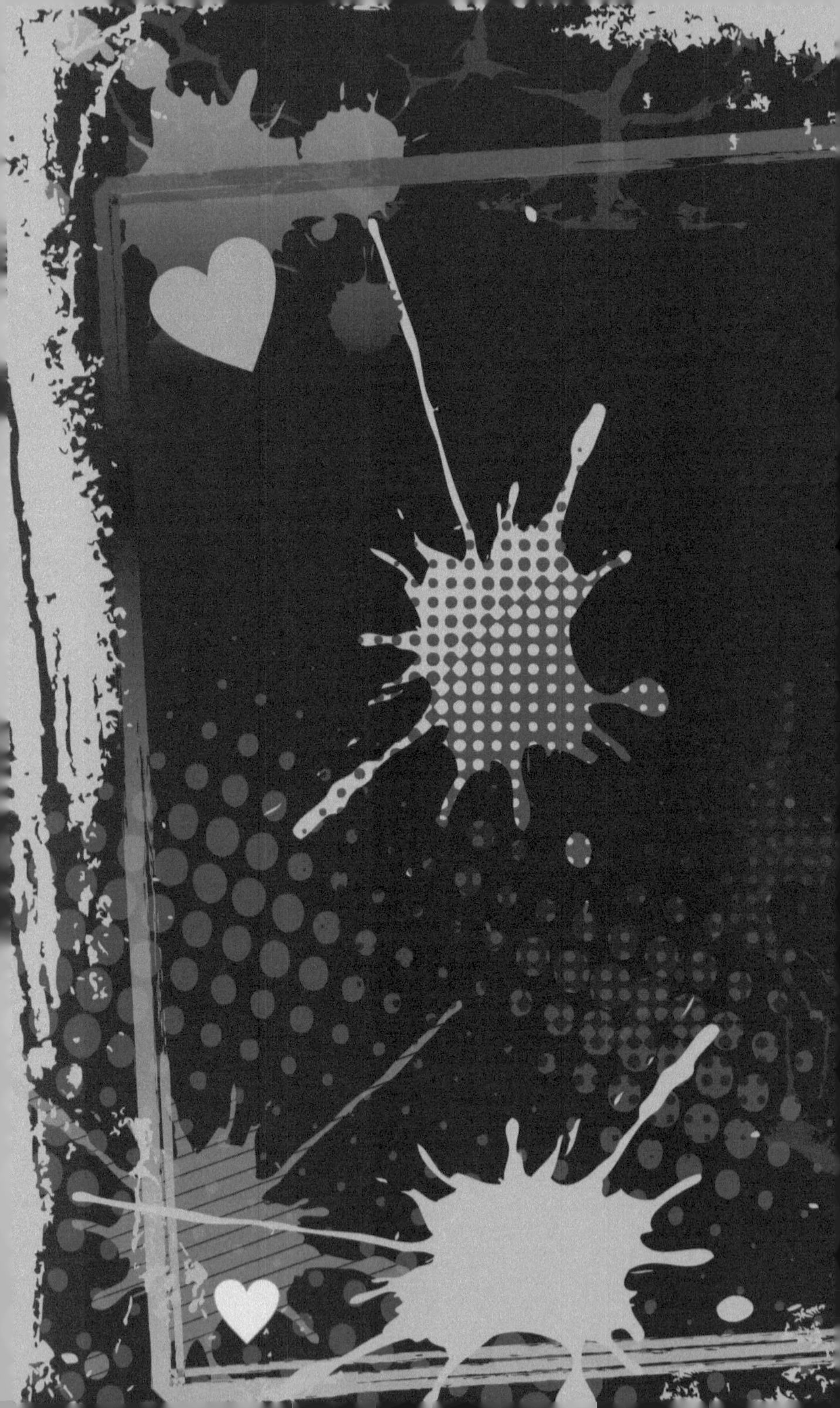

"It's not going to be as bad as you think. Kelly's family is great and I'm sure they are going to love you," Dad said as we drove towards our new home in the small town of Smith's Peak.

"I'm just worried about school, Dad. I'm sure I'll get along with her family," I reassured him. I really did like Kelly. She was genuinely nice and best of all, she made my dad happy. My mom had died eight years ago and it was only in the past year, since he met Kelly, that Dad had been smiling again.

Dressed casually in jeans and a tight-fitting t-shirt that accented his muscles, even I had to admit Dad looked handsome today, although I thought the thin shirt an odd choice to meet Kelly's family in considering the cool weather.

"I'm sure you'll thrive at the new school; getting a brand-new start, making new friends. I'm confident you'll do great!" Dad said after a minute of silence.

"Right."

He didn't like the fact that I'd experimented with some alcohol and drugs, snuck out a few times and gotten in a few fights. I wasn't really a bad child, but I also wasn't an innocent one either. Maybe things would be better at this school. Maybe I'd actually have a choice of boys to date, who weren't losers, here. I was going to miss my bestie whose family despised technology, so I couldn't text or call her. She had been the only one to keep me out of trouble, but we couldn't really stay friends being half a state apart.

We stopped in front of a large, two-story house, and Dad turned to face me. "She has two kids that live with her, but she also has a large number of others who visit her. I'm not sure how many will be here today, so I wanted to warn you."

"Why do so many people visit her?"

Dad looked down at his hands a moment before saying, "Most of her family isn't actually blood related. They're more like friends or adopted kids who don't have any blood relatives so they formed their own family."

Oh. Well, that sounded like a better family anyways, one you could divorce. A sudden tap on my window made me jump in surprise.7 I turned and found a boy about my age smiling at me.

"Go on," Dad urged me and bumped his elbow into mine.

I could be nice long enough to escape to my room. Swallowing hard, I unbuckled my seat belt and opened my door. "Hi, I'm Chloe," I said to the cute guy standing in front of me.

He held out his hand. "I'm Ethan."

I shook hands with him and chastised myself for feeling afraid of him when he was smiling and being nice. Why was I reacting so strangely to him? I didn't usually have this issue.

Ethan walked to the back of the truck and opened the hatch and tailgate. I reached in around him and grabbed my box which was labeled "personal".

Ethan took it from me. "I'll carry this for you."

My pulse jumped, and I quickly took the box back. "Thanks, but I'll carry this one." As I pulled the box into my arms, I heard the glass bottles inside clinking together.

Ethan's eyebrows raised, but he just shrugged. "Okay."

I walked up to the porch steps where Kelly stood holding the door open. I relaxed as she hugged me. "Hello, Chloe. Let me show you to your room." I walked inside the house and stopped in my tracks. At least ten people were standing and sitting in her living room, some my dad's age, but most my age or younger. I quickly followed Kelly up the stairs and away from all of the people staring at me.

Kelly opened the last door and moved aside. "Welcome to your new room."

I stepped in and forced myself not to groan. The walls were completely white and the room only had a dresser, a nightstand and a bed. I had a lot of decorating to do. "It's great," I murmured as I walked in and set my box on the nightstand before sitting on the bed.

Kelly said, "I know this is tough for you, but I promise to do everything I can to help make this easier. If you need anything just let me know."

I smiled. "Thanks, Kelly."

She smiled back and walked away, leaving me alone. I knew I should probably help my dad, but judging by the number of men downstairs, I thought I would just get in the way. I looked longingly at the box on the nightstand, but knew I had to wait until all of my boxes were upstairs.

Ethan stepped into the doorway with two of my boxes. "Knock, knock."

I rushed forward and took the top box from him. "Let me help you, those are probably heavy."

He set the other box down on the floor and smiled. "Thanks. What do you have in here, weights?"

I opened one of the boxes and showed him the contents. "Books." I scanned the room again and sighed. No bookshelf. I started unpacking the books and setting them on the floor along the wall. Ethan tried to help, but he didn't know what order they went in so he left to help finish unpacking the truck.

A younger boy came up a moment later with a box of my clothes. I asked him his name, but he just barred his teeth at me and ran out of my room.

"That was strange," I mumbled as I unpacked more of my books.

Ethan set my largest and final box on the floor and smiled. "That's everything. Dinner will be ready in about thirty minutes."

I smiled at him and walked him to my door. "Thanks."

He nodded, gave me a smile, and walked away.

I shut the door and locked it with a soft sigh. "Finally."

I walked to the nightstand and opened my personal box. Two bottles of coconut rum sat nestled in my underwear for safe keeping on the ride here. I took out one bottle and stroked it. "It's alright. You made it safe and sound." I opened the lid and took a large gulp, relishing in the liquid burn as it slid down my throat. "Much better."

It only took me twenty minutes to unpack everything since I didn't keep much. People who kept everything were odd to me. I rubbed coconut lotion on my hands and arms and then walked down the stairs to find the dining room. I just followed the sound of the people talking and laughing from the entryway down the hallway and into a giant dining room where three long tables filled the space. Dad and Kelly were sitting at the heads of one of the tables. I scanned the tables and realized they were separated by age group. The table Dad was sitting at had all of the adults, the second table had the teenagers, including Ethan, and the third table had all of the young kids. Ethan waved at me and gestured to the empty seat beside him.

At least I'd made a friend already.

I started towards the empty chair when Kelly stood up. "Everyone, I'd like you to meet Chloe."

I waved and hurried on my way to the empty chair as everyone said hello. I sat down, and Ethan patted my shoulder. "Don't worry, it'll get better in a few days when you've gotten to meet everyone."

I nodded and then looked at the end of the table. To say he was handsome was an understatement. He was one of those people you see and think, "They can't be real. They have to be genetically engineered to be so beautiful." He had golden hair and emerald green eyes. And I was staring at him in front of all of the other teenagers.

I turned away from him to the other end of the table where a beautiful, thin girl was sitting. "Hi, I'm Chloe."

She smiled. "I'm Amy."

Ethan cleared his throat and began the introductions, starting with Amy and then going to her left to a nerdy kid with glasses and a pocket protector named Alex, to a muscular and tough-looking girl named Emma, to the beautiful boy named Dylan, and then to my right where a shy girl named Lisa was sitting, and beyond her was a hard looking guy with tattoos named Tom.

I smiled politely at each introduction but found my gaze straying to Dylan repeatedly, and would have to quickly refocus it on the other people around me. Dylan barely looked at me, only glancing up when Ethan had said his name.

Distracted as I was, the dinner they served was delicious. However, I just wanted to go back to my room.

I leaned closer to Ethan and asked, "Do I need to ask to be excused or can I just leave?"

Ethan smiled. "You can leave if you want."

I smiled in thanks and walked out of the dining room to the sound of my dad and Kelly's laughter and hurried upstairs to my room. I pulled out a small flask I'd stolen from a store and filled it with the coconut rum before hurrying back downstairs and outside. The light was fading, but I needed to get out and besides, I wasn't afraid of the dark, just groups of people.

I walked around the edge of the house and found a beautiful garden with tall hedges. The perfect place to hide. I wandered inside and found a concrete bench facing a small pond which had koi fish swimming lazily around it. It was beautiful in the moonlight and I instantly felt safe and relaxed. I sat down and took a drink from my flask.

"I know we've barely met, but I doubt you're old enough to drink that," said a deep voice.

I turned and found Dylan sitting on the opposite side of the pond, watching me.

"I…"

He stood and walked slowly towards me. "And just so you know, the lotion doesn't help mask the stench of the alcohol." He held out his hand and smiled. "Don't worry. I won't tell anyone, as long as you give me the flask."

"Why should I? How do I know you won't just drink it?" I spat.

He sat down on the bench beside me and exhaled. "I didn't

want the first time we talked to be like this. I'm not trying to be a jerk, but if Kelly or one of the other adults finds that on you, you'll get in a lot of trouble. Please."

I sighed and handed him the flask. "Whatever."

"Thank you," he whispered.

"Dylan?"

"Yes?"

"Are you one of Kelly's blood relatives?"

He shook his head and smiled at me. "No. I'm just one of the strays she found a home for."

I wasn't sure what he meant by that, but instead of embarrassing myself any further I headed out of the garden. I walked back to the house and up to my room feeling like a scolded child. Sadly, if my father had caught me, I wouldn't have felt bad, but having Dylan find me and take my flask made me miserable. I plopped down on my bed and sighed. Hopefully tomorrow would be better.

I WAS RIGHT, it was better. Ethan showed me around the property and even took me to a trail I could walk down through the woods that butted up against the back of the property. After the grand tour, I was forced to sit in the living room and be introduced to each of Kelly's extended non-blood family. They were all really nice, and Dad was smiling. It was the least I could do to make him happy.

The introductions ended, and we gathered in the dining room to eat dinner together again. I sat down beside Ethan and tried to focus on eating, but my eyes were constantly drawn to Dylan, who didn't glance my way once. I felt like someone was looking at me the entire meal, but then again, people probably were since my dad and I were new to the family.

I went to my room as soon as I finished my plate and tried to fall asleep as fast as I could. Tomorrow was the first day of school, and I didn't want to go with bags under my eyes.

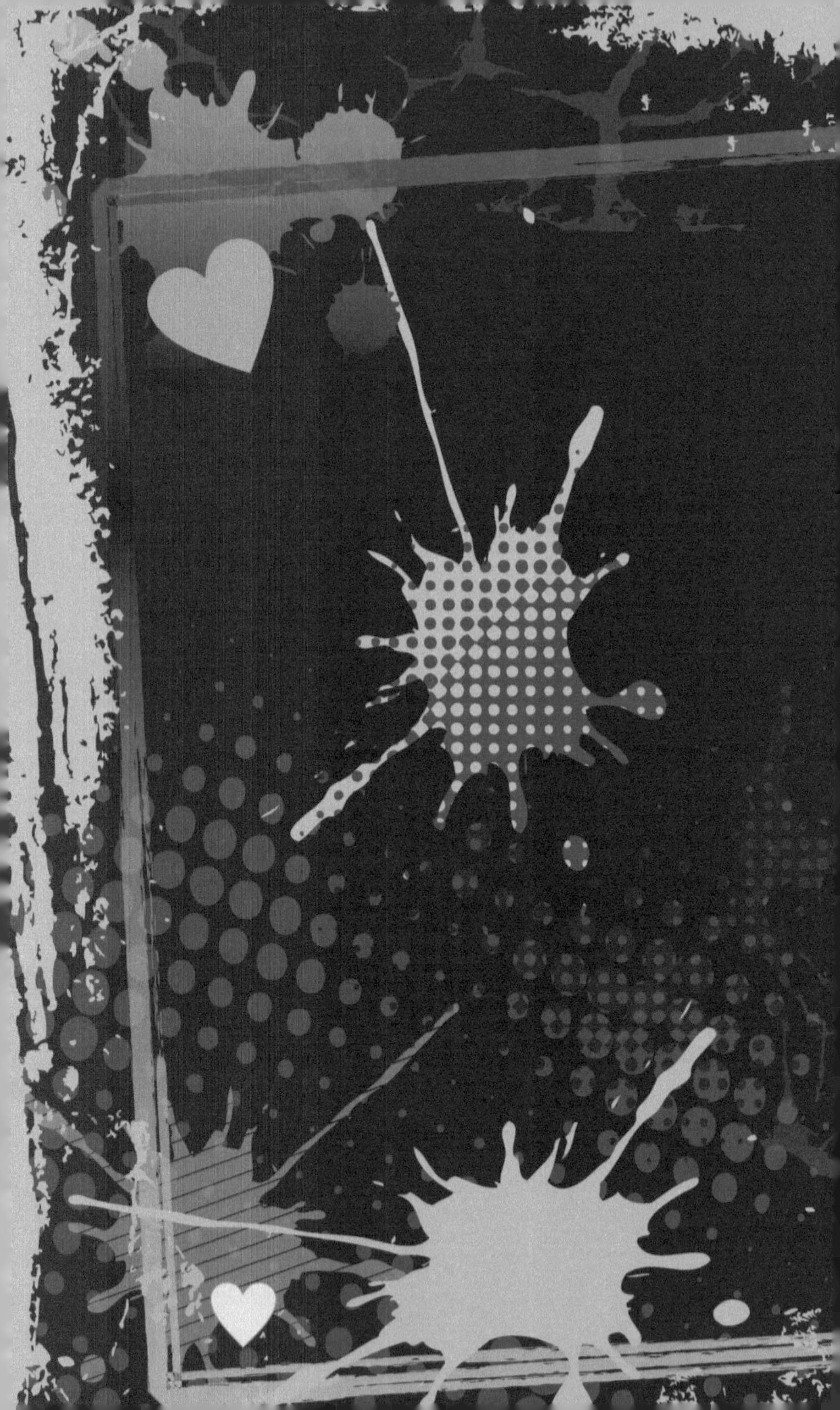

TWO

The school ended up being only two miles away from the house, so instead of cramming myself into the car with the other kids, I walked. The cool misty air felt refreshing against my skin and helped me wake up a little more. Things hadn't really started off well, but I was determined to make it better.

The school came into view, and I smiled. I had been expecting a small dilapidated building, but it looked just like my old school had, well except this school didn't have gates surrounding it to keep us in. I walked past all of the staring students to the office.

"Excuse me, I'm Chloe Smith. I need my schedule," I said to the three chatting secretaries. The office was very small with a large L-shaped desk that the three secretaries all shared and three small offices on the sides where the principal, vice principal, and the nurse were all sitting at desks reading newspapers.

I shook my head. I hadn't realized anyone read those anymore.

One of the secretaries pulled out a packet of papers from in front of her and handed it to me. "Here you go, darling. Let us know if you need anything else."

Schedule, campus map, and school policies. "Looks like I have everything. Thank you." I walked out of the office and sat down on the planter outside of it to plot out my classes on the map. English, algebra, physical education, lunch, and animal science were the classes I had been assigned. The warning bell rang just as I finished labeling my map. First period was two buildings down from the office. I folded up the map and slid it in my back pocket before heading towards the first class.

The class was so boring I had to keep pinching myself to stay awake. I was glad that Dad had waited until the new school year started for us to move so that I wasn't coming in late, but I still felt like the outcast as everyone already knew each other in the small town.

On the way to third period, I passed by Dylan. I smiled and waved. "Hey, Dylan." He looked at me a moment, nodded once, and then continued on his way with a couple of too-pretty girls keeping pace with him, snickering as they walked by.

Why hadn't he talked to me? Did he not want people to know we knew each other? Or maybe he just didn't want to associate with me anymore than he had to. I'd met people like him before so I would treat him like he had me and ignore him too.

At lunch I bought my food and looked around at the crowded cafeteria. Dylan was sitting with everyone from Kelly's including Ethan, the shy girl, the tough girl, and the pretty girl. I was having an awful time remembering any of their names. I really did want to sit with them, but since I was supposed to be ignoring Dylan, I decided instead to go eat outside, away from everyone. I didn't want to intrude on their group anymore than I already had by joining the family and invading Kelly's house anyways. And obviously Dylan didn't want me to sit with him.

I sat down against the side of the English building where a couple of soda machines were and ate my lunch. I pulled out a book I'd brought to read and was flipping to the place my bookmark was holding when someone cleared their throat. I looked up to find an ugly girl standing over me with her arms crossed. "Can I help you?" I asked.

"Yeah, get out of my spot," she said in a gravely voice.

I put my book away and looked at the wall behind me. "It doesn't have your name here."

"Look, new kid, just get out of my spot unless you want me to beat your brains out," she said angrily.

That was mistake number one for her. No one threatened me. I stood up and put my hands on my hips. "Back off. This is my spot now. So, just go find another place to hide."

Her fists clenched at her side at the same time her jaw clenched and then she lifted one to poke a finger into my chest. "I don't usually hit new kids before giving them a warning, but you're pushing me over the edge."

Mistake number two for her. I hated people poking me in the chest. "Get your filthy finger off of me. If you touch me with it again, I'll break it," I said through gritted teeth as I slapped her hand away.

Somehow, we'd already gained an audience. Kids were gathering now to watch our ordeal, hoping for a fight, which I knew was likely to come. I tried to rein in my anger, but it had a mind of its own.

She smirked and started to reach forward again with her

dirty finger. I grabbed her finger and twisted it to the side until I heard it crack. She screamed in pain and swung at my head with her other hand. My adrenaline pumped fast through my body, but I kept the smile off of my face. This bully had obviously not been put in her place yet. I blocked her hit and punched her once in the stomach before punching her in the face. She stumbled backwards and fell on her butt, holding her finger to her chest and her cheek with the other hand.

"I told you not to touch me. Now you listen here. You may be tough, but I hate bullies and have a reputation for turning them into sniveling wimps. You should think about that next time you try to mess with someone you don't know." I picked up my bag and walked away from her, shaking the pain from my knuckles.

Dylan and the rest of Kelly's kids were standing across the walkway watching me. Dylan shook his head and turned away from me, the other kids following behind him.

"Great. Not only did I hurt my hand, but now I've made a worse impression with him. Could this day get any worse?" I grumbled as I walked to my next class.

Ethan and Dylan were already sitting in chairs in my animal science class when I walked in, whispering to each other. I ignored them and sat down in the back chair, farthest away from them. Ethan turned around and waved to me, smiling. I smiled back at him and waved; glad someone wasn't mad at me. Dylan had to know that I couldn't have backed down to that girl. If I had she would have bullied me the rest of the year and I would have been seen as a coward. He had to understand, didn't he?

I didn't pay attention during class, my thoughts completely consumed by Dylan. I'd never been so strongly attracted to a guy I'd just met before. Of course it was my luck that he didn't want anything to do with me. The bell rang and I hurried out of the class before Dylan and Ethan.

I made it two feet away from the classroom when someone grabbed my arm. "Chloe? What are you doing here?"

I turned and repressed a sigh when I recognized the person holding me as someone who went to my old school. "Hey, Steve," I greeted. Steve had tried to date me, but when it became clear he was only after one thing, I stopped talking to him. Then he'd moved and apparently come here to this school.

"When did you start going to school here? Wait, did you get expelled?" he asked with a smirk on his face.

I shook my head and pulled my arm out of his grip. "My dad remarried and his wife lives out here."

Steve smiled. "Well, I'll have to remember to thank him. You look great." He reached out to run a hand down my side, but I stepped back.

"I told you before, Steve. I'm not interested in dating you."

Steve smiled wider and stepped closer to me, making me back up towards the wall of the building. "Oh, come on. You know you and I could be great together. Remember how much fun we had that one time when we did acid together?"

"Everything alright, Chloe?" asked Dylan who had somehow materialized beside us.

"I'm fine, Dylan."

Dylan glared at Steve a moment before turning back to me. "You want a ride home? We don't have much room, but we can make some for you."

Why was he suddenly being nice to me? He'd ignored me the rest of the day, but now he was trying to be nice?

"No, I don't want to *bother* you," I said angrily as I stepped away from both Dylan and Steve.

Dylan glared at Steve one more time before walking away.

Steve laughed and looked at me. "Your dad married Kelly Wisdom? You're part of the family of freaks!"

I glared at him. "It's none of your business who my dad married and if anyone is a freak here, it's you." I walked away from him without a glance back. My heart was pounding against my chest as I walked out of the school and down the road back towards Kelly's house. No, my home.

Why had Dylan done that? Did he care or was he doing it out of obligation for Kelly? And what did Steve mean about them being the family of freaks?

I was deep in thought and didn't notice the car next to me until the window rolled down and the ugly girl I'd hit snarled at me. "Hey, new girl."

"Come for a second broken finger?" I asked her as I continued walking.

The car came to a stop and ugly girl and two uglier girls got out. Ugly girl smiled at me. "No, I've come to repay you."

"Just leave me alone, alright? I didn't want any trouble, but you had to push it. If you had just left me alone, I wouldn't have had to break your finger."

The three girls surrounded me with evil grins spreading across their faces. I'd been jumped before, a few times actually, so I knew what was coming. I also knew that no matter how well I fought, three against one always resulted in me getting bruises. I slipped my backpack off one of my shoulders and waited patiently.

Ugly girl glared at me. "You're not scared?"

I shrugged. "You think you're going to frighten me so that all I will do is cower and let you kick me. I'm not scared, which means I'm going to fight back and you're going to get just as many, if not more, bruises from me. If you'd rather not fight me, I'm fine with that. I'd rather not have to hurt you anymore than I already have."

"What a cocky twit!" Uglier number one said from behind me.

I smiled. "We going to stand here and chat or we going to fight so I can kick your butts and get home in time for dinner?"

Ugly girl rushed me in anger. I swung my backpack, now full of textbooks, and slammed it into the side of her head, sending her stumbling sideways, clutching her head. Uglier one and two grabbed for me, trying to hold me so the other could hit me. I ducked and dodged towards the road, but uglier one grabbed my arm. I spun and punched her in the face, but uglier number two was there too and punched me in my face. Ugly girl came back and punched me on the other side of my face. I kicked uglier one in the shin and she dropped my arm, letting me free to move out of their circle to better fight. I punched uglier two in the back of her head, making her drop to her knees. Ugly girl punched my cheek, splitting the skin. The blood was cool against my hot cheeks and the pain made my head spin slightly. Dad had trained me to fight and now I was using everything I'd learned from him, minus the killing techniques since those were only to be used when my life was in danger. I broke another of Ugly girl's fingers and dislocated uglier one's knee before grabbing my backpack and running as fast as I could the last mile to Kelly's. My head and face were throbbing, but other than bruises and the one cut I was fine.

I held the tears in, saving them for when I was alone. I opened the front door and heard voices in the dining room. I shut the door quietly and ran up the stairs to my room before anyone could see me. I threw my backpack on the bed and looked in the mirror. My face was already swelling, but the cut on my cheek was small and had stopped bleeding. Overall, I'd survived pretty well.

I heard footsteps and peeked my head out. Ethan was heading towards the stairs. "Ethan," I whispered loudly before pulling my head back in.

Ethan walked to my room and tried to peer in, but I hid behind the door. "What's wrong?"

"Can you do me a huge favor? I hate to ask, but it's really necessary."

Ethan smiled. "Sure. What's up?"

"Can you get me my dinner and bring it up here?"

Ethan frowned. "What? Why?"

"I just don't want to deal with everyone right now. Please, Ethan. I'll owe you."

Ethan sighed. "I'd really like to, Chloe, help you I mean, but the number one rule here is that everyone eats together. If I try to bring your plate out of the dining room, they're going to ask questions and then come see you."

"Oh. Well, thanks anyways," I said as I sagged against the wall.

Ethan was quiet a moment and then sighed loudly. "What if I bring you back some bread and meat in a napkin? It won't be much."

I perked up and smiled, causing my cut to split open and bleed again. "I don't eat much anyways. Thank you, Ethan. Thank you."

He walked away, and I closed and locked my door. I didn't want Dad stopping by and opening the door without knocking.

I grabbed three pain pills from the bottle in my dresser drawer and swallowed them. The adrenaline was starting to wear off, and I was not looking forward to tomorrow. I knew I couldn't hide from Dad until the bruises were gone, but I could hide for as long as possible.

Two knocks on my door woke me from a half sleep. I walked to the door and asked, "Who is it?"

"Ethan."

I unlocked the door and opened it just wide enough for his face to fit through, while I hid behind the door so he couldn't see me.

He held out a napkin filled with food and said, "Here, this is all I could get. No one stopped me, but I need to get back."

I took the food and whispered, "Thank you."

Ethan said, "If you want to talk about something or if you're in trouble, we're all family here and I'll listen or help if I can."

Tears formed in my eyes and I blinked them away. It wasn't time for crying yet. "Thanks Ethan. I'm just...I'm just trying to deal with the first day of school."

Ethan laughed. "Well, you did make quite an impression today."

I sighed. "Yeah, but not the best one I could have made."

"I've got to get back, but do you want me to come see you after?"

"No. No, it's alright. Thanks, Ethan. I really appreciate it."

"No problem. Anything for family."

I waited until he was back down stairs before grabbing my jacket, a flashlight, and the food and rushing downstairs and outside. I knew if I stayed in my room that Dad or Kelly would probably come and insist that I talk with them, so I headed around the house and out into the forest. The trail led to a lake where Kelly had put some benches. The benches overlooked the lake which reflected the stars beautifully. I sat down and ate the food as I listened to the nocturnal animals waking up as the sun finally set and darkness consumed the world. I finished the last of the meat, cheese and bread Ethan had pilfered and hugged my jacket tighter around myself before letting the tears flow. The last time I'd cried was three years ago and now three ugly, stupid bullies were making me cry tonight.

My face was hot and one of my eyes was beginning to swell shut. I couldn't go to school looking like this tomorrow. I'd be a laughing stock. The tears finally stopped, and I shivered in my jacket and sniffled.

"You shouldn't be in the woods at night," said a familiar deep voice.

I rubbed at my nose and eyes, only to gasp in pain as I touched my swollen face. "I just needed to get some fresh air."

Dylan sat down beside me and inhaled deeply. "I love the forest at night. It's my favorite place to think…or hide."

There was a new moon so the forest was complete dark. I could barely see the outline of Dylan's face as he turned to look at me. "Are you crying because of that boy?"

I laughed and shook my head. "No, Steve's just an idiot. I wouldn't cry about him."

Dylan leaned towards me and asked, "Why do you smell like blood?" He turned on his flashlight and the light blinded me as he pointed it at my face. I swore I heard a growl, but then Dylan lowered the light, causing it to turn towards him so I could see his face, and asked, "Did he do this? Did he hit you?" He was so angry and so handsome. Dylan reached out towards my face, but I stood up and moved away from him.

"Why are you being nice to me?" I asked.

"Should I be mean?" he asked in an amused voice as he shut off the light.

I sighed. "Look, I know me and my dad joining your family probably rubs you the wrong way and I get that I'm already a thorn in your side so you don't want to associate with me at school, so why are you here now?"

"I heard you sneak out and wanted to make sure you weren't alone in the woods. Like I said, the woods are dangerous at night." He paused for a moment and said, "And you aren't a thorn in my side. I didn't intend to make you feel like I don't like you."

Great, now he thought I was a whiny, clingy idiot. "I don't care if you want to act like you don't know me at school. I just want to know why you're being nice now. Is it just because you feel obligated?"

"Who hit you, Chloe?"

"It doesn't matter, I take care of myself. I don't need you or anyone else to fight my battles for me."

"Just tell me if it was that boy. Please."

Each time he said please, it was as if part of my willpower dissolved. "No, it wasn't Steve, or any other boy."

"Do you want to talk about it?"

"No. I got what I deserved and they got what they deserved too."

"They? More than one person hit you?" he asked, angry again.

I sat down on the bench next to him again and sighed. "Yes, it was that ugly girl who tried to bully me at lunch and two of her friends."

"You should have just walked away from her," he said.

I laughed. "Right, and then I would have been labeled a

sissy who lets people walk all over her. No way. I've dealt with bullies before and I never back down."

"We should get back to the house, before they start to worry."

"Amy's really pretty. She's your girlfriend, right?" He would know I was trying to change the subject, but I was curious.

Dylan laughed. "No. She wanted to be when we were younger, but she's more like a little sister to me and there's no way I could date her. Besides, she has someone else she likes now."

"Oh, so one of the two girls I saw you with at school is your girlfriend then?" I knew he would guess why I was asking, but in the dark I could hide the blush covering my cheeks.

"No, I don't have a girlfriend."

"Oh."

We sat in silence a few minutes before Dylan stood up. "Come on, we need to get back."

"Dylan?"

"Yeah?"

"Thank you."

"For what?" he asked as he turned his light on and led the way back to the path and out of the woods.

"For being nice and coming out here to find me."

"Chloe?"

"Yeah?"

"Don't come out here alone at night again, please. There are bears and wolves that inhabit the woods, and I wouldn't want to find your body instead of you sitting on the bench."

There was that please again and what seemed like an admission of caring. I knew it was too early for him to really care, but it still made me smile. "Alright, I promise. Will you promise me something?"

Dylan stopped and turned to face me. "What?"

"Don't tell anyone about my face."

He laughed softly and said, "Alright, I promise."

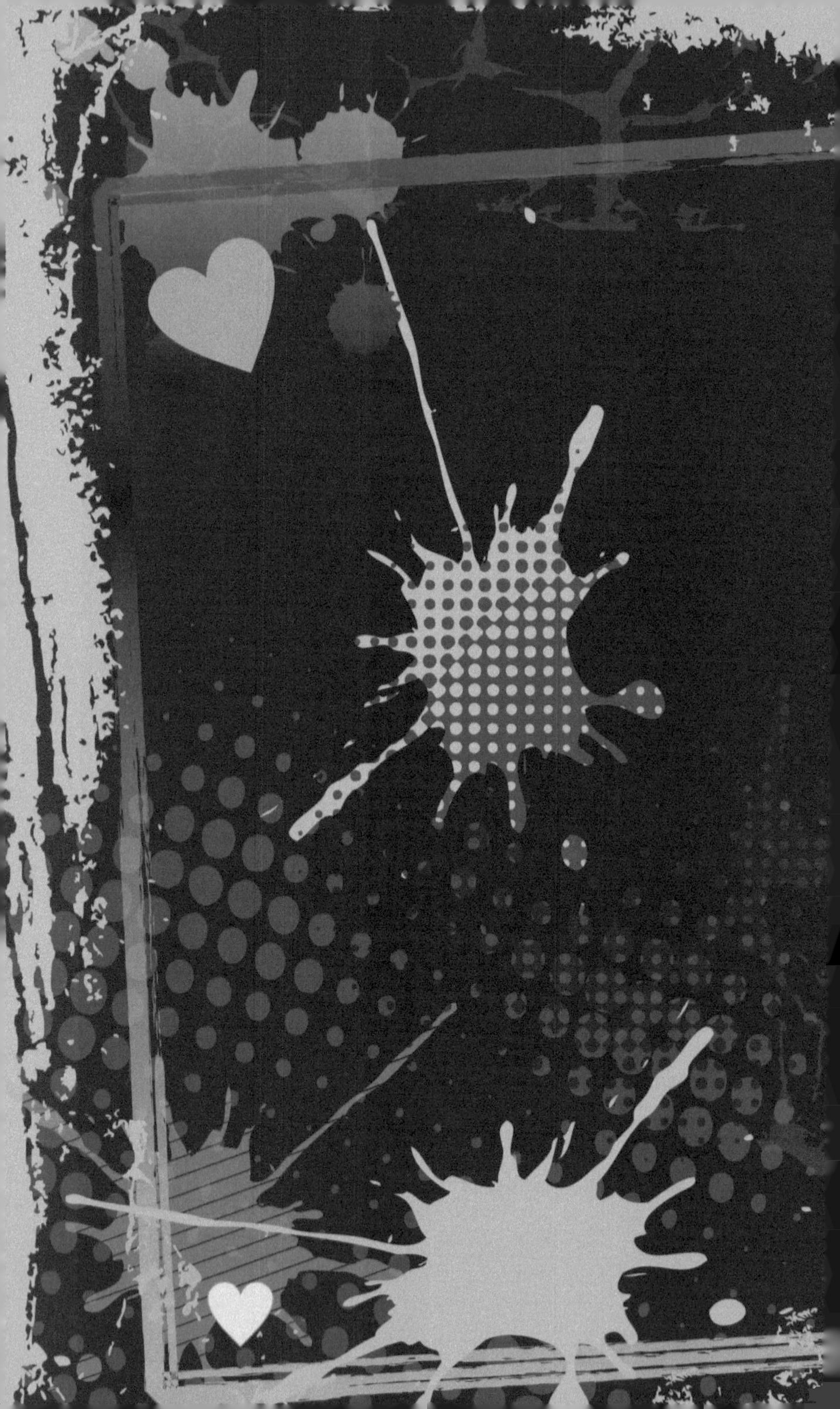

THREE

Neither Kelly nor Dad even checked to make sure I went to school, so I stayed home alone and tended to my wounded face and pondered over my encounter with Dylan.

I knew I shouldn't make more of it than it was, but I felt like I had connected with him last night. And knowing he wasn't interested in Amy made my day that much brighter. At noon I made myself a sandwich and was just sitting down to eat it when someone knocked on the front door. I set the sandwich down and walked to the front door, peering through the glass. I'd met him the second night, but I couldn't remember his name. Eric, Sean, no, Adam. I opened the door and hid my face. "Um, hi Adam. No one's home right now."

He tried to look around the door at me, but I stayed back. Adam smiled. "I'm sorry. I'm not trying to scare you. I was just trying to find Kelly."

"She's not here. I think she went to show a couple a house in Lakeston." Kelly was a realtor and was gone most of the time.

"Oh. Right. Well, could I come in?"

I bit my lower lip and exhaled. "Can you promise me something first?"

Adam arched an eyebrow in question. "Um, it depends on what it is?"

"I'll let you in if you promise not to tell anyone, including my Dad and Kelly, about my face."

Adam frowned for a moment before asking, "Have you discussed whatever the problem is with Dylan?"

"Yes." Why did that matter?

He nodded. "Alright."

I opened the door and stepped back to let him in. Adam walked in and then stared at me with wide eyes and raised eyebrows. "Please tell me whoever did this has a black eye to match?"

I laughed. "Yeah, a black eye, lump on the head and two broken fingers. The other two just have black eyes though."

I headed back towards the kitchen and sat on the barstool to eat my food.

Adam opened the fridge then looked at me in shock. "The other two? What did you do yesterday, take on a family?"

I shrugged. "One girl tried to bully me at lunch, and I punched her and broke her finger, then after school she brought two friends to jump me."

Adam pulled out all the fixings for a giant sandwich. "Well, at least you hurt all three of them. I'm surprised a girl your size can fight, though."

"Dad has been teaching me since I was old enough to walk to defend myself."

Adam smiled. "Yeah, your dad is quite the fighter."

I stopped chewing and looked at him. "You've seen my dad fight?"

Adam nodded as he lathered mayonnaise on a piece of white bread. "Yeah, he practices with us from time to time."

"Wait, you guys practice fighting?" I asked in shock.

Adam laughed. "Sorry, I forget that you haven't been coming here with your dad. Our family is really big on staying fit and being in the best shape possible. We spar with each other every weekend. You're more than welcome to watch, or even join."

I thought about practicing with Dylan watching, but didn't want to embarrass myself. Adam and I ate in companionable silence and then he looked up at me.

"Has Kelly talked to you yet?" he asked softly.

I frowned. "What do you mean? About the fight at school? She doesn't know—"

Adam shook his head. "About our family."

I shook my head. "No, Dad just told me a little bit before we got here about how you are mostly not blood relatives, but nothing besides that. Why? Was she supposed to?"

Adam sighed. "I'm sure she plans to talk to you soon. I'm going to go for a walk in the woods. I'll be back."

"Could I come with you? I like the woods and—"

"No!" Adam said urgently. I blinked at him in shock and he sighed. "I'm sorry. I just...I need some time alone and...just stay in the house, please."

Why did everyone have to say please? "Okay."

Adam looked like he wanted to say more, but he cleaned up his mess and left. I sat in the kitchen a little bit longer before heading up to my room to hide from everyone.

I napped for a few hours until someone knocked on my door. I sat up and my head throbbed in pain. "Who is it?" I asked as I walked towards the door.

"Dylan."

My heart rate doubled as I moved the last few feet to the door and pulled it open, but hid behind in case someone walked by. "Um, hi."

"Can I come in?"

I shrugged. "Sure." I shut the door behind him, and he gave me a strange look. "I just don't want Dad or Kelly barging in and seeing my face."

He nodded and then squatted down to look at my books. "I saw the girls who jumped you today."

"You didn't say anything to them, did you?" I asked.

Dylan stood up and walked around my bed towards my dresser. "No, but I'm impressed with how much damage you inflicted on them."

I smiled and then grimaced in pain. I popped open the pain pill bottle on my nightstand and put four in my hand. Dylan frowned at me. "I think you're only supposed to take two."

I popped all four in my mouth and swallowed them with a gulp of water. "Well, I'm in pain."

Dylan stopped next to my dresser and frowned. "You still have alcohol."

How did he know that? The bottles were closed. Unless one of them opened up and was leaking. I rushed around my bed and pulled open my dresser, trying to block Dylan's view and check my bottles. "Uh, maybe."

Dylan tried to reach around me, but I slammed the drawer shut and turned so my back was pressed against the dresser. The position put me incredibly close to Dylan though and my heart beat faster as my mouth went dry.

Dylan's emerald eyes were mesmerizing, and I swore little flecks of gold started to appear in them the longer I stared. "Chloe, give me the bottles."

I shook my head and broke my stare. "No."

Dylan frowned at me. "You don't need them and it's bad for you."

"It's my body and thus my choice to decide what I put in it," I said and shook my head as my anger rose.

Dylan's frown turned into a scowl. "I don't want to fight with you, Chloe. Just give me the bottles."

I sighed and turned around. I really wasn't in the fighting mood. I opened the drawer and pulled out the first bottle, staring at the liquid inside. Dylan had taken a step back to give me room to open the drawer, so he didn't see me unscrew the lid. I got three good gulps in before he yanked the bottle from my hand.

"What do you think you're doing? You could kill yourself by taking pain pills and mixing it with alcohol!"

Honestly, I'd forgotten I'd taken the pain pills. "Who cares? I'd just be saving you the trouble of dealing with me. I'm sure you'd be happier without me around to bother you." I hadn't meant to say it, but it had come out anyways.

"You don't know anything about me," he said with a growl as he took the second bottle out of my drawer and headed towards my door.

"I'm sorry. I'm not usually like this," I said softly as he pulled open the door.

He stopped and shut the door before turning to me. "I'm not either. This transition is hard on all of us, but we'll work it out. Please, just stop trying to hurt yourself."

I looked in the mirror and laughed. "Right, I have enough people trying to do it for me."

"Just between you and me, she had it coming and I'm glad someone from our family did it."

"Dylan?"

"Yeah?"

"Can we start over? Forget all of this?"

Dylan set the bottles on the floor and held out his hand. "Hi, I'm Dylan."

I shook his hand and shivered at how warm it was. "Hi, Dylan. It's a pleasure to meet you. I'm Chloe."

We smiled at each other a moment longer and then I watched as he left my room, shutting the door behind him. I sunk onto my bed and groaned. "Could I have been a bigger idiot?"

"Chloe!" Dad yelled from downstairs.

"Great. He takes the bottles and rats me out," I grumbled as I walked to my bedroom door. "Yeah, Dad?"

"Why didn't you go to school today?"

"Uh, I'm not feeling well."

"Come down here and don't make me shout."

I sighed and walked down the stairs, preparing for the worst. Dad stared at my face, eyes wide and jaw dropped, for a moment before stepping forward and probing it.

Kelly walked in the front door and gasped, "Who hit you?"

"Bullies at school."

"Dylan!" Kelly yelled.

Dylan walked out of the kitchen. "Yes?"

Kelly pointed at my face. "You aware of this?"

Dylan nodded. "Yeah."

Kelly arched an eyebrow. "And you didn't tell us, because…?"

"She made me promise not to," he said softly.

Kelly sighed. "Fine, but did you deal with who hit her?"

Dylan smiled at me and shook his head. "No, she did."

Kelly turned to me, and my dad asked, "Who hit you?"

"I told you, a bully at school."

Dad shook his head. "You have too many bruises for one girl to have done this."

"The one girl brought two friends to jump me after school."

Dad groaned. "That's it. We're changing your training for multiple opponents."

Kelly blinked at my dad. "That's it? You're not going to ground her?"

Dad shrugged. "Chloe doesn't pick fights so the other girl must have started it and if three girls took her on and she survived this well then the other girls are more damaged. Plus, would you go to school looking like this?"

Kelly frowned and then turned to me. "From now on you're riding with the other kids to school."

"There's not enough room, and I don't—"

Kelly gave me the mom stare and I stopped talking. "You will ride with them. Dylan, you can drive the Suburban from now on and you make sure that she doesn't get hurt again. You understand?"

"I can take care of myself! I don't need you telling him to protect me, like I need a bodyguard. I'm not a poor defenseless girl," I yelled angrily.

Kelly sighed. "If that were true, then you wouldn't have a single bruise on your body."

"Dad!"

Dad shrugged. "I think it's a good idea for Dylan to look out for you."

My jaw must have been touching the floor. "Can I be dismissed?"

Dad nodded and I stormed out of the house and around the back to the garden. I plopped down on the bench and watched the koi fish swimming around. Dylan was going to end up hating me now for having to be my new watcher. I had to make sure I fought my fights away from him. I was not going to be *protected*.

The next morning, I climbed into the Suburban with the rest of the kids and slumped in the back seat. My face wasn't swollen anymore, but the bruise on my cheek and eye were a disgusting pale green color. I tried to hide it with concealer, but it didn't help much.

Dylan drove to school in silence, and I realized I was taking it out on everyone when I shouldn't have been. "Do we ever get to do anything fun?" I asked lightheartedly.

Dylan looked up in the rearview mirror a second before focusing back on the road. Ethan turned around and said, "Well, we get to go on family camping trips and the town has a festival in October."

A festival sounded fun. I used to love the mini fairs that came to town with rides and carnival games.

Dylan parked the SUV, and we all climbed out. As we started towards the school entrance, I saw Steve leaning against a wall. He smiled at me and started to walk my way. Dylan walked faster until he was keeping pace next to me and glared at Steve. I rolled my eyes and stopped walking, but Dylan stopped with me. "Dylan, I can handle this myself."

Dylan smiled. "I'm sure you can, but Kelly wanted me to make sure you didn't get hurt again."

"He's not going to hurt me."

"There's more pain than physical."

I stared at him a long moment and then pushed around him to walk to Steve. "What do you want, Steve?"

"Is it true you busted up the Kurtis family?"

"You mean the ugly girl whose finger I broke?"

He nodded. "Yeah, rumor is that her and her two sisters jumped you, but you whooped them."

"Oh, well yeah, that's true."

"I think that's really hot," he whispered as he moved closer to me.

I stepped back and shook my head. "I told you, Steve. I'm not interested in you."

Steve looked behind me and asked. "Is it because of that freak, Dylan?"

I looked behind me. Dylan was standing with his hands at his sides, opening and closing them into fists. He looked pissed...and so hot.

"No, I just wouldn't ever sleep with you. I'd rather die."

Steve tore his gaze from Dylan to glare at me. "You just might have to rethink that, Chloe. One day, you might have a choice between death and—"

"Are you threatening her?" Dylan asked from beside me.

I jumped and turned to glare at him. How did he always sneak up on me like that? "Dylan, I told you. I can handle this."

Dylan didn't take his eyes off of Steve. Steve smiled at me. "I'll see you around, Chloe."

Dylan started to reach out towards Steve, but I stepped between them and pushed Dylan's chest. "Stop it. You are not my bodyguard, goddammit. I can take care of myself."

Dylan's jaw was clenched tightly and after a moment of staring into my eyes, he sighed and walked away from me.

I felt bad for yelling at Dylan and pushing him, but I didn't want him trying to protect me all of the time.

I couldn't focus in my classes again because of Dylan. At lunch I got my food and headed to sit in the spot I'd claimed from the Ugly Kurtis girl, only to find Dylan and the others sitting there. "Um, what are you guys doing here?"

Ethan smiled. "Family always eats together."

Emma said, "And we figured if you fought so hard for this spot, we might as well take advantage of it."

"You guys don't have to…I mean I don't want to inconvenience you guys."

"Sit with us, Chloe," Dylan said, looking up from his lunch.

I swallowed and nodded. "Okay. Um, thanks guys."

Ethan and Amy moved over so I could sit down against the wall between them. I had just taken a bite from my pizza when Ugly Kurtis walked up. "What do you freaks think you're doing?"

Her face was still swollen and both eyes were black. The two fingers I'd broken were in splints and seeing it all brought a satisfied smile to my face.

"We're eating lunch," I answered.

"This is my spot. Get the hell out of it," she yelled, her face turning bright red.

Dylan and everyone were ignoring her so I decided to do the same. She tried to step between Dylan and Lisa, but Dylan stood up and blocked her path. "Your stench is interfering with our meal. Beat it."

Ugly Kurtis glared at him before looking at me. "This isn't over."

I shrugged. "I can give you and your sisters another thrashing if you'd like. Though, you might want to bring more than two of your sisters since I only got one swollen eye out of the mess from the three of you."

Ugly Kurtis glared at the group before stomping away.

Lisa said, "You shouldn't egg her on like that."

I shrugged. "I'm not a passive type. Plus, as long as she really doesn't bring more than three of them, or guns, I'll be fine."

"You have a lot of confidence in your fighting abilities," Emma said.

I laughed. "I didn't say I'd make it out without a scratch, just that I'd make it out."

We ate in silence the rest of the lunch period, but for the first time I felt accepted and didn't mind the silence. Dylan, Ethan, and I made our way to animal science, still in silence. I wished I could figure out some way to start a conversation so Dylan said something to me besides, "sit with us." We made it into the classroom and they sat in their seats beside each other and I continued on to the seat in the back of the room. Dylan didn't even watch as I walked to sit away from them.

The teacher droned on about the difference between mammals and reptiles and amphibians. My mind droned on about how I was never going to have a chance with Dylan. He was too perfect and I was...well me.

Class ended, and I wished I had a bottle of alcohol. I was already obsessed with a guy I'd known only a few days. It was beyond pathetic, and I vowed from now on not to care. If only it were that simple.

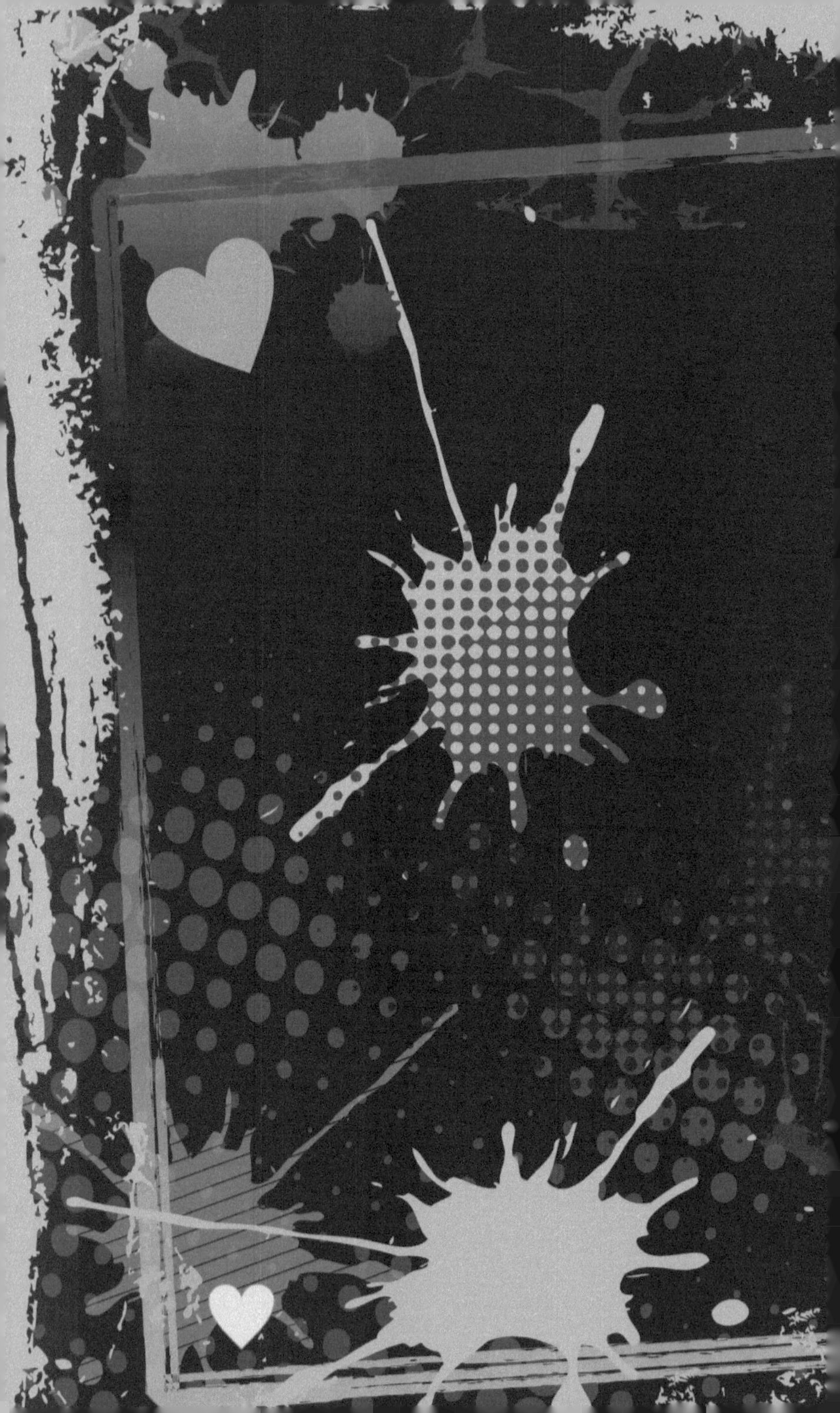

FOUR

I tried the next few days to find a guy to take my attention off of Dylan, but he was the hottest guy at the school. By the time Friday came, I was completely frazzled and upset because he was back to being standoffish. It took a while, but I finally talked my dad into letting me take his car to go to the mall that was forty miles away with a promise to have my cell phone on at all times. I was determined to find a guy, someone to take my mind off of Dylan.

"Chloe," Dylan called as I walked towards my dad's car.

I clenched my teeth and turned around. "Yeah?"

"Where are you going?"

Kelly must have put him up to this. "The mall. Dad gave me permission."

"Do you mind if I come?" he asked.

Part of me wanted to say that of course I minded because the whole point was to find a guy to forget about him, but the other part really wanted him to come. It would be nice to have a few hours of alone time with him.

"I don't need a bodyguard," I told him as I unlocked the door.

"I know that. I need to get something from the mall though," he said as he stood at the passenger side door.

What should I do?

I stared at him for a few minutes and then straightened my spine and said, "I'm sorry, but I want some alone time."

He walked around the car and stared into my eyes. "You look like you want to find some trouble."

"I want to find some clothes and a new book," I said as I met his gaze.

"Look, I know we don't always get along, but I am a nice guy and I promise to leave you alone if you want, once we get there."

I couldn't really argue with that. "Fine. We will ride together and that's it. I don't need you keeping an eye on me or trying to be a bodyguard or anything else ridiculous."

He smiled. "Agreed."

I knew I was probably going to regret this, but I climbed in the car and unlocked the door for Dylan. I read over the directions Kelly had given me quickly and then started our drive. I felt on edge with Dylan beside me, and I really wanted to find a way to apologize for how I was acting, but my brain couldn't come up with anything to discuss. So, we drove the forty miles in uncomfortable silence and I almost sighed in relief when we finally made it to the mall.

"So how about we meet at the food court at one?" I suggested.

He nodded. "Okay."

I locked up the car, and we headed into the mall. He didn't seem upset so I decided not to apologize and turned in the opposite direction as him, heading towards the skate shop where I was hoping to find some cute guys shopping. The mall was full of people, which hopefully put my odds of finding a cute guy higher. I finally made it to the store and my luck was finally prevailing. A famous skateboarder was at the store posing with shoppers in pictures for publicity. I took a deep breath and walked into the store, instantly met by stares from guys, many of them cute.

I pretended not to notice their stares and walked to the girl's section of the store and searched through the pants and shirts with various labels. It didn't take more than two minutes for one of the hot guys to approach me. "Hey," he said with a smile. "You need any help?"

I held up a pair of cargo pants. "I'm trying to decide if these would flatter my figure or not."

The guy looked to either be a senior in high school or a recent graduate. He couldn't be over nineteen. He had gauged ears and messy, but sexy hair. "I think you should try these on," he said as he walked to another rack of clothes and then held up a pair of jean shorts.

I took the shorts and eyed them. They were going to be pretty short, but still super flattering. "Well, these are cute, but it's getting to be winter so I'd better stick with pants this shopping trip."

He nodded and walked to another rack and then handed me a pair of jeans and then a t-shirt of the same brand. "Then this would be a nice Fall outfit."

I took the outfit and smiled. "That is nice. I'll try them on then."

He led the way to the fitting rooms and said, "Let me know if you need any more help."

"Maybe you could just wait for me to try them on to tell me if it's cute?"

He nodded. "Sure thing."

I closed the door and changed quickly into the new clothes. The outfit fit well and the shirt hugged my chest nicely. I stepped out of the changing room and turned slowly. "What do you think?"

"Very nice," he said with an approving smile.

"I think I need some shoes to match," I said as I stepped back into the fitting room to change.

"Ones that match your outfit or your personality?" he asked from outside.

I stepped out with the shirt and pants folded in my hand. "You think you can find ones to match my personality?"

He looked me from head to toe and then nodded. "I think I can try."

We had just started towards the shoes when a second sexy guy stepped into my path. "Hello, you're new to this area, aren't you?"

"I just moved to Smith's Peak," I said with a smile. This guy was attractive than the worker, with black spiked hair and super blue eyes. He was dressed in all skater brands and held a skateboard under his arm.

"I'm Bo," he said with his hand extended.

"Chloe," I said as I shook his hand.

I turned around and the guy who had been helping me was at the shoe wall, scouring over the section. "Do you live near here?" I asked Bo.

He nodded. "I live about twenty minutes from Smith's Peak. Maybe we could meet up for coffee sometime?"

This was what I'd been looking for. "Sure," I said with a smile.

He held out his cell phone. "Can I have your number?"

I typed in my name and number as a new contact and then

handed it back. He smiled. "It was nice to meet you, Chloe," he said as he took a step back.

"You too, Bo." I turned around and walked quickly to the sales guy. "Any luck with my personality?" I asked him as I sat down.

He turned around and smiled, apparently having missed my whole exchange with Bo. "I have two I'm debating between."

"She's definitely the black with pink accents," said a guy behind me. I turned around and stared in disbelief at the famous skateboarder who had been taking pictures and signing boards.

"Why do you say that?" I asked him with what I hoped was a nice smile, though I was in shock at the moment.

He smiled at me. "I'm good at reading people," he said as he handed me the shoe to look at. "I'm Rob."

It was a pretty shoe. "Do you have it in a size seven?"

"If they don't, I'll have one personally delivered to your house," Rob said.

"We actually only have it in six and a half or seven and a half," the sales guy said, sounding disappointed.

Rob smiled. "Looks like I'll be making a trip back down this way."

"You don't really have to do that," I said, stunned by his offer.

"I never go back on my word, especially to beautiful women," he said as he took out a super fancy cell phone. "If you aren't comfortable giving me your address, you can just give me your number and we can meet up for dinner."

"How old are you?" I asked curiously.

He stepped closer and whispered, "Nineteen. You?"

My age was probably going to be a deal breaker. "Sixteen. Seventeen in December."

"I'm a December birthday, too," he said with a bright smile. "Do you get cheated on presents like I used to because of Christmas?"

I nodded, took his phone, and put my number in it. "Yes. I always get necessities for my birthday."

"Rob, break's over," a guy in his forties said from the front of the store where more fans had lined up.

Rob sighed and took the phone back from me. "Work calls, but I'll give you a call when I get your shoes."

"Okay," I said with a smile.

He turned and then said, "And Mark, put those clothes on my bill for the day."

"What?" I gasped.

He smiled. "I'll be calling you real soon, Chloe."

Mark, the sales guy said, "Wow, I've never seen him flirt with a girl before."

"So, he doesn't do this often?" I asked.

Mark shook his head. "No. I mean he does buy less fortunate kids, clothes and stuff sometimes, but he doesn't ever flirt with the girls. He must really be interested in you." He stared at me a moment and then said, "Well, let's get these written down under his tab. You're one lucky girl."

I followed Mark, but kept looking over at Rob who was signing and smiling in pictures with fans. Nineteen and he had a bunch of money and a fan base. Was he really a nice guy or a player? I had to hope he was a nice guy. Otherwise, I'd be right back on the Dylan wagon.

"Dylan!" Rob said happily. "How you been, man?"

I turned around and stared in shock as Dylan and Rob gave each other the one-armed guy hug.

"I'm good. You're obviously doing well," Dylan said with a smile.

Rob shrugged. "I'm doing alright. It'd be better if I got to see you more."

"I'm always up for weekend visits," Dylan said.

Rob smiled wide. "Maybe I'll just do that."

"Are you coming tomorrow?" Dylan asked.

Rob nodded. "Yeah, I'll see you tomorrow for sure."

"Rob," the older man said.

Rob nodded. "Yeah, I know back to work."

"See you tomorrow," Dylan said as he headed into the store, closer to me.

"Alright, you're all done," Mark said and then handed me the bag of clothes.

"Thanks," I said with a sincere smile.

"Come back soon," Mark said seriously.

I laughed. "Okay."

I was trying to slink out of the store without Dylan seeing me, but he stepped right in front of me as I rounded the last rack of clothes. "Hey."

I tried not to look surprised and said, "Hello. Done with your shopping already?"

He held up three bags. "Yep. You?"

I nodded. "Yeah, now I'm starving though. Time for the food court."

Dylan smiled. "Okay."

I headed out in front of Dylan and Rob waved to me. "Bye, Chloe."

I waved back. "Bye and thanks."

He winked. "Anytime. And I'll see you soon."

"I'm looking forward to it," I said as I continued walking.

Dylan waved to Rob behind me and then walked faster to catch up. "You know Rob?" he asked.

I shrugged. "Yeah. So, are burgers okay for lunch?"

Dylan wanted to ask me more, but he refrained and said, "Yeah, I can always eat a burger."

We walked in silence a moment and then I asked, "So, what did you get?"

"Just a couple shirts and a gift for Lisa for her birthday."

"Oh, I wish I had known her birthday was coming up. I don't really know what I would get her though."

"Don't worry about it," he said. "She knows you don't know our birthdays yet."

"Yeah, but I'm part of the family now and—"

"Don't worry about it," he said seriously. "She'd probably feel awkward if you got her something so soon. Just wish her a happy birthday. She's not big on presents anyways."

"Okay," I said quietly. I stopped at the end of the line to the burger place and felt my cell phone vibrate against my leg just before the tone for a text message played. I opened it and stared at the unfamiliar number with the message.

Unknown Sender: *Found a pair that I can pick up tonight.*

I RESPONDED and asked who it was, wanting to be sure.

UNKNOWN SENDER: *Rob.*

I SMILED.

· · ·

ME: *How'd you find them so soon?"*

IT WAS ABOUT two minutes before my phone vibrated again.

Rob: *I'm that brand's number one sponsored athlete. I have a lot of pull.*

ME: *That's awesome. So, when's the next time you'll be down this way?"*

I WAS ACTUALLY REALLY HOPING he'd be able to come soon. It would be nice to go on a date.

"What would you like?" the cashier asked.

"A double cheeseburger meal with a chocolate shake, please."

The cashier looked about my age, but she obviously didn't like her job. "Anything else?"

"What do you want?" I asked Dylan.

"Two double cheeseburgers," he ordered.

I pulled out my cash, paid, and then moved to the left to wait for our food. My phone vibrated and I pulled it out.

ROB: *I'll be down tomorrow actually. Is that too soon?*

Me: *Tomorrow sounds great.*

MY HEART FLUTTERED at the thought of seeing him so soon and getting to go out on a date with him.

"How long have you known Rob?" Dylan asked as he grabbed our tray of food and walked towards an open table.

"A short while, why?" I asked as I grabbed my burger.

"Where did you meet?" he asked as he took a bite out of his burger.

"At one of his signings," I said as I ate mine. It was delicious. My phone beeped again.

ROB: *Do you want to meet me somewhere or can I pick you up for dinner?*

"ROB'S A GOOD GUY, but he travels a lot," Dylan said.

I looked at him and tried to judge his mood. "He seems like a fun guy, though."

Dylan sighed. "Yeah, he is. He'll be coming over tomorrow." He was looking down at his phone and then started typing on it. Probably a text message.

"Really?" I asked in shock. "To Kelly's?"

I instantly wrote back to Rob.

Me: *I think it's safe to give you my address.*

I ALMOST LAUGHED OUT LOUD, but I held it in and typed my new address.

"Yeah. He's coming to Kelly's and then he has a date for dinner or something," Dylan said as he looked at me.

"Cool," I said. "Since you guys don't get to hang out much, I'm sure you'll have a lot of fun."

"We always do," Dylan said with a smile. He looked at my phone when it beeped again.

. . .

ROB: *You live with Kelly?*

Me: *My dad married her a month ago and I just moved to her house a week ago.*

I FINISHED my burger and leaned back in my chair feeling full and satisfied. "That was a great burger."

"It was okay. Adam makes the best burgers though. You'll have to ask him to make you one some time."

ROB: *Oh I see. Well I used to live with Kelly so I know the way. I'll be hanging out with Dylan and the rest of the family during the day and then I'll take you out to dinner. Is that okay?*

Me: *Sounds great to me.*

Rob: *Great, see you tomorrow. Getting yelled at to stop texting while I'm working. :-)*

I PUT my phone away and smiled at Dylan. "I'll do that."

"Are you ready to go?" he asked me.

I stood up and nodded. "Yep."

We walked out of the mall in silence again, and I realized I needed to apologize to him for how I had acted now. "I'm sorry about being rude to you earlier."

He looked at me and then shrugged. "It's okay. I understand needing your space sometimes."

"Still, I shouldn't have been rude to you. It's not fair of me to take my stress out on you."

"Stress?" he asked.

"School… and trying to fit in. You all know each other so well, and I barely know anything about any of you."

"I can help you study if you need it, but Alex is the smartest of us. And you just need to hang out more instead of hiding in your room."

I stopped at the car and gaped at him. "I don't hide."

He smiled. "Don't get defensive. And yes, you do. As soon as you finish eating, you run upstairs instead of staying to talk and hang out with us."

He was right, but I wasn't doing it to hide. "I just get a little overwhelmed being around that many people I don't know."

I unlocked the doors, and we climbed inside. "You won't ever get to know them if you keep hiding."

He was right. Dang I hated when I was wrong. "Okay, you have a point. I'll try to be more social." We drove back to the house in silence again, but this time it was comfortable. I was really glad he'd asked to come with me because now I felt a little more at ease around him. We stopped at the house, and I stared at the vast number of vehicles parked there. "What's going on?" I asked.

"Your dad didn't tell you?" he asked.

"Tell me what?" I asked back as I looked at all the people walking around the property.

"Tomorrow is our family reunion. There'll be three times as many people as there usually is."

I felt my heart start to race and turned my head away from him. I wasn't a fan of big crowds after an incident at a concert where I'd almost been trampled.

"Chloe?" Dylan whispered. "Are you alright?"

A group of twenty men and women walked towards the house from cars that they'd just parked. It was too many. There were too many people. I tried to respond to Dylan, but my body wasn't working how I wanted it to. I tried to unbuckle myself, but my fingers kept fumbling with the button and my fear began to grow.

"Easy, Chloe," Dylan whispered. "Let me help."

I jerked away from him as he reached down and unbuckled me, and then I bolted from the car, racing as fast as I could towards the forest. At least fifty people were standing in the backyard around a barbecue talking, but as soon as I ran by, all eyes turned to me.

"Chloe!" Dad yelled.

I ignored them. I needed space. I needed air. The trees whipped by me, and I tried my hardest not to trip on roots or rocks. I wasn't sure if I was on the path anymore or how far I even was, but it wasn't far enough. My heart was beating faster than ever, and I continued to run. My breathing became erratic and then I started to hyperventilate. I slowed down and dropped to my knees as I fought for breath and tried my hardest to calm myself. It was a stupid fear, I knew that, but my body didn't.

Spots started to appear in front of my eyes so I rolled onto my side and tried to calm down and relax.

I'm safe and alone. I'm safe and alone.

Warm hands touched my shoulder, and I would have screamed if I'd been able to. "Easy Chloe. Everything's alright. It's just me," Dylan whispered as he leaned me up so I was leaning against his legs and chest. He wrapped his arms around me and his warmth felt incredibly good. "Your dad didn't tell us you had a phobia of groups," he whispered in my ear. "If I had known, I would have prepared you better before we got here."

My breathing was returning to normal, and my heart was slowing its chaotic race.

"What happened?" he asked me. "Why are you afraid of groups?"

I swallowed and then shivered against him. "Concert," I managed to whisper. "Trampled." I knew I needed to get away from him, but being held by him felt too good.

"This group is very different from a concert," he whispered. "Here, we all respect each other's space. No one will hurt you here, Chloe."

My breathing and heart rate were finally back to normal and despite how incredible it felt to be in his arms, I sat up and moved away from him. "I'm sorry," I whispered. "I thought I'd gotten over it since I could handle school."

"You have nothing to apologize for. I'm not comfortable in crowds of people I don't know," he admitted.

"Chloe," Dad called from nearby.

"Over here," I answered.

He stumbled through the forest and then came into view. "Are you alright?"

"Yeah, I just got freaked about the crowd. I'm good, you can go back."

"You sure?" he asked, his brows furrowed.

I nodded. "Yes, sorry. I'll be there in just a minute."

He nodded and then walked away, leaving me and Dylan alone again. He was determined to let me work out my own stuff. It was great sometimes, but other times I wished he was a little more hands on.

"You should go visit," I told Dylan.

"I'm not leaving you alone. Come on. We can walk back together."

"Everyone's going to think I'm crazy now," I whispered in embarrassment.

"Everyone there is already crazy in one way or another. Come on."

I didn't want to face the crowds, but I would feel better if he was with me instead of going alone. "I don't know if I can."

He grabbed my hand and pulled me up. "If you start to get scared again, you can race up to your room and hide."

I glared at him. "You think this is funny?"

He shook his head and looked at me seriously. "I was being honest. If you get scared you can go up to your room and no one will bother you."

I was definitely out of my element with him. "Okay."

He patted my back and smiled. "Good choice."

He started to walk away, and I grabbed his hand, making him turn to face me. "Dylan, thank you."

He smiled. "Any time."

He led the way out of the forest and towards the even larger group of people in the backyard. I stopped and stared at the large group and felt my heart start to speed up. Dylan stopped with me and waited silently beside me. I'd never been to a family reunion before or been around so many people who knew each other, besides school.

Emma, Lisa, and Amy walked towards us and stopped a few feet away. "Hey, Chloe," Lisa said with a smile. "I have some people I'd like you to meet."

I looked at each of their smiling faces and didn't want them to see how scared I really was. I took a shaky breath and then smiled. "Okay."

Dylan whispered something to Emma as we walked towards the group. Lisa linked arms with me and smiled happily. "Everyone is really looking forward to meeting you."

"How many people are in your family?" I asked softly.

"Over two hundred," Amy said. "But we rarely get everyone together like we are this weekend."

Over two hundred!

"Just breathe," Emma whispered. "We're all family here. Everyone just wants to meet their new sister."

Sister? I hadn't really thought of it like that. I hadn't thought of these girls as my sisters. Hearing them say that made my fear evaporate and a smile split my face.

Adam walked up to us and smiled. "Hey, your face is looking a lot better. Green definitely didn't suit you."

I laughed and started to truly feel happy. "Thanks, Adam."

Lisa led me to a small group of teenagers and said, "Everyone, I'd like you to meet Chloe."

The group all smiled at me, except for one girl who scowled, then one by one, they introduced themselves. There were so many names and so many new faces that I didn't stand a chance of remembering them all.

"How're you handling things so far?" one of the guys asked me.

His name started with a P, but I couldn't remember the rest of it. "Honestly there are just so many people that I have a really hard time remembering anyone's name."

One of the girls with a super thick head of hair said, "It gets easier the more often you spend time with the group."

"It'd be easier if everyone wore name badges the first month," I said with a laugh.

Everyone laughed with me, and my tension completely eased. I could work through this. I could make it through the crowd without being overwhelmed. A breakthrough, even if it was a small and sort of dumb one.

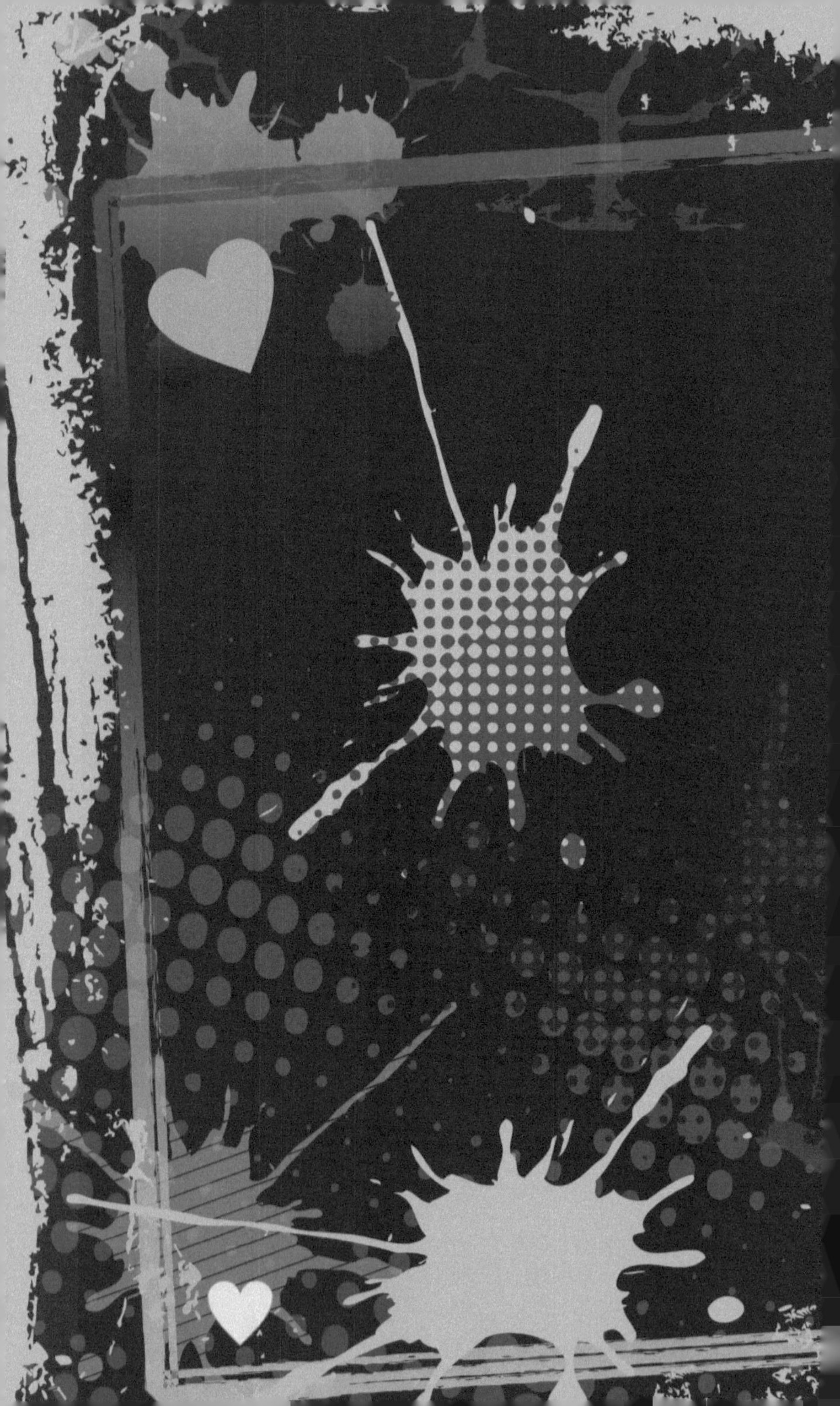

CHAPTER

FIVE

"Food's ready!" Adam called from the barbecue.

The group spread out to form a single file line, and I stood beside Amy and Lisa as we waited. Dad and Kelly were at the front of the line with Dylan right behind them. He turned around and scanned the line until he found me and then waved at me to come forward. I shook my head and kept my spot.

"Dylan wants you up front," Lisa whispered.

"It's okay. I can wait in line with you guys," I said.

Dylan stepped out of line and walked back towards me. "Chloe, come on up here and get some food."

"I can wait," I said.

Some of the others around us started to watch me which was embarrassing. The girl who had glared at me earlier was staring outright, without even trying to hide it.

Dylan grabbed my hand and pulled me forward before I could object. "I told you, you have to try Adam's burgers and if you aren't one of the first in line you'll get stuck with a hot dog."

I gaped at him, not sure why he was being so persistent, but let him lead me up to the front of the line behind my dad. Dylan handed me a plate and smiled happily at me.

This Dylan was completely different from the one I usually saw at school. He was so happy and so nice. Was it because his family was here? Dylan got a burger from Adam and then said, "Make sure you give her a good one, this is her first time tasting one of your burgers."

Adam smiled at me. "Well, these aren't my famous burgers, but they're still pretty good. I'll make you my famous burgers when I'm over on Wednesday if you want?"

"That'd be great," I said with a sincere smile.

He put a burger on my bun and said, "Make sure she doesn't ruin it with ketchup," to Dylan.

We continued down the line to get chips and salad and I asked, "What did he mean about the ketchup?"

Dylan bit a piece of a chip off and said, "He uses his own sauce so you don't need ketchup. I add mayo but that's just how I prefer it. You'll probably like it plain."

I put some ketchup and mayonnaise on my plate on the side in case I wanted to put it on the burger and then grabbed a soda from the ice chest before following Dylan towards the large, open grassy area. He sat down, and I sat down beside him, chewing on a cheesy-flavored chip.

I lifted the burger and took a small bite. Flavor exploded in my mouth, and I moaned in pleasure. "This is great."

Dylan laughed. "I told you so."

"It's like a hundred times better than the mall's burger place."

"And that's not even his best burger," Dylan said.

I ate my food slowly, enjoying being able to be around so

many people and Dylan's company. Lisa, Amy, Ethan, Tom, Emma, and Alex sat down with us to eat as well.

"What do you think of the burgers?" Tom asked me.

"They're incredible," I said honestly. "The best I've ever had."

"Hey guys, did I miss anything?" Rob asked as he walked over to us with a plate of food.

Everyone stood up and hugged Rob, all very obviously pleased that he was there.

He looked at me and smiled. "Hey, Chloe."

"Hi, Rob," I said with a pleasant smile.

"I thought you weren't coming until tomorrow," Dylan said. I wasn't sure if he sounded pleased or sad about it.

"Manager let me off for the weekend for good behavior," Rob said and then everyone laughed.

"When's your next competition?" Alex asked.

"Next weekend," Rob answered. "In San Diego."

"Dang," Emma said. "If it was close, we could go, but San Diego is too far."

"We'll just wait and go to another one," Dylan said.

"You guys could stay in the hotel with me!" Rob said enthusiastically. "It's been so long, and I know Kelly wouldn't mind if you guys went for the weekend. Come on. What do you say, Dylan?"

"Oh please, Dylan!" Lisa begged. "I've always wanted to see him skate."

"Please!" Amy said as she leaned towards him.

"I'll ask Kelly," Dylan said.

"Yes!"

"Alright!" everyone in the group said happily.

I felt bad that I was intruding on the group's time together so I stood up and was about to head to the house to go to my room, but Amy stood up and asked me quietly, "Where're you going?"

"I feel like I'm intruding," I told her honestly. "You guys don't get to see Rob often, and I just thought it'd be better if I let you guys enjoy him being back."

"You're part of the family now, too. We enjoy you being with us as well," she said with a smile.

I hugged her and whispered, "Thanks, but I think I'll still leave." She looked at me strangely, but then just shrugged and sat back down with the others. I walked through various groups of people, smiling at everyone as I made my way. Everyone seemed really nice, and I had been having a good time. Dylan had been right that I just needed to hang out more.

"I don't know what you're trying to do or what your game is, but it won't work," the teenage girl who had glared at me said as I walked by her.

I blinked at her. "I don't know what you mean. I'm not playing a game."

"I see how you look at him. You think him taking you to the front of the line meant anything?" she asked with a sneer.

"Look, I barely know Dylan and he was the one who dragged me to the front of the line. I didn't ask him to."

She glared harder at me. "Keep your hands off him. He's mine."

Now I understood. "Look, Dylan doesn't like me that way, okay? He made it clear that we're just friends so back off. I don't like being threatened."

She smiled and laughed. "This isn't me threatening you. Trust me, girl, when I threaten you, you'll know because you'll be crying for your daddy to come save you."

Now I was pissed. No one called me a coward. "I fight my

own battles, twit, and you don't scare me. I'm not the type to be easily manipulated or pushed around. So, next time you think about threatening me, remember that I fight back."

"Everything alright?" Adam asked as he walked towards us with an armload full of utensils from the grill and table.

"Let me get the door," I said to him as I walked passed the girl and held it open.

"Thanks," he said as he walked by.

I looked at the girl and said, "I'm just trying to be part of the family. I don't want any trouble and I don't want any fights. So, just go find Dylan and have fun flirting with him. I don't care."

I shut the door behind me and walked into the kitchen, grabbing a bottle of water and holding it against my forehead where a headache had started. "Everything alright?" Adam asked again from the sink where he was washing dishes.

"Nothing I can't handle," I answered.

"Be careful of Cynthia," he said.

I lifted a brow. "Who?"

"The girl you were talking to. She's a little bit crazy and unstable. Just watch your back if you're alone with her, okay?"

I sighed. "Great. Thanks."

He laughed and patted my shoulder. "It's not so bad. You'll be fine."

"I'll be in my room," I told him as I walked out of the kitchen and towards the stairs.

I closed my door and took three pain pills before flopping down on my bed and closing my eyes. I'd already made an enemy and I hadn't even done anything wrong.

"Knock, Knock," Rob said as he pushed open my door slowly.

I sat up and smiled. "Hey."

He looked around my room and said, "Wow, you are in desperate need of a decorator."

"Yes, I need about two gallons of purple paint and a very large bookshelf," I said as I crossed my legs on the bed.

"So, why did you run away?" he asked me as he turned to face me.

"I didn't run away," I said, shaking my head.

"Is it because of Dylan? Are you and him an item and you just didn't want to turn me down?" he asked.

My jaw dropped. "What? No. No. You have the wrong idea. Dylan and I are just friends. And I came up here so everyone could have time with you without me being around."

"You didn't have to do that," he said as he sat down on the bed next to me.

Being this close to him made my heart beat faster in a very pleasant way. "I know, but they're your family and you don't see them often. I was just trying to be nice."

"Well, we all appreciate it, but we'd like it better if you came down. Everyone is worried about you."

I doubted that. "Well, as you can see, I'm fine."

"Do you want to talk about whatever happened?" he asked.

"Huh?" I asked, blinking at him.

"You're obviously upset about something and you weren't before you left our group." He scrunched his eyebrows together. "You look like this right now."

I laughed and shook my head. "No, it's alright. I'll get over it."

"So, do you still want to go out to dinner tomorrow?" he asked.

"Of course I do," I said.

"Your shoes are in my car. You want to walk down with

me to get them?" he asked as he stood up.

"No, we can get them later. You should go back and hang out with everyone."

He grabbed my hand. "Okay."

"What are you doing?" I asked as he pulled me up.

"Going back to hang out with everyone," he said with a smile.

"I didn't mean me," I said with a laugh as he tugged me out my bedroom door.

"You are part of everyone," he said as we walked down the stairs.

"You're not going to let me stay in my room, are you?" I asked as he reached for the back door.

He smiled. "Nope."

The door opened, and I pulled my hand out of his in case it was my dad. Kelly looked at Rob and then me. "What's going on?" she asked cheerfully.

"Rob's forcing me out of my den to join the rest of the group instead of isolating myself," I answered.

Kelly kissed Rob's cheek and then walked past us. "Good for him."

Rob pushed my back gently, forcing me out the door and then followed beside me back towards the group.

Amy winked at me and smiled, like she knew something I didn't. I sat down beside her and she asked, "So are you going with us too?"

"Where? For what?" I asked.

"You didn't ask her?" Dylan asked Rob.

Rob shrugged. "I thought it was your place to ask her," he said to Dylan.

Dylan and Rob stared at each other a minute and then Dylan shrugged. "Kelly already said yes."

"You have to come!" Lisa said excitedly. "Please."

"What are you guys talking about?" I asked. "I'm totally out of the loop."

Dylan said, "We are all going to San Diego next weekend to watch Rob skate at a competition."

"Really?" I asked.

"Yeah," Amy said. "Please, Chloe."

"Yeah, please Chloe," Rob said with a cute smile.

"If everyone is alright with me going then I guess I can't say no," I said with a smile.

Lisa jumped from her spot and hugged me. "I'm so excited!"

I hugged the usually shy girl back and laughed. "It's not like I'm going to prom with you Lisa."

The group laughed and Lisa said, "I know, but it'll be the first trip with you and I can't wait."

Amy's stomach growled, and she groaned. "I'm so hungry."

"We just ate," I said with a laugh, but then my stomach growled too.

Amy laughed. "See you're hungry too."

"I want ice cream," Emma said with a pouty face.

"That does sound good," I said. "A warm brownie with ice cream sounds even better."

"With sprinkles on top!" Lisa shouted.

Several of the other groups of talking people turned to look at us and we all laughed.

"So, let's go get some," Rob said.

"We can't," Amy said sadly. "No moola."

"Um, hello? Famous skateboarder who makes lots of moola from contracts is sitting right here. I'll pay," Rob said.

"Really?" Lisa asked excitedly. She jumped up and ran over to Kelly who had just walked outside.

Lisa was so full of energy, unlike at school where she barely talked and moped around. Why was everyone so different here at the house? Lisa ran back and tossed the Suburban's keys to Dylan. "Let's go!"

Everyone stood up and headed towards the front of the house to go. I followed behind them, but felt sort of out of place. Rob had already bought me clothes and shoes. I didn't want him to buy me ice cream too.

"Why so glum?" Emma asked me.

I slowed down so we were farther away from everyone. "Promise to keep a secret?" I asked her.

She smiled. "I love secrets. Yes, I promise."

"I met Rob in the mall today and he didn't know I lived with you guys, but he bought me the clothes I was going to purchase and a pair of shoes and so I feel like I'm taking advantage of him if he gets me ice cream, too."

Emma frowned in thought. "I see where you're coming from and I can understand it, but it's Rob's money and this time it's not just you he is buying for." She stared at me a moment then asked, "Do you like Rob?"

I didn't want to talk about this right now. "He's sweet and really hot, but I don't really know him yet."

"What about Dylan?" she whispered.

I felt my heart plummet and I whispered back, "He's made it pretty obvious to me that he isn't interested in dating me."

"Really?" she asked, eyes widening.

"Come on guys!" Amy called from the Suburban.

"Don't worry about it," I told her cheerfully, "Let's go get some ice cream."

"We'll talk later," she said seriously and then we jogged to the SUV. Emma found a spot in the middle, which left only one spot in the very back between the window and Rob.

"So, Friday you'll leave school right after third period and drive to the airport. I'll meet you guys at the airport and we'll ride to the hotel and hangout."

"I'm so excited!" Lisa said happily.

"We couldn't tell," Tom teased her.

We all climbed out at the ice cream shop and filled up the small store. I looked at the various flavors as I tried to decide what to get. "Any favorites?" Rob asked me.

"I have too many favorites," I said with a laugh. "What about you?"

"He likes cheap, easy girls, which explains why he's hanging out near you," Cynthia said with a sneer before walking over to Dylan.

My blood was boiling, and I wanted to hit her in that stupid face of hers.

"Don't let her get to you," Rob said. "She's just jealous. My favorite is strawberry. So, what would you like?"

"I don't know," I said sadly. "I'm not really in the ice cream mood anymore."

I started to walk away, but he grabbed my arm and stopped me. "Don't let her win."

"It's not about winning," I said. "It's about ruining the day." I pulled away from him and walked out of the ice cream shop to sit on the raised wooden walkway. I didn't even know her and she was already trying to ruin my time with the family. Why? I hadn't even been near Dylan.

"What's wrong?" Dylan asked as he walked out of the shop and stood next to me.

"Nothing, go on back inside," I said as I pulled my knees up and put my chin on them.

Dylan sat down and leaned around me to meet my eyes. "You're a terrible liar."

I sighed and stood up. "I know not everyone is going to like me, but I hate when people instantly hate you for a dumb reason."

"Who hates you?" he asked.

"Dylan, our ice cream is ready," Cynthia said with a sweet smile as she held up two cups of ice cream.

"I'll be inside in a minute," he said to her. "Chloe, you know you can talk to me. I can help."

"Your ice cream is going to melt," Cynthia said a bit more sternly.

"Go eat," I told him and then whispered, "I don't need her to have another reason to hate me."

Rob walked past Cynthia and handed me a cup of vanilla ice cream on a brownie with rainbow sprinkles. "Here you go."

I took the ice cream, but refused to look at either of them. "Go inside, Cynthia," Rob said angrily, "Leave her alone."

"What happened?" Dylan asked.

"Nothing, right Chloe?" Cynthia said with a sweet smile.

I was embarrassed and pissed at the same time, but couldn't pick an emotion to stick with. "Chloe, we saved seats for you and Rob," Emma said as she walked outside.

"Those are the last spots," Cynthia said. "Those were for me and Dylan."

"I'm fine outside," I said as I sat down again and took a bite of my brownie.

"See, she prefers to be outside where the rest of the garbage is," Cynthia said bitterly.

"Leave her alone, Cynthia. She hasn't done anything to you," Rob said angrily.

"Of course she hasn't. If she had, she wouldn't be here right now."

"Back off," Dylan said seriously to her.

"I haven't done anything. Have I, Chloe? I have behaved and kept my hands to myself."

"Apologize," Dylan said.

Cynthia laughed. "Are you drunk? Why on earth would I apologize when I've done nothing wrong? Have I said anything that's not true?"

That was the last straw. I stood up and handed my ice cream to Rob. "Thanks for the ice cream, but I've lost my appetite." I walked down the stairs and headed back towards the house.

"See, she's leaving like a good pup," Cynthia said. "She knows she's not one of us and knows she's not ever going to fit in. She's weak."

"Shut up!" Rob yelled. "You are being rude for no reason."

"Don't yell at me," she said angrily.

"Cynthia, shut up," Dylan said.

"You're taking her side?" Her voiced ticked up at the end of her question.

I walked faster to get out of earshot of their conversation and wished I could have just punched her in the face instead of walking away. I'd thought about it, but I'd probably just disappoint Dylan.

"Chloe!" Amy yelled as she caught up to me. "Don't go."

"I can't stay there with her," I said. "I'm going to end up punching her."

Amy laughed. "That would be fun. I've thought about it a few times."

"I don't care that she calls me names or whatever, but she doesn't even know me."

"She's always had a big crush on Dylan and seeing a pretty

girl living with Kelly who Dylan pays attention to is scary for her."

"I told her Dylan isn't interested in me, so I don't see why she's trying to upset me still. It wasn't my fault he came outside to check on me."

"Come back," Amy said. "Please."

I shook my head. "Sorry. I can't go back now."

"If I punch her in the face will you come back?" she asked with a smile.

I laughed. "That would be awesome, but no. Thanks, but I'll just walk home."

"It's going to be dark soon. You can't walk alone."

"Amy, go back and hangout with them. I'll be fine."

She shook her head and linked arms with me. "Nope, I'm staying with you wherever you go."

I stopped and stared at her. "I don't want to ruin your fun."

"Then come back," she said with a cheerful smile.

"No."

She shrugged. "Alright, then let's keep walking."

"Chloe, wait up!" Lisa yelled as she ran after us.

I groaned. "Not you, too. Go back."

She linked arms with my other arm and said, "We're family and besides, it's always better for girls to travel in groups together."

"Wait up!" Rob yelled as he ran towards us with Emma, Tom, Ethan, and Alex.

"What is wrong with you people? You can't all follow me," I said, my voice wavering as my heart squeezed.

Rob smiled. "Well, we weren't having any fun being with Cynthia so we followed you."

"Great, now I ruined everyone else's night," I muttered.

Lisa pinched my arm. "No, you didn't. Cynthia ruined her

own night. Now she's getting scolded by Dylan as he drives her home."

"Right, I'm sure she's really upset about being alone with Dylan."

Tom laughed. "Dylan is so not into Cynthia."

"No one is into Cynthia," Alex said. "She's too angry and mean."

"And rude," Ethan said.

"And way too full of herself," Rob said.

"She's your family though," I said as we kept walking.

"Yes, but like family, there are some you like and some you'd like to punch," Emma said.

The group laughed, and I whispered, "I hope I don't end up being the second one to more than Cynthia."

Amy and Lisa squeezed my arms and Amy said, "Trust me, you're not."

Dylan and Cynthia passed us in the SUV and Cynthia glared at me as they drove by. "It's not even my fault. She's the one who started it," I said defensively.

"Well, don't worry. She won't be coming with us to San Diego," Rob said from behind me.

"Would she have normally gone?" I asked.

"No," the group said in unison and then started laughing.

We made it back to the house and found the rest of the family around a campfire with marshmallows on sticks. "S'mores!" Emma yelled excitedly. "I love s'mores."

I tried to break away to go to the house, but Lisa and Amy kept their arms through mine and forced me to go to the large fire with them. Amy detached from me long enough to grab three sticks and put marshmallows on the ends of them. "Here," she said as she held out two, one for me and one for Lisa.

I took the stick and stood with the girls by the fire, letting my marshmallows get toasted and brown. Rob walked around and mingled with the rest of the family, looking incredibly happy.

I followed Amy to the table where the rest of the s'mores fixings were and finished making mine. I was about to put it in my mouth when Cynthia snatched it from my hand and took a bite. "Thanks."

That was crossing the line. I slapped the s'more out of her hand and glared at her. "What the hell is your problem?"

"Cynthia," Kelly said in her motherly tone. "What's going on?"

"Chloe made me a s'more and then when I took a bite, she slapped it out of my hand."

"You're a fat-mouthed liar," Amy said angrily. "You stole her s'more and took a bite. She didn't make it for you, and you know that. You've been giving her a hard time all night. Just back off already."

"Didn't Dylan just scold you?" Lisa asked.

"Shut it, Lisa," Cynthia said, glaring at her.

"Cynthia, you're out of line," Kelly said in a harsh tone.

"Why are you all taking her side?" she whined. "She's not one of us."

"She is one of us," Kelly said. "The sooner you learn that, the better."

Cynthia turned and pushed me in the chest, making me stumble backwards. "She's weak. She's too weak to be one of us."

Now I was pissed. She turned, completely ignoring me, and I punched her in the side of the face as hard as I could. She stumbled sideways, clutching her cheek. "I've had enough of your mouth," I said.

Lisa laughed. "That was awesome."

Cynthia turned and met my eyes with crazed ones. "You're going to pay for that."

"I'm not afraid of you, Cynthia," I told her honestly.

"You should be," she said in a creepy voice.

"Cynthia," Kelly said in the mom tone. "Go to the house, now."

"You'll find out real soon what it means to be scared," she started again.

Emma yelled, "Shut up!" and punched Cynthia in the head, knocking her out cold.

Several of the others cheered, including the adults and Amy and Lisa.

"Dylan, take her up to the house. She and I are going to have a very long talk," Kelly said.

I hadn't even seen Dylan come up, but he stepped out from behind me to pick up Cynthia's unconscious body. Why wasn't Kelly upset that we were fighting? Why hadn't she stopped me or scolded me for punching Cynthia? What type of family was this? I really shouldn't have punched her and yet they weren't getting angry at me or telling me I was wrong. It was…weird, but awesome.

I really just wanted to go to my room, but Rob handed me another stick with a marshmallow. "That was a nice punch."

"Thanks," I said softly as I watched my marshmallow cook.

"Maybe you should keep your distance from her tomorrow," Adam suggested.

I nodded and handed him my stick. "Yeah." I headed to the garden and sat on the cool grass, watching the fish swimming lazily. The sun was almost gone and my day had been half good and half bad.

"I thought you weren't going to hide anymore?" Dylan

asked as he sat down on the other side of the pond.

"I need a new hiding spot," I mumbled. "I'm not really having a good day."

"I'm sorry she was so mean. She's never been very nice, but I didn't think she'd attack you like that."

"Whatever. It's not your fault," I said as I stood. "I'm going to go to bed."

"It's seven o'clock," he said with a frown.

"Good night," I said as I walked past him towards the house.

"Chloe," he whispered, "did you at least have a little fun today?"

"Yes," I answered. "I did. At least until she accused me of trying to take you from her and was under the false impression that you liked me."

"What?" he asked, his eyes widened and his mouth dropped open a tad.

"I told her you weren't interested in me, but she didn't believe me for some reason."

"Wait, what?"

"Night, Dylan," I said and walked away from his baffled face. Boys were confusing, but it was obvious Dylan wasn't interested in dating me. Hopefully, tomorrow would be better and tomorrow night on my date with Rob would be three times better. I just had to figure out my outfit.

I walked into the house and listened, but didn't hear Kelly or Cynthia so I hurried up to my room and grabbed a towel before heading to the shower. I could hear the family outside laughing and talking around the campfire. I did want to go back out there, but now I was too embarrassed and honestly, I felt exhausted. I showered quickly and then climbed into my bed, dreaming of brownies and rainbow sprinkles.

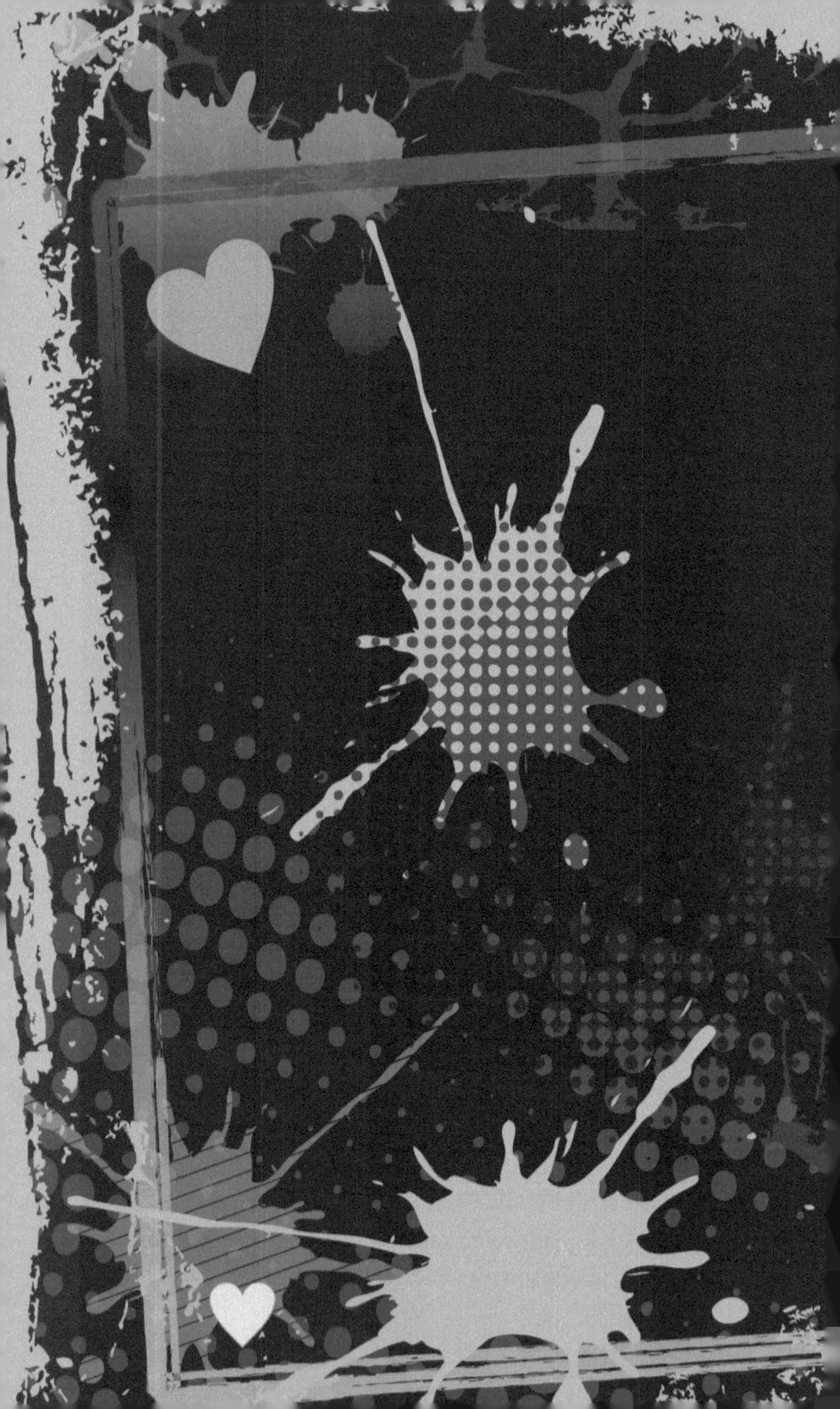

I spent the next day inside, and the family left me alone. Even more people showed up for the reunion so I was actually glad I wasn't being forced to be outside. At lunch, Adam made burgers again, but I didn't want another incident so I made myself a sandwich and ate it in the kitchen. As I was putting the dishes in the sink Adam walked in and frowned at me. "Did you not like my burgers yesterday?" he asked.

"Your burgers were great," I told him.

"Oh, so you're hiding?" he asked.

"No, I'm just refraining from engaging in family activities."

He smiled. "You're hiding."

I sighed. "Yes."

"You have no reason to hide. You stood up for yourself and actually were very brave. Cynthia is the only one who should be hiding. She made a complete ass of herself."

"Yes, but she picked on me in front of everyone," I whispered.

"And you stood up for yourself. You have no reason at all to be embarrassed."

"Thanks, but I still can't go outside."

He shrugged. "I'm not going to force you. I'm just telling you that we all think you're awesome. Not everyone would have stood up for themselves like you did."

I watched him leave and wondered if he was right. Did everyone think I was strong for standing up for myself? Or was he in the minority? I went back up to my room and opened the book I'd started re-reading. I was so engrossed in the story that I lost track of time. When I finally looked at the clock again, it was only three minutes until Rob and I were supposed to leave for dinner. I ran into the bathroom and went to work on my hair and makeup, hoping he wouldn't be mad if I was a little bit late. I finished in record time and ran to my room to change.

I was just adjusting my outfit when he knocked on the door. I opened it and stared in shock at Dylan, not Rob. "Oh. Hi, Dylan."

"Hi, um, you look nice," he said as he scanned my outfit.

"Thanks," I said as I fidgeted with the dress. "Did you need something?"

"I just came to check on you," he said as he continued to stare at me.

"There you are," Rob said with a wide smile. "Are you ready?"

I nodded and then turned back to Dylan. "Did you need something else?"

He shook his head. "No."

"Don't wait up for us," Rob said to Dylan as he followed me down the stairs.

I felt bad leaving Dylan like that when he'd come up to check on me, but there wasn't really anything I could do. Plus, there was no reason for me to apologize for going on a date with a guy that actually wanted to date me.

"Where are we going to eat?" I asked Rob as we walked outside.

"There's a really great steak house about thirty minutes from here that I thought you'd enjoy," he said as he stopped beside a red Ferrari.

"This is your car?" I asked him.

"One of my cars, yes," he said with a smile, opening the passenger door.

"One of? You have more than one?" I asked as I sat down.

He shut my door and walked around the driver's side. "Yes, I own four vehicles."

"Wow," I said, seriously impressed. He started driving and the sound of the car was even more impressive. "Do you have a favorite?" I asked him.

"This is my favorite," he said. "What about you? What car are you planning on getting?"

I laughed. "I won't be getting a car. Dad's job isn't exactly very lucrative. Don't get me wrong. I don't mind, but it means I won't be getting a car when I get my license."

"Well, if you could have a car, what would you get?"

I hadn't really thought about it. "I don't know honestly. Maybe an older Mustang or Camaro. Or an import that gets really good gas mileage."

"That's very practical of you," he said with a laugh. "But I'm asking if you could get any car, what would you get?"

"I'm not much of a car person. Something fast, cool sounding, and pretty. Something that guys would drool over," I said with a smile.

"Nice."

"So, how often do you get to visit with Kelly and the family?" I asked. It was actually a very important question since I needed to know if there was a chance at this relationship going anywhere.

"The past few years I haven't been able to come as often as I'd like. I've only been able to come twice a year, but now that my publicity tour is over, I'll be able to come up at least once a month."

"Oh, that's good," I said as I thought about his answer. Once a month. Could you have a relationship when you only saw each other once a month?

"What's your favorite type of music?" he asked.

I smiled. "I bet you can't guess."

"A challenge?" he asked. "I accept." He glanced at me then said, "Hm, I think most people would assume you're a rock girl, but that's too stereotypical. Country would be their next guess, but I don think you're into that either."

I refrained from laughing as he tried to deduce what I liked.

"You're obviously a non-conformer and don't follow trends so you aren't a punk lover or a hip-hop fan. Hm."

We drove a few minutes in silence and I asked, "Do you give up?"

He shook his head. "No, I'm just working out the final choices."

"Okay," I said, "but you have three more minutes."

He drove silently those three minutes and then said, "Blues."

My mouth dropped open. "How'd you figure it out?"

He smiled victoriously. "I told you I'm good at reading people."

"Wow. Okay, what's your favorite?" I asked him.

"Bet you can't guess," he said with a sneaky smile.

I turned and stared at the profile of his face and then said, "Techno."

He laughed. "Who told you?"

I shook my head. "No one. I can just sense that you're a techno lover."

"Really?" he asked.

I nodded. "Yep."

"That's impressive."

"I try," I said and then laughed.

We finally exited the forests and entered a small-town teeming with people. Rob parked in front of a large, brick building and shut off the engine. "Here we are." He climbed out of the car and then walked around to open the door for me.

"Thank you," I said after he shut the door and locked the car.

He smiled. "You didn't think a skater would have manners, did you?"

I smiled in embarrassment. "Well, I have to admit that you've definitely made me see that you can't judge a book by its cover."

"Likewise," he said before kissing me on the cheek. "You look beautiful in that dress."

I smiled. "Thank you."

He opened the door for me and waited as I walked inside. The hostess sat us immediately and a busboy brought us water and bread. I looked over the menu, deciding on the prime rib and then set it down.

"So, why don't you have a girlfriend?" I asked.

Rob set his menu down and sighed. "That's a complicated story, but basically I haven't found the right girl for me. Plus, I was traveling so much that it was impossible."

"Are you going to live with Kelly again?" I asked.

He shook his head. "No, I have a house just on the other side of the forest from hers. It'll be nice to finally get back to it."

"Are you ready to order?" our waiter asked.

We placed our orders then Rob asked, "Why don't you have a boyfriend?"

"Well, I did have one, but he turned out to be a douche so I dumped him and then I found out we were moving so I didn't get another one. Plus, there aren't many good choices."

"No guys at school caught your eye?" he asked.

One, but I couldn't tell him that. "No," I said. "None of the guys at school."

"Well, that's lucky for me," he said with a smile.

"Why me?" I asked him. "The sales guy at the skate shop said you never flirt with girls."

Rob studied me a moment then said, "Well, you're beautiful and I could just sense that you were a good match for me. Don't ask me to explain it because I can't even explain it to myself."

His answer really shocked me and made me want to get to know him even better. "So, how come none of the girls in the family caught your eye?"

"Some caught my eye, but they weren't a good match."

"I bet Amy caught your eye," I said with a teasing smile.

He shrugged. "She catches everyone's eye, but she's taken."

"What?" I asked in shock. "By who?"

He smiled. "You don't know?" I shook my head and he laughed. "Well, I'm not going to spoil it. You'll have to ask the girls who they are paired up with."

"Here's your salad, miss," the waiter said as he set a salad on the table in front of me.

"It's cruel to make me wait," I told Rob as I took a bite out of the salad.

He shrugged. "I can't ruin it for you. The girls love the shocked look on people's faces."

"Now I want to know even more," I said.

"So, what type of books do you read?" he asked as he snatched a crouton off my plate.

"I read a little of everything, but I love fantasy stories."

"Like vampires?" he asked with a teasing smile.

I shrugged. "I have read some of those, but I prefer fairies and witches."

"Really?" he asked. "Why not vampires?"

"There are just too many vampire stories out there. I still read some, but I try to avoid the mass hysteria over a specific series. Usually, I end up disappointed." Plus, I'd had a run in or two with vampires, but I wasn't going to admit that to anyone. That was a secret between me and the friend I'd experienced it with.

"Do you have any other hobbies?"

"I like hiking and camping. What about you? Do you have any hobbies besides skateboarding?"

"The usual, cars, the outdoors, and sports."

The waiter came and took my empty salad plate and refilled our waters. "I'm sorry about yesterday," I said finally. I'd wanted to apologize to him yesterday but I'd been too embarrassed.

"Sorry about what?" he asked.

"About leaving the ice cream shop after you were so nice and took me with everyone. I don't usually act like that, but I've never had someone despise me so much when they don't even know me."

"And it didn't help that you were still trying to find your

place within the family," he said with a serious expression. "You have no reason to apologize to me. Cynthia is the one who should apologize." He reached under the table and set his hand on my knee. "You can always come to me and talk to me about your problems."

"Thank you," I said as I enjoyed the warmth of his hand on my leg.

Our food arrived, and he sadly pulled his hand away. The food was delicious and filled me up.

"How was it?" he asked as we headed outside.

"It was great. I've never had such tender meat before. It just melted in my mouth."

"I'm glad you enjoyed it. Are you ready for our next adventure?" he asked with a cute grin.

"Of course," I said with a smile. He pushed open the door and the cool night air blew over me, making me shiver. "I should have brought a coat," I said as I wrapped my arms around myself.

Rob draped his left arm across my shoulders and rubbed my left arm with his hand. "I have a sweater in the car you can put on."

He was incredibly warm, and I moved closer to him to steal more. "You're so warm," I said through chattering teeth.

"You're very cold," he said as he rubbed my arm faster. "Let's get in the car so I can crank up the heat."

"T-t-thanks."

We climbed in the car and he started it, turning the heat on full blast. I shivered for a minute until the car warmed up and then sighed in contentment. "Better?" he asked.

I nodded. "Yes, thank you. You can turn it off now."

He turned it off and wiped his head. "Thanks, I can't stand the heat much." He turned sideways and reached behind me, putting his face really close to me. He inhaled and said, "You smell good."

"Thanks," I said as I restrained myself from trying to kiss him. "So, what are we doing now?"

He leaned back, pulling a sweater from behind the seat and set it on my lap. "Now I'm going to take you to my favorite spot in Smith's Peak. Buckle up."

I put the sweater on first and then buckled my belt. "How long did you live with Kelly?" I asked him.

"For as long as I can remember. My parents abandoned me on Kelly's doorstep when I was a baby, and she took me in."

"Wow, I'm sorry," I whispered.

He turned and smiled at me. "Don't be. I love being part of Kelly's family."

He drove out onto the street and headed past the town we'd been in and deeper into the forest. No lights or houses were visible, yet I felt like someone was watching us. I'd never been a chicken about the dark before, so I wasn't sure why I had the bad feelings that I did, but I kept my eyes peeled in case anything was out there.

Rob pulled off onto a small gravel road that I hadn't even seen as we were driving and parked his car. "There are a lot of deer out here and I'd prefer not to scare them away so we'll have to walk the rest of the way. I'll get your shoes for you."

He climbed out of the car and around to the trunk then handed me the box with the shoes he'd gotten specifically for me. "They're great," I said as I slipped off my heels and put on the sneakers.

"I'm glad you like them," he said with a smile. I stood and wrapped the sweater tighter around myself before shutting the car door and following him down the road. "No talking until we get there, okay? And only whispering beyond that."

I nodded in understanding and together we walked into the dark, silent forest towards something unknown. My heart was beating a little faster than normal in anticipation, but I trusted Rob. I could barely see where we were going so I had to walk carefully to avoid tripping and embarrassing myself. We started climbing up a hill, which was even more difficult in the dark.

Rob walked beside me with his hand on my lower back to help me up. "We're almost there," he whispered softly into my ear.

I shivered at the touch of his warm breath and stayed silent as we continued up the hill. Hiking in the dark was definitely a new experience for me. If only I had a flashlight this would be a lot easier. We finally made it to the top of the hill, and Rob motioned for me to lay down on my stomach. I wasn't sure why he wanted me to and I really didn't want to get the dress dirty, but I also wanted to see what he brought me here for. He laid down on his stomach, scooting close to the edge of the hill, and I followed his example, thankful I was wearing his sweater.

I was about to ask what we were looking for when I saw them. Wolves, about fifty of them, ran around down below in the valley playing. I'd never seen wolves in person before and especially never seen so many playing together. It was incredible and awesome, and I was extremely grateful for Rob bringing me here.

He leaned close to me and whispered, "I like to come watch them sometimes and I thought you might enjoy seeing them."

I nodded and continued watching as the group played together. "They're beautiful," I whispered.

"Not nearly as beautiful as you," Rob whispered from right

beside me. I turned to look at him, and he kissed my lips softly. "You're the first person I've ever shown this to."

"Thank you for showing me," I whispered and then kissed him back.

He was so warm and so gentle that it drove me mad. I wrapped my arms around his neck and pulled him closer to me as we kissed. He tasted different from any other guy I'd ever kissed and that only excited me more. He rolled on top of me and kissed my lips then my jaw and then my neck. I ran my hands through his hair and then ran them down his back where I could feel his taut muscles through his shirt.

Is this what it would be like to kiss Dylan?

"What's wrong?" Rob asked as he leaned back to look at my face.

I hadn't realized I'd dropped my hands from him until he'd leaned back. I smiled and leaned up to kiss his lips. "Nothing."

"I'm moving too fast for you, aren't I?" he asked.

"Maybe a little," I said as he sat back and helped me sit up.

"I'm sorry. You should have just said something. I don't want to make you uncomfortable."

"It's okay, really," I said as I wrapped my arms around myself. With him away from me it was really cold up on the hill. I turned around and looked back at the wolves. Most were still playing, but one was standing completely still in the middle of the others, looking right up at me. For some reason I felt embarrassed that the wolf had witnessed me kissing Rob. Why on earth would I feel that?

Rob turned my face back towards his and leaned in to kiss me again. "Wait," I said softly. "Shouldn't we leave now that the wolf has seen us?"

He looked down at the wolf and whispered, "Oops."

I turned back, and the wolf was still staring at us. What was he doing?

"Time to go," Rob said softly as he tugged on my hand.

I let him lead me back to the car in silence. As we started back towards home I said, "Thank you for taking me to see the wolves. It was really cool."

"You're welcome."

"It was weird how that wolf was looking up at us," I commented.

Rob shrugged and then a devious smile crossed his lips. "He probably just heard us and was trying to see what was happening."

We stopped at Kelly's house and all of the lights were off. It was only ten o'clock so people should have still been up.

"Where is everyone?" I asked Rob.

He shrugged. "I don't know. Do you want me to stay with you until they come home?"

Part of me wanted to say yes, but I shook my head and smiled. "Thanks, but I'm tired and I think I'll just go to bed."

He leaned across and kissed my cheek softly. "I had a great time tonight."

"Me, too," I said as I started to take off his sweater.

"No, you keep it. It looks better on you anyways," he said with a cute smile.

"Okay. Thanks again for the shoes."

"You're welcome. I'll see you Friday, right?"

I looked at him. "Friday?"

"Yeah, everyone's coming to San Diego, remember?"

I'd forgotten about it actually. "Oh, do you want me to come?"

He laughed. "Of course I do. Will you please come?" he stuck out his bottom lip in a pout, which made me laugh.

"Alright, I'll come."

"Great!" he said, his pout replaced by a wide smile.

I climbed out of the car with my heels in hand and smiled at him. "Good night, Rob."

"Good night, Chloe."

I turned around before I did something dumb and walked up to the house. The door was unlocked so I walked in and called out, "Anyone home?" No one answered me so I went up to my room and changed into pajamas. I loved pajamas and bare feet more than anything. The house was incredibly empty feeling, which was a nice change from the crowded feeling I usually felt when inside.

I walked to the kitchen and took out all the ingredients for cookies. Baking chocolate chip cookies always helped me think clearly. I measured out the flour and poured it into the bowl and then quickly went through the other ingredients, having them memorized.

Tonight had been fun, but there just wasn't that super spark between Rob and me. Not like the one I felt for Dylan. Why couldn't Dylan like me? It would make things so much easier. It wasn't fair to Rob to compare him to Dylan, but when being honest with myself I really wanted Dylan. There had to be some way for me to change his mind. I didn't usually try to get a guy that didn't want me, but there was just something about Dylan, something mysterious and sexy.

"Have fun tonight?" Dylan asked from the doorway.

I screamed and dropped the egg I was holding. "Holy crap. You scared me," I said as my heart beat triple its normal speed. I grabbed a paper towel and mopped up the broken egg.

Dylan walked over to help. "I'm sorry. I assumed you heard me walk inside."

I shook my head. "No, I was thinking. When I think, I tune

everything else out." I looked up and met Dylan's eyes. "Where is everyone?"

He walked to the trash and put the napkin in it. "Everyone's out playing around. I figured you would be back by now and wanted to make sure you weren't alone."

"Thanks," I said as I went back to mixing the cookie dough. "But you could have stayed with everyone else. I'm okay by myself."

"You want me to go?" he asked, turning towards the door.

"No," I said a little too loudly. "I mean, I'm okay, but I'd rather have someone here."

He sat down on a barstool and watched me. "How was your date?"

I really didn't want to talk to him about this, but since he'd asked. "It was fun, but I don't know. I don't think Rob and I are a good match."

"Why not?" Dylan asked.

I set the spoon down and looked at him. "He's a great guy and any girl would be lucky to have him, but there's just not a strong enough connection between us."

"It was only your first date. Sometimes connections take longer to build," he said.

"It seems like you're pushing me towards Rob. Why?" I asked him as I finished up the cookie dough.

"I'm not pushing you to him," he said defensively.

I wanted to confront him about it, but I dropped it. He was probably just trying to ensure that I didn't try to come back to him. Maybe I did need to give Rob another chance. We had fun, and he was a great kisser. "So, are you excited about next weekend?" I asked to change the topic slightly.

"Of course. It's been too long since I've seen him compete."

"It sounds exciting. I've never been to a skating competition before. I can't wait to be there."

"You're going?" he asked with shock evident in his voice.

"Rob invited me to go," I said softly. "I don't have to if you don't want me to."

"Of course I want you to go," he said with a smile. "I just thought that you wouldn't want to since you just said that you and Rob aren't a good match."

I shrugged. "Maybe you're right. Maybe I just need to give him another chance."

He stared at me with the weirdest look on his face and then looked towards the door just as it opened. I put the dough on the cookie sheet, in the oven, and then hopped up on top of the counter to wait.

"Hey, Chloe," Lisa said with a wide smile as she came in. "How was your date?"

"Good," I said with a smile back at her and then looked down at my hands because Dylan was watching me still.

"I'm going to bed," Dylan said a bit sharply as he stood up. "Don't stay up too late, Lisa. We have school tomorrow."

"Yes, Father," Lisa said sarcastically.

Dylan pointed at her and then walked out. Lisa hopped up on the counter next to me and leaned her head on my shoulder. "Not a great night?" she asked softly.

I sighed. "The date was okay. Rob's a great guy, but..."

"But you are into Dylan," Lisa said.

"Which isn't fair to Rob, especially since Dylan doesn't even like me."

"Chloe, I think—"

"I decided to give Rob another shot, though. I'm going to go with you guys next weekend and see how things go with him."

Lisa sighed and shook her head. "Boys are so complicated."

"As if girls aren't?" Tom asked as he walked in and leaned against the counter opposite of us. He looked at my face and the smirk he'd had disappeared. "You okay, Chloe?"

I rubbed my face with my hand and then smiled. "Yeah, I'm just tired. I should have waited until tomorrow to bake the cookies."

He didn't look convinced, but he said, "Lisa and I can finish them up if you want to go to bed."

"Will there be any cookies left?" I asked with a laugh and then hopped down. "Thanks, Tom, but I'll finish them."

"Is that cookies I smell?" Ethan asked as Amy and he came inside.

"Maybe," I said as I grabbed an oven mitt and walked to the oven.

"What's wrong?" Amy asked in a whisper as she came over to me.

"Same thing as usual," Lisa whispered to her.

"Lisa," I said with a groan.

"I'm sorry," Amy said. "You want to paint each other's nails and talk about it?"

I shouldn't have been surprised at the girls' camaraderie, but it made me extremely happy. "Thanks, Amy, but after I make these, I think I'm just going to go to bed." I pulled out the cookie sheet and everyone in the room inhaled loudly. It took two minutes to get the cookies off the sheet and onto a cooling rack and then put more dough on the sheet and back into the oven.

"I don't want to go to school tomorrow," Lisa pouted.

"Me neither," I said with a sigh.

"You think the Kurtis girls will try to fight you again?" Emma asked as she walked inside the kitchen with Alex.

"I don't know," I said honestly, "but if they do, I'll handle it."

"You're such a tough ass," Cynthia said sarcastically as she walked in the kitchen.

I ignored her and took some raw dough from the bowl and nibbled at it.

"What's up, Cynthia?" Alex asked calmly.

"On my way out and wanted to say bye," she said as she started to walk towards me.

"Bye," Amy said as she stepped in front of her. "It was *so* great to see you again."

"Bye, Chloe. It was great meeting you," Cynthia said as she turned away.

"Same to you Cynthia," I said with a bright smile.

She glared at me once and then walked out of the house. I leaned against the counter and closed my eyes. This was turning out to be a very strange weekend.

"So, what did you do on your date?" Tom asked as he ate one of the cookies from the cooling rack.

I didn't really want to talk about it, but everyone was trying really hard to be friendly. "He took me out to dinner and then took me to this place way off the road that overlooks a valley." I wasn't sure if he wanted me to tell them about the wolves, but I didn't think it would hurt.

"A valley?" Emma asked.

"Yes. There was a really large pack of wolves playing together down in the valley. It was really awesome."

Everyone gaped at me. "He took you to see the wolves?" Lisa asked softly. I nodded and she smiled. "Wow, he really must like you then. That's his super secret spot. None of us have ever been able to see it."

The shock on their faces felt like jealousy, but that didn't make sense because none of them were interested in him. I felt bad even though I hadn't done anything wrong. "Well, we didn't stay long. One of the wolves spotted us."

"Oh," Tom said with a slight smile.

"What?" I asked.

He shook his head. "Nothing. I think I'm going to head home. The cookies are great, Chloe. Try and save some for tomorrow."

"Okay," I said quizzically.

"We should all head home," Lisa said with a pout. "We'll see you in the morning, okay?" she said to me.

I nodded and watched all of them except Amy leave. She walked to me and patted my shoulder. "It is late. Maybe we should put the rest of the dough in the fridge and finish tomorrow?"

I looked at the clock and gasped. "Is it really eleven-thirty?"

Amy nodded and then yawned. "Yep."

"Okay, you're right. I'll just take these out of the oven. Can you put the dough in the fridge?"

Amy nodded, grabbed the bowl, and headed towards the fridge. "Do you want to talk about Dylan?" she asked softly as I pulled the cookie sheet out.

I shrugged. "Not much to talk about. He made it clear tonight that he would rather I set my affections toward Rob."

"What?" Amy asked, stopping mid-step.

"I told him that I didn't think Rob and I were a good match because there wasn't a serious spark between us and he told me that it was only our first date."

Amy sighed and shook her head. "Rob and he are like brothers. He's probably just trying to look out for him."

"Well, I'm going to give Rob another chance in San Diego.

I am attracted to him and if I push Dylan out of my head, I did have a great time with Rob."

Amy put the measuring cups and spoons in the sink and grabbed a cookie off the cooling rack. "That's smart," she said around her bites. We both headed up the stairs, and she said, "I'm really happy you're coming with us next weekend."

"Me too," I said with a happy smile. Even with the dumb boy issues, I was happier here and it was all thanks to Kelly's family making me welcome. That was really all I craved, to feel wanted.

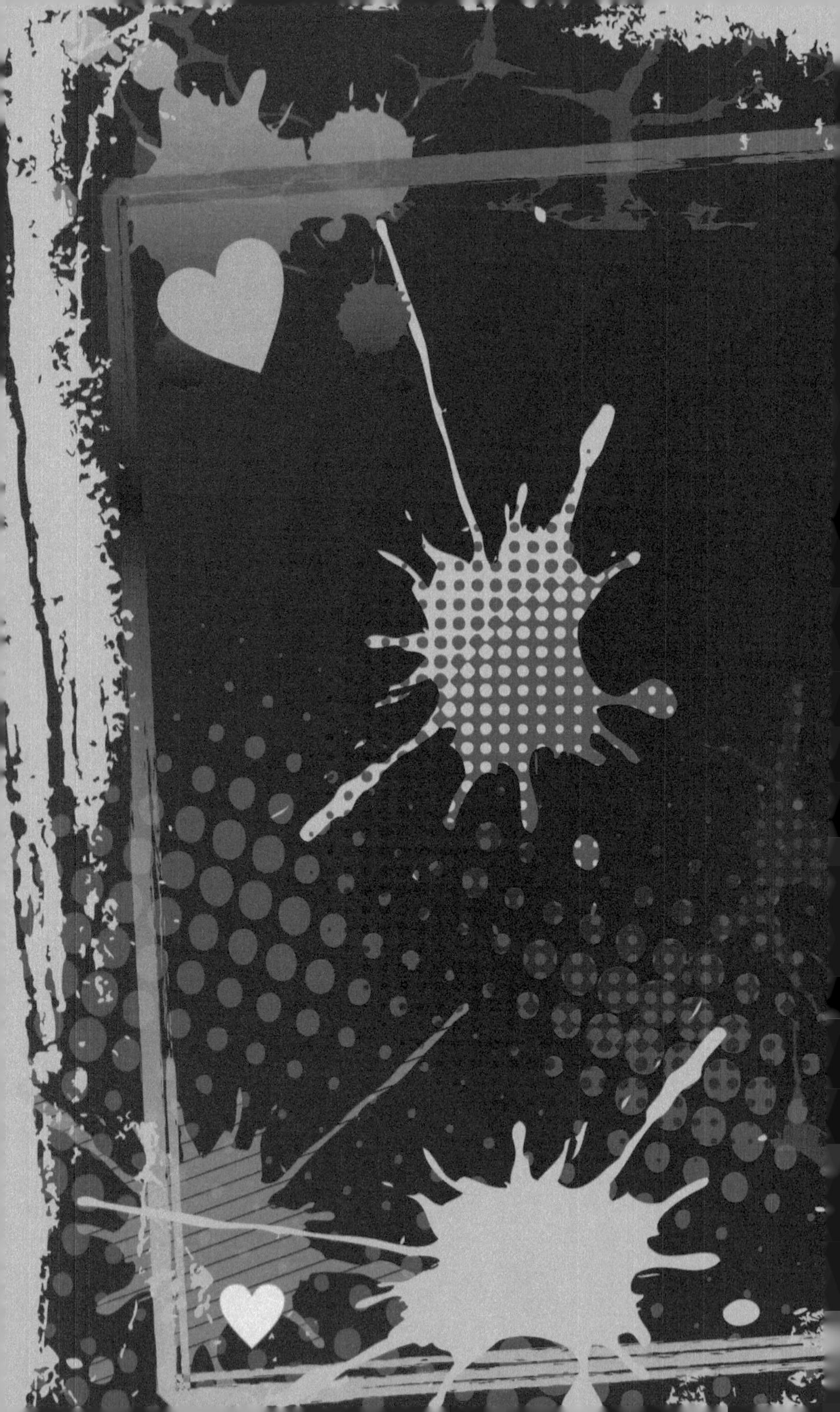

SEVEN

The next week was uneventful and boring in every way. Dylan was just as passive as ever, and we didn't talk unless it was necessary. At meals he sat with us, but kept silent and never looked at me. I'd been spending most of my time during and after school with Amy, Lisa, and Emma and really enjoying myself. They were each so different from me and the types of friends I usually made and yet we got along so well.

On Thursday after school, we decided to make a trip to the grocery store to pick up some more makeup and to start Lisa on wearing some before we left for San Diego the next day. Amy and Emma were walking in the front while Lisa and I walked behind them as we made our way down the side of the road towards town.

Kelly's place was close to town and it was a nice fall after-noon so we decided to walk. Plus, Dylan and a couple of the guys were on some mysterious trip and were using the Suburban so we couldn't drive even if we had wanted to.

I kicked an empty soda can at the back of Emma's heels,

which made Lisa laugh hysterically. Emma turned around and rolled her eyes at me, but I could see the sides of her mouth pulling up in a smile.

"So, who do you have a crush on, Amy?" I asked. I'd been dying to ask her that question since we'd started hanging out, but figured I should give it a few weeks before I pried.

Amy turned around to face me, walking backwards as she talked. "You don't know?"

I shrugged. "I don't really pay attention to who you girls are making googly eyes at when we are all hanging out."

Lisa giggled. "Amy likes Ethan."

I blinked at Lisa and then at Amy. "Ethan? Really?"

Amy nodded and sighed dreamily. "He's just so sweet and so strong. If you had ever seen him fight you would be making googly eyes at him, too."

Emma gasped. "I've got a great idea! Let's spar tonight. We haven't in a long time, and I know Chloe has been working in secret with her dad this week to face multiple opponents. Plus, then we can watch the guys spar, too."

"Who do you like Emma?" I asked, equally curious to find out who her crush was.

"I bet you couldn't guess." Emma said smiling at me.

"Tom," I said confidently.

They all laughed loudly, and Emma shook her head. "No way. Elliot's my guy. Oh, he's so cute with those glasses and fast fingers flying across the keyboard."

I shook my head in disbelief. "I've been wrong about every one of your crushes. Okay, Lisa. Who do you like?"

She blushed and looked down at her hands. "Tom."

My mouth dropped open. "Tom? Big, tattooed, Tom?"

Lisa giggled. "Yes. Oh, I love his tattoos. Have you seen

them all? He has one of a white wolf cub howling up at the moon on his shoulder and he says that it reminds him of me." Emma and Amy glanced at Lisa and then turned away. Lisa looked at the ground in embarrassment. "Well, I mean, he says it reminds him of me because I'm so small and cute."

"Well, we'd ask who you like, but it's pretty obvious," Emma said, a smile back on her face.

I looked at the ground as I walked, kicking rocks with the toe of my shoes. "Well, obviously he doesn't have any interest in me so that's a pretty moot point," I said sadly.

Amy, Lisa, and Emma shook their heads and sighed in unison.

"Why the creepy unison sighs?" I asked with my hands on my hips.

Amy said, "You have a lot to learn about Dylan."

"What does that mean?" I asked in frustration.

Emma shook her head. "Sorry, Chloe, that's one subject you're going to have to research on your own."

"Do you think things will work out between you and Rob?" Lisa asked softly.

I shrugged. "I don't know, but I'm going to try my hardest to push Dylan out of my head and focus on Rob fully to see if it could work or not. It'd be dumb for me to focus on a guy that isn't interested in me and give up a guy that is."

We started walking again and the discussion turned to deciding how the fighting would go tonight. Just the mention of seeing Dylan sparring with the other guys made me shiver in delight. I could still look and drool, right?

We finally made it to the store and headed straight to the makeup aisle. Lisa kept trying to pick neutral colors for her makeup, but Emma and I took all of the items she'd chosen and put them back on the shelves. I took out bright colors to accent her blue eyes while Emma got black eyeliner. She tried to argue with us, but when Amy suggested that Tom might like it, she stopped arguing.

I grabbed some more eyeshadow, mascara, and eyeliner to refill my supplies at home and then decided on a set of bright purple eyeshadows for fun.

After grabbing smoothies, we started back towards home. We sipped on our smoothies and swung our bags of new makeup items. I was finally happy and felt like I was truly home. The kids at school called Kelly's family freaks, but they were the nicest family I'd ever met. I was starting to be proud to be in their family.

Lisa kicked the same empty soda can at the back of my feet that I'd kicked at Emma, which made us all laugh, until we saw the car stopped in the road ahead of us.

I recognized the car instantly and sighed. "You guys go on home. I'll deal with this."

Ugly Kurtis and five other girls got out of the car and started to walk our way.

Emma asked. "You think you can handle six?"

I shrugged. "I guess I'll find out, but this isn't your fight." I set my smoothie and bag down and Lisa, Amy and Emma did the same. I frowned. "No. I don't want any of you to get hurt because of my big mouth."

Lisa stretched out her hamstrings and laughed. "You think we're going to let you have all the fun?"

Amy pulled her right leg up and stretched her quadriceps. Emma squatted down and then stretched out her arms.

Ugly Kurtis walked up to us with her ugly family and smiled. "Why if it isn't the freak girls out for a stroll? How convenient that we found you here."

I turned to Amy, Lisa, and Emma and asked, "Are you guys sure about this?"

Lisa bounced up and down on the balls of her feet. "Are you kidding? I haven't had a fun challenge like this in a long time! Besides, we're family and family always sticks together, no matter the circumstances."

Emma and Amy nodded their agreement.

Lisa yelled, "Let's kick their butts!" She charged forward and slammed her small fist into the side of one of the girl's heads in the most graceful charge I'd ever seen. The girl stumbled backwards, first eyes wide and then a grimace of pain.

Amy moved almost too fast for me to track and had a girl on the ground and was punching her face multiple times. Emma grabbed the biggest girl and tossed her over her shoulder before spinning and kicking her in the chest and sending her flying down the road.

I'd never seen anything so incredible and so crazy. There was no way I was going to fight any of them!

Ugly Kurtis came at me, and I sidestepped her wild swing and punched her in the side of the face. She yowled and tried to backhand me. I dodged and punched her in the stomach, making her double over, and then kneed her in the face as hard as I could. Bones crunched and I felt warm liquid soak into my jeans.

I turned just in time to block a punch from another girl and punched her back in the face. Ugly Kurtis collapsed to the ground. I turned and kicked the girl attacking me in the stomach, making her lose her breath. She stood up and swung at me, hitting me on the cheek and opening a new cut. I cursed and doubled my attack, hitting her in the face and kicking her on the inside of her legs just to cause her pain. She dropped to her knees, and I roundhouse kicked her in the face, knocking her out.

Another girl punched me in the back of the head, making my eyesight waver and causing me to stumble forward. I turned to defend myself from her next attack, but the girl was lying on the ground a few feet away, and Lisa was holding her hand out to me. "You have to remember to watch your back."

I stood up and rubbed the back of my head. "Right." I looked around at the six unconscious girls lying randomly on the road and in the ditch and turned to my friends. "You've all been holding out on me. You never said you guys were crazy good fighters."

Amy shrugged. "You never asked us what our fighting capabilities were."

Emma and Amy checked all of the girls and moved the ones in the road to the ditch and then we grabbed our smoothies and bags, ready to head home.

The sound of a truck engine made us turn back towards the road, praying it wasn't the cops. Kelly's Suburban stopped, and Dylan, Ethan, and Tom climbed out.

Tom whistled. "Wow. Did anyone videotape it?"

Lisa laughed. "No. We were a little busy fighting."

Ethan approached Amy and inspected her split lip where a girl had hit her and caused her to bite it. "There were only six, one of you could have sat out and videotaped it for us."

Lisa skipped over to Tom and smiled. "So, what did you get me?"

Tom smiled coyly at her. "What makes you think I got you something?"

She moved closer to him and said, "Because whenever you go to Wolf Creek you get me something."

Tom wrapped his arms around her and said, "Well, you'll just have to wait until tonight to find out what I got you."

Lisa groaned and stepped out of his arms. "I hate waiting."

Dylan walked to each of the unconscious girls and double checked them before walking back to me. "You alright?"

"Yeah, I'm fine. Just a goose egg on the back of my head and a cut on my cheek. The girls here did most of the work though."

Emma shook her head. "No, we each took two. Lisa was toying with one of hers though so her second one got around her just long enough to knock you in the back of the head."

I groaned. "Yeah, I know I have to watch my back. My dad's always telling me that."

Dylan reached forward and probed my head for the bump. I hissed in pain when he hit it and his warm hand rested on the back of my head a moment. "There's no blood, but we should have Doc check you to make sure you didn't get a concussion."

In the movies this would have been the time that the main girl made a witty comment and the two shared a laugh. But I wasn't witty and all I could do was focus on the feel of his hand on my head and his body so near mine.

Dylan stepped back from me as though he just realized who he was touching and dropped his hand. He turned to the others and said, "Let's get home before the sherriff happens to drive by or the girls start waking up."

I stepped back farther away from him and turned so he wouldn't see the tears forming in my eyes. I headed down the road, and Dylan called out to me to come back, but I ignored him.

Emma caught up to me and opened her mouth, but by

then tears had already started down my cheeks, so she just put her arm around my shoulders and walked in silence with me.

I shrugged off Emma's arm and then smiled at her. "Thanks."

She smiled back at me. "You're welcome."

We made it back to the house, and the Suburban still hadn't shown up. Adam and Kelly gasped at the sight of our faces.

Adam asked, "How many were there this time?"

"Six," I answered as I tossed my empty smoothie cup in the trash.

"Where are Lisa and Amy?" Kelly asked.

"The guys happened by after we'd finished so they gave them a ride back. Chloe and I felt like walking instead of driving though," Emma said.

Kelly looked like she didn't believe us, but then she just shrugged her shoulders. She was the weirdest "mom" I had ever met, but I really liked her for it.

"I'm going to take a shower," I told Emma before walking upstairs and into the bathroom. I stripped and groaned at the blood on the knee of my pants. I hoped Kelly had something to get the stain out because they were my favorite pair of pants. I turned the shower on and stood under the hot water, letting it relax my muscles. I hissed in pain again as the water run over the bump on the back of my head.

The water wasn't nearly as warm as Dylan's hand had been. I dropped to the ground in the shower and cried. No matter how hard I tried not to think about him, it was impossible since he was always around and the only one my mind focused on. Everything about him confused me though. One minute he acted like he cared and then the next he acted repulsed by me.

Amy said I had a lot to learn about him, but how could I learn anything if he kept pushing me away?

"Chloe? Are you alright?" Dad asked.

I sniffed and wiped my eyes and nose. "Yeah, just coming down from my adrenaline rush." I quickly washed my hair and then dried off. I hadn't brought clothes with me so I wrapped the towel tightly around my body and grabbed my dirty clothes before heading to my room.

I dropped the dirty clothes in my laundry basket and grabbed clean ones from my dresser. I walked down the stairs towards the kitchen, but at the sound of Dylan's angry voice, I stopped and listened.

"She needs to know!" Dylan said angrily. "It's not safe for her to be kept in the dark."

"He's right, Kelly. We're in the middle of a war and she can't protect herself if she doesn't know what she is up against," Dad said.

Kelly sighed. "I know. I was just trying to give her time to get to know everyone before we told her. It's not going to be an easy thing for her to deal with."

"You think I don't know that?" Dad asked, sounding angry himself. "I'm well aware of the feelings and thoughts she's going to have once she finds out."

"I don't like hiding things from her," Dylan said. "It's hard enough to be near her. I can't even act like myself because until she knows what I am, she won't understand why I act that way. I don't want to jeopardize her safety. You made me leader of the teens for a reason. I'm telling you that we need to tell her. Please." Dylan stopped talking a moment and then whispered, "Please, Kelly. For me."

Kelly sighed. "Fine, we'll show her soon, but not until after the San Diego trip."

I backed up slowly and silently until I was at the stairs and then clomped down a couple of the steps before walking into the kitchen. Everyone looked at me and I asked, "What?"

"How's your head?" Dad asked with a smirk on his face.

I groaned. "I know. I know. Always pay attention to your blind spots."

Dylan turned to walk away and I said, "The girls and I were thinking about having some fights tonight. None of us got seriously hurt in the fight today and I obviously need to learn a few more things."

Dylan nodded. "Yeah, that sounds like fun."

I turned to my dad. "Do I get to watch you fight for once?"

Dad laughed. "Sure, kid. I'm sure one of the guys will spar with me."

I walked to the fridge and grabbed a bottle of water.

"Oh, and Doc's on his way here to check on you," Dylan said.

I groaned. "I don't need a doctor. I'm fine."

Dad shrugged. "Dylan's right that it never hurts to be sure."

Thirty minutes later I'd finished making the cookies and was sitting on a bar stool while a tall man with hands as large as my head probed my lump. "Well, the lump isn't very big and…" he flashed his penlight in my eyes. "She doesn't have a concussion, so I think she's fine."

Dylan had been leaning against the wall with his arms crossed, but once he heard the doctor's prognosis he walked out of the room. Doc patted my hand and smiled.

Lisa waved at me from the back door. "Thanks, Doc." I left the kitchen and followed her out the door. "What's up?" I asked.

She leaned close to me and whispered, "Dylan's in the garden. I thought you'd like to know."

I folded my arms over my chest. "Why should I care?"

She smiled. "Go talk to him."

I exhaled and nodded. "Alright, but if this goes bad, I get to punch you once on the shoulder."

She laughed. "Deal."

I took a deep breath and walked out into the garden to the koi pond where I guessed he would be. "Hi," I said when I saw him sitting beside the pond, feeding the fish.

He looked up and then back down at the fish. "Hey."

I sat on the bench and watched the fish snapping up the pieces of food. I could play silent if that's what he wanted.

"Who are you going to spar with tonight?" he asked me without looking up.

I shrugged. "I don't know. I'm obviously outmatched by everyone, including Lisa, so I don't know. Maybe I'll just watch."

"I think you and Lisa would be a good match."

"Who are you going to spar with?" I asked.

He smiled. "Tom. We have an ongoing rivalry."

"Really? I figured you and Elliot would be a better match."

Dylan's head shot up and he looked at me liked I'd called him a dirty word. "Me against *Elliott*!"

I laughed. "I was just joking."

Dylan smiled and stood up. He walked over and sat down beside me on the bench. "So, how much of the conversation between me, Kelly, and your dad did you hear?"

I looked at my hands. "I don't know what you're talking about."

Dylan laughed. "Come on. How much?"

I shrugged. "Not much. Just that you're all hiding something from me and I'm going to find out after the trip."

"Are you scared?"

I looked up at him and asked, "Should I be?"

He leaned towards me, staring in my eyes and asked, "Do I frighten you?"

I swallowed the lump in my throat. "If you mean, am I scared that you'll hurt me physically, then no." I was terrified that my already hurt emotions were going to get worse.

He leaned closer and inhaled loudly. "You used my shampoo."

I blushed and turned my head to the side, away from him. "I didn't have any. I'm sorry. I didn't know it was yours. I'll buy some tomorrow."

"I'm not mad. I like the smell on you," he said in a deeper than normal voice.

I turned back to face him which put our noses centimeters apart. "I like it more now."

He rubbed the tips of our noses together softly and then jumped up and away from me. "I'm sorry. I…I didn't mean…"

"Why do you do that?" I asked, my hands fisting.

He froze as he looked at me, eyes wide. "What?"

I stood up, my fists at my sides. "Why do you get close to me and then jump away and act like you're horrified that you touched me? If I repulse you so much, then why do you touch me in the first place?"

"Chloe, it's not…"

"I'm tired of your stupid games, Dylan. If you don't like me then just tell me. Just tell me you think I'm ugly and disgusting and I'll leave you alone."

Dylan blinked at me, but said nothing.

"Whatever. Give me the silent treatment again. I'm used to it by now." I stormed away and slammed the door shut behind me as I walked into the house. I walked into the kitchen and found Lisa, Tom, Ethan, Amy, Kelly, and my dad snacking on the cookies. I was on the verge of tears, but I refused to cry yet. I walked up to Lisa, punched her on the arm and then walked up to my room. I slammed my door and collapsed on the bed, but the tears disappeared and all I was left with was a throbbing headache. I rolled onto my side, pulled the blankets up, and went to sleep.

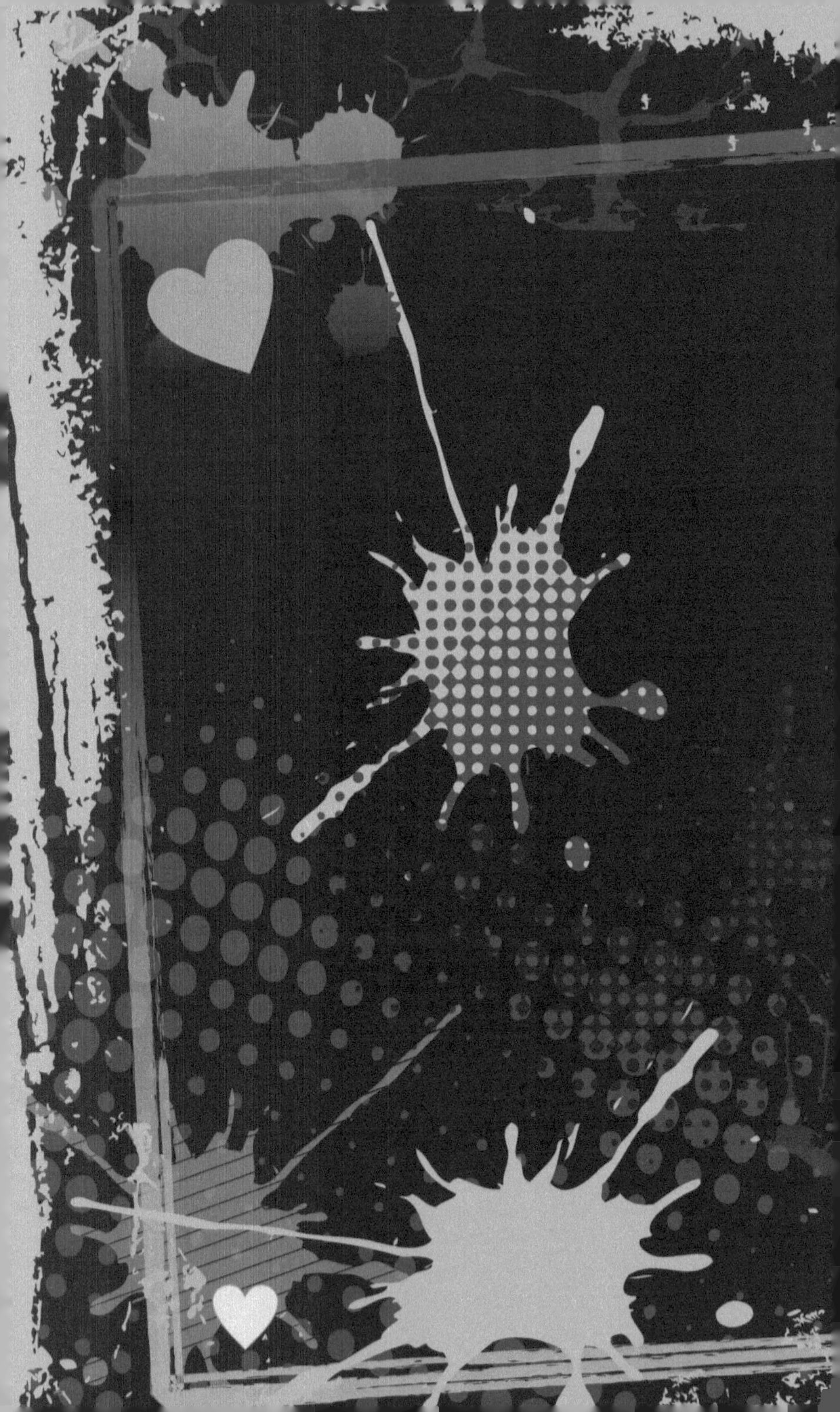

EIGHT

"Chloe, wake up. It's time for dinner."

"I'm not eating," I grumbled.

"You have to eat otherwise you won't get to spar with us."

"I'm not doing that either," I said as I rolled over and pulled the blankets up.

My blankets were ripped away faster than I could grab them.

"Get out of bed right now. You are not going to snivel up here all night."

"I'm not sniveling—I'm sleeping," I said, finally figuring out that it was Amy talking to me.

Amy put her hands on her hips and arched one of her perfect eyebrows. "Wash your face, put some makeup and some loose-fitting clothes on and let's eat so I can kick your butt." I stared at her for a moment and then she said, "That's not a request. Let's go."

I groaned and did as she asked. She did my makeup for me, saying I had no taste in color even though I thought I'd done a good job. We walked down the stairs, arms linked and into the dining room where everyone was already gathered. Amy nudged Emma who waved her hands so everyone moved over and I could sit between the girls. Dylan was looking at me, but I made sure to avoid looking at him. I needed to be done with him.

We ate dinner in silence and then Kelly said, "Alright, the girls thought it'd be a good idea to have some sparring and I agree. Everyone meet in the gym in ten minutes."

I followed Lisa and Amy, not knowing where the gym was. To my surprise we walked outside and to the large barn, but instead of dirt and hay, the floor was completely lined with mats. They had their own personal dojo!

"Chloe, you want to work on multiple opponents?" Lisa asked.

I shrugged and started stretching with them. The guys and all of the grown ups filed into the barn and started stretching too. It was weird how everyone just showed up from wherever they lived within minutes to the house. Did everyone just live super close?

I nodded at Lisa, and we faced each other. Emma and Amy stood on opposite sides so that we formed a square. I took a deep breath and then nodded again. Lisa ran forward and kicked out at me. I jumped over her leg and tried to punch her, but she'd already moved and was behind me. I dropped down and rolled to the left, but that put me right next to Amy. She punched down at me, but I rolled again, and she punched the mat. I got to my feet just in time to block a punch from Emma. I heard Lisa running at me so I ducked down and swiped her legs out from under her and then Amy punched me in the face.

Emma's hand whizzed by my face as she tried to punch me while I was off balance. I grabbed her wrist and twisted as hard as I could. She yelled in pain, but I couldn't take advantage of the situation because both Amy and Lisa were attacking me at once. I pulled Emma forward by her wrist and then spun around her to jump on her back. I got her in a headlock and held on as tightly as I could. Amy tried to punch me in my side, but I kicked out with my leg and knocked her a few feet away to land on her butt. Lisa jumped up, trying to climb onto me, but I used my elbow and caught her in the jaw. She fell onto her butt and growled.

Emma tried to pry my arms off, but I held on as tightly as I could. Amy and Lisa came at me at the same time, but I kicked both of my legs out, doing the splits, and caught them both in the chests. Emma dropped to the ground and tapped the mat twice. I released my hold on her and backed up to face off with Amy and Lisa who were both smiling. Never a good sign.

Amy and Lisa rushed me again, heading straight for me. I ducked down, but instead of colliding together, Amy vaulted up and over Lisa and landed, facing me. She punched me in the face, sidestepped, and kicked me in the back, knocking me flat on the mat. I tried to roll away, but Lisa sat on my back and wrapped her arm around my throat.

I tried to buck her off, but Amy sat on my lower body, completely immobilizing me. I tapped the mat twice and both jumped off of me.

"So not fair," I said when I regained my breath.

Lisa patted my back. "That's the point of the exercise, sometimes people fight unfairly. Like the Kurtis girls."

I reached up and prodded my tender face. "You could have been a little more gentle, Amy."

Amy shrugged. "I believe full force is the best way to practice. Your enemies won't go easy on you so neither will I."

Emma helped me stand up and smiled at me. "I'm impressed, Chloe."

I smiled back at her. "Thanks."

We moved off of the mat and Ethan and Elliot walked on to it. We sat down against the wall of the barn to relax, and Amy sighed. "I love this part."

To say Ethan and Elliot exceeded my expectations is putting it mildly. They were using moves I'd never seen before and moving faster than I thought possible. Ethan did look good when he was shirtless, covered in sweat and fighting, but the next fight is what really got my attention.

Dylan walked out to the middle of the mat and stretched his legs and arms.

Tom walked to Lisa and squatted down. "Kiss for good luck?"

Lisa said, "Beat him, and I'll give you that kiss."

Dylan laughed. "Looks like you're not getting a kiss tonight, Tom."

Tom rotated his neck around and smiled. "Tonight, is the night you're going down, Dill."

Dylan rolled his eyes. "You say that every time we spar and every time, I whip your butt."

Tom nodded and faced Dylan. "Yeah, but tonight's the first night that Chloe's watching you."

Dylan's head swiveled in my direction, and Tom launched himself at Dylan. I wanted to look away, to make Dylan think that I didn't care and wasn't watching his fight, but the truth was that I was mesmerized. Dylan and Tom flew at each other again and again and their fists made contact more times than I could count, but neither backed down. Dylan ripped his shirt off and my breath caught in my throat. He was hot. Model hot.

Amy leaned over to me and whispered, "Gorgeous, isn't he?"

I didn't know what to say to her and I was afraid if I opened my mouth drool would leak out, so I just nodded.

Dylan and Tom were tiring and their movements were slower, but the fight was just as intense. Their bodies were covered in sweat which made it impossible to wrestle. Tom punched Dylan in the nose, and the bone crunched. I gasped unintentionally, and Dylan looked over at me. He wiped the blood under his nose with the back of his hand and then turned to face Tom who was smiling victoriously. Tom never had a chance to block Dylan's punch. One moment Tom was smiling and the next he was on his back on the mat. Tom tapped the mat and clutched his now broken nose.

I almost yelled in excitement for Dylan winning, but caught control of myself at the last second and turned to find my dad. He caught me looking at him and nodded. He stepped out onto the mat and said, "Chloe requested to see me fight. Who wants to spar with me?"

A tall man called Samson stepped forward. "I'll spar with you."

Dad smiled. "Alright."

I looked around for Dylan, even though I shouldn't have been looking, but he and Tom were gone. Probably to tend to their busted noses. I relaxed against the wall and watched as Dad and Samson squared off. Samson was obviously the more physically equipped, but I wasn't sure how much fighting experience he had.

A blue bag of ice appeared in front of my face. "Here." I looked up and Dylan smiled at me. "For your face."

His nose looked completely fine, except for the cotton he'd shoved up inside of his nostrils. "Thanks," I said softly, pressing the ice to my face and turned back to watch my dad's fight.

Dylan sat down beside me and the heat from his body relaxed me. Why was he always so hot?

Dad nodded and the fight started. I'd always thought my dad was a great fighter, but Samson was amazing. My dad was better than I thought, and I couldn't believe my eyes as I watched him using various martial arts moves he'd never taught me.

"He's really good," Dylan said softly.

I turned to look at him. "Who?"

He smiled. "Your dad."

I turned back and ignored him to watch my dad, but the fight was over with Samson pinning Dad to the ground, and Dad tapping out.

Dad stood up and shook hands with Samson. "Great match, Sam."

Samson smiled. "You, too. You're getting better. I think the training with Marcus is helping."

I smiled at my dad and clapped my hands. "Good effort." He rolled his eyes at the line he always used for me when I lost.

A few others started fighting, but I couldn't watch them. I could only feel Dylan looking at me.

I turned and our eyes met. "What?" I asked with a frown.

"Why are you mad at me?" he asked.

My mouth dropped open and I gaped at him. I couldn't even form words. I stood up and walked out of the barn. How could he even ask me that?

The air outside felt incredibly cold, and I shivered as I walked from the barn to the house.

"Chloe," Dylan called as he ran up to me. "Wait."

"I need to get packed for tomorrow," I said without looking at him. "Thanks for the ice." I tossed the bag sideways to him, not bothering to look, and walked into the house. I knew I was being rude, but he had really pissed me off. Why was I mad at him? Ugh! As if he didn't know.

I grabbed three cookies before storming up to my room and slamming my door. My anger was beginning to simmer, but I didn't really care anymore. I grabbed a duffel bag and put clothes and necessities in it for the weekend trip to San Diego. I just had to get through one more day at school then we'd be on our way and I'd use Rob to distract me from Dylan. It was going to be pretty hard to ignore Dylan since he was going to be there too, but I had hope. Hope that I could stop this ridiculous infatuation with a guy that didn't like me back.

Why couldn't I get him out of my head?

Someone knocked on my door and I repressed a sigh. "Who is it?"

"Emma."

"Come in," I said as I folded another shirt and put it in the bag.

She sat down on the bed and looked around my room. "We need to paint your room," she said with a frown. "It is way too boring."

"I agree completely," I said with a smile.

She stared into my eyes and asked, "What's up? Why'd you leave?"

"I don't want to talk about it," I said as I jammed a pair of socks into the bag.

"If you let things bottle up, you're going to explode."

I turned and studied her. She looked like a tough girl, one I would not want to meet in a dark alley, yet she was smart and kind and completely not like I'd thought she would be.

"He did that thing again where he touches me and then jerks away and looks horrified. So, I got mad at him and yelled and left and then in the barn he asked why I was mad at him. Hello! Maybe it was you treating me like I'm sour milk," I said and sounded much more hurt than I realized.

"I'm sure he didn't mean to hurt your feelings."

"I just wish he would tell me exactly how he feels and get it over with. I just want to know whether he thinks I'm disgusting or if he actually does like me. I mean if he thinks I'm disgusting then stop trying to be nice. I know we're supposed to be family or whatever now, but that doesn't mean he has to play nice. He could just ignore me like he does half the time."

"He isn't very good with girls he doesn't know," Emma said softly. "You just have to give him time to get to know you."

"How is he supposed to get to know me when he freaks out if he touches me?"

"He isn't like most guys, Chloe. He was raised in a family unlike any other and he has trust issues from his birth parents abandoning him. You really need to cut him some slack."

I sighed. "I'm trying, but I can't keep taking the rejection and pain he makes me feel when he does something nice and then acts disgusted that he did it."

"Life has been very different recently, and I'm sure he is just trying to figure it all out. I know he doesn't mean to hurt you. He'd never mean to do that."

"Well, he is," I said softly as I folded a pair of pants and put them in the bag. I was done packing so I zipped it up and tossed it next to the door. "What war is happening?"

"What do you mean?" Emma asked with wide eyes.

"My dad, Kelly, and him were talking and they mentioned something about a war and me not being safe."

Emma sighed. "Oh. Well, our family has this really long-term rivalry with another family. Basically, it's a family feud, like the Hatfields and McCoys."

"Oh," I said.

"Emma," Dylan called through the door. "Can I talk to you?"

"Thanks, Emma," I said as she stood to go.

She smiled. "Anytime."

I turned away from the door so I wouldn't see Dylan as Emma left to talk to Dylan and changed into pajamas. Hopefully tomorrow went by quickly and I could have fun for the weekend.

"THE DAY IS DRAGGING ON," I moaned quietly in second period. If it had been any other class besides Algebra, I probably wouldn't have cared, but math being dragged on slowly was torture. I set my head on my desk and sighed softly. Only a couple more classes after this and then freedom.

"Are we boring you, Chloe?" the teacher asked.

That was a totally trick question. If I answered honestly, I'd get in trouble. "My head hurts. Can I go to the nurse's?" I asked as I lifted my head slowly up.

"Go."

I grabbed my bag and hurried from the classroom. The weather was starting to get chillier, and I really needed to invest in a coat. I walked around the school yard, stopping at the soda machines where we usually ate lunch to sit down until the bell sounded. I closed my eyes and enjoyed the silent school.

My phone vibrated, and I pulled it from my pocket to find a text from Rob.

ROB: *Only a few more hours until I get to see you again.*

I REPLIED IMMEDIATELY.

ME: *I know! I'm looking forward to hanging out with you and everyone. Gotta go, teacher is watching me.*

I PUT my phone back and closed my eyes again.

"Hey," Dylan said softly from in front of me.

My eyes flew open, and I stared at him while trying to calm my racing heart. "Damn, you scared me again. I didn't hear you walk up."

He sat down and smiled. "Sorry. I guess I need to start stomping when I am coming near you."

I wanted to leave, but I did need to play nice. "It's okay."

"Are you excited?" he asked.

I nodded. "You?"

He laughed. "Of course I am. It's been a long time since I've been out of the house for a weekend and it's been even longer since I've been able to hang out with Rob."

"I'm sure you'll have a lot of fun," I said as I closed my eyes.

"You're still mad at me, aren't you?" he asked.

This was not a conversation I was ready to have. I stood up

and slung my backpack onto my shoulders. "I don't want to talk about it."

Dylan stood up and grabbed my arm. "Chloe, please talk to me."

"Yes, I'm upset, Dylan. You really hurt my feelings and upset me. I don't want to talk about it, though. Not now. I don't want to ruin our trip by talking about it. Let's just pretend it didn't happen and if you want to talk about it when we get back, we can talk about it then. Okay?"

He let go of my arm and sighed. "Okay."

Emma and Amy walked up to us with wide smiles. "You guys left class early too, huh?" Amy asked.

"Yeah, too excited," I said with a wide smile.

"Can't we leave now?" Emma asked Dylan. "It's only one more class period. Please."

Dylan smiled. "Sure. Go round up everyone else and meet in the parking lot." Amy and Emma trotted off, leaving me alone with Dylan again. "Chloe, I'm sorry I hurt you. I would never want to hurt you."

"Drop it," I said fiercely. "I told you we can talk Sunday night if you want, okay?"

"Okay."

I walked away from him, heading to the parking lot and tried not to get emotional. I hated being a girl sometimes. Dylan walked behind me, but thankfully wasn't trying to talk anymore about it. I leaned against the SUV and closed my eyes as I refocused on Rob. This weekend was about giving Rob another chance and I couldn't do that if I was thinking about Dylan.

"Sleepy?" Alex asked from beside me.

I opened one eye and looked at him. He never talked to me. "Yes. I couldn't sleep last night."

He smirked. "I never sleep at night."

"He sleeps in all of his classes and still somehow aces them," Tom said bitterly. "It's infuriating."

"Have you been using the word-a-day calendar I bought you?" Alex asked Tom.

Tom glared. "Maybe."

"Doors are open," Dylan said.

I pushed myself off the vehicle and turned to open the door, but Alex already had it open for me. "Ladies first."

"Well then by all means, go in," Tom said to Alex.

"Be nice, children," I said to them with a chuckle as I climbed inside.

"Nice is overrated," Tom said as he climbed in behind me.

"Sometimes that's true," I said with a laugh.

"What are we laughing about?" Emma asked as she and the rest of the gang climbed in.

"About how being nice is overrated," Tom said.

Lisa snuggled up against Tom. "You're always nice to me."

"That's because I like you. I'm not nice to people I don't like," he said as he put his arm around her shoulders.

I realized that I was in the center seat and messing up the couples being able to sit next to each other so I climbed out and said, "Emma sit up here by Alex," before walking around to the front passenger seat.

"You didn't have to do that," Emma whispered as she climbed in.

I buckled myself and closed my eyes. "Wake me up when we're at the airport."

"Yes, ma'am," Dylan said as he started the engine and turned on the radio.

I tried to sleep, but I was too excited and too aware that I was next to Dylan. I thought about getting my phone out and texting Rob, but just kept my eyes closed and tried to release the headache that was building bigger and bigger.

"Chloe, are you alright?" Dylan asked a few minutes later. "You look like you're in pain."

"Headache," I whispered back.

"I have medicine," Amy said as she started unzipping her backpack.

"You do?" Dylan asked, shock evident in his tone.

I opened my eyes and turned around to get the pills. Amy smiled. "Chloe's been getting headaches a lot lately. I wanted to make sure I was prepared."

"Thanks," I said sincerely. "I never remember to bring pain meds on trips." I held out my hand, and she put three in my palm.

"You're only supposed to take two of those," Dylan said seriously.

"Two to four," I replied as I popped the pills in my mouth and stole Emma's water bottle from her hand and took a gulp. I handed her the bottle back and she rolled her eyes.

"The label says two," Alex said.

"Guys, relax. I've been taking pain meds my entire life. Two or three or four doesn't matter. I'm not going to die from overdosing on a couple extra pain meds."

"It's still not safe," Dylan whispered.

"Driving a car isn't safe," I snapped at him. "Neither is flying in a plane or walking down the road or eating uncooked cookie dough, but I do all those things and I'm still perfectly safe and healthy."

"And a little bit crazy," Tom said.

I laughed. "Pot calling the kettle black?" I asked him with a smile.

Lisa laughed. "Burn!"

Everyone except Dylan laughed, and I closed my eyes again, this time with a smile. Sadly, it wasn't long before we arrived at the airport and my nap was ruined. I hurried to the back of the vehicle with everyone else to grab our bags. I watched as each guy grabbed his girl's bag and felt jealousy and sadness creeping up. I went to grab my bag, but Dylan grabbed it before I could.

"I can carry it," I said softly so the others wouldn't hear.

"No worries. We always carry the girls' bags. It's called manners," he said with a smile.

"Thanks," I said.

"We're friends, Chloe," he said and then patted my back. "Friends help each other."

"Right," I said blinking at him.

Amy grabbed my hand and pulled me towards the airport entrance. "Come on!"

We checked in and then the guys took our bags to get checked in as well. There wasn't much security since it was a smaller airport, but I was shocked at how many people were there.

My phone rang, and I answered it without looking. "Hello?"

"Hello, beautiful," Rob said cheerfully.

"Hey, Rob. What's up?" I asked.

Dylan looked at me a moment and then turned back around.

"I was about to ask you that," Rob said.

"We're at the airport, just waiting for our plane," I told him as we found our terminal and sat down in super uncomfortable plastic seats.

"Great! Well, I just wanted to talk to you before you boarded your plane. I can't wait to see you."

"Same here," I whispered.

"I'll see you at the airport when you arrive. Bye."

I hung up the phone and exhaled. It was weird to have a guy like me so much and me only be a little interested. I needed to focus. Dylan's a friend and Rob's more than a friend.

"Chloe, you're frowning," Amy whispered.

I shook my head and smiled. "Sorry. So, Rob just called and he said he can't wait to see everyone."

Amy smiled. "Are you guys going to go on another date?"

I shrugged. "We hadn't talked about it. Honestly I figured we were all just going to hang out as a group."

"We don't mind if you guys want to go out on another date," Tom said.

I didn't know what to say to that so I just closed my eyes and relaxed as we waited for the plane.

An announcement came over the loudspeaker, but it was muffled and hard to understand.

"That's us," Dylan said and stood.

I turned my phone off and followed the group, my excitement building and the fight with Dylan forgotten. It was the weekend, and we were getting out and away from adults. It was time to party!

We boarded the plane, and I moved down the rows looking for my seat, shocked to find that I was sitting next to Dylan. Had he done it on purpose or had it just turned out that way since everyone was already paired off as couples? I didn't want to ask so I sat down beside him and buckled my seat belt. I closed my eyes and slept until the jarring of the plane landing woke me.

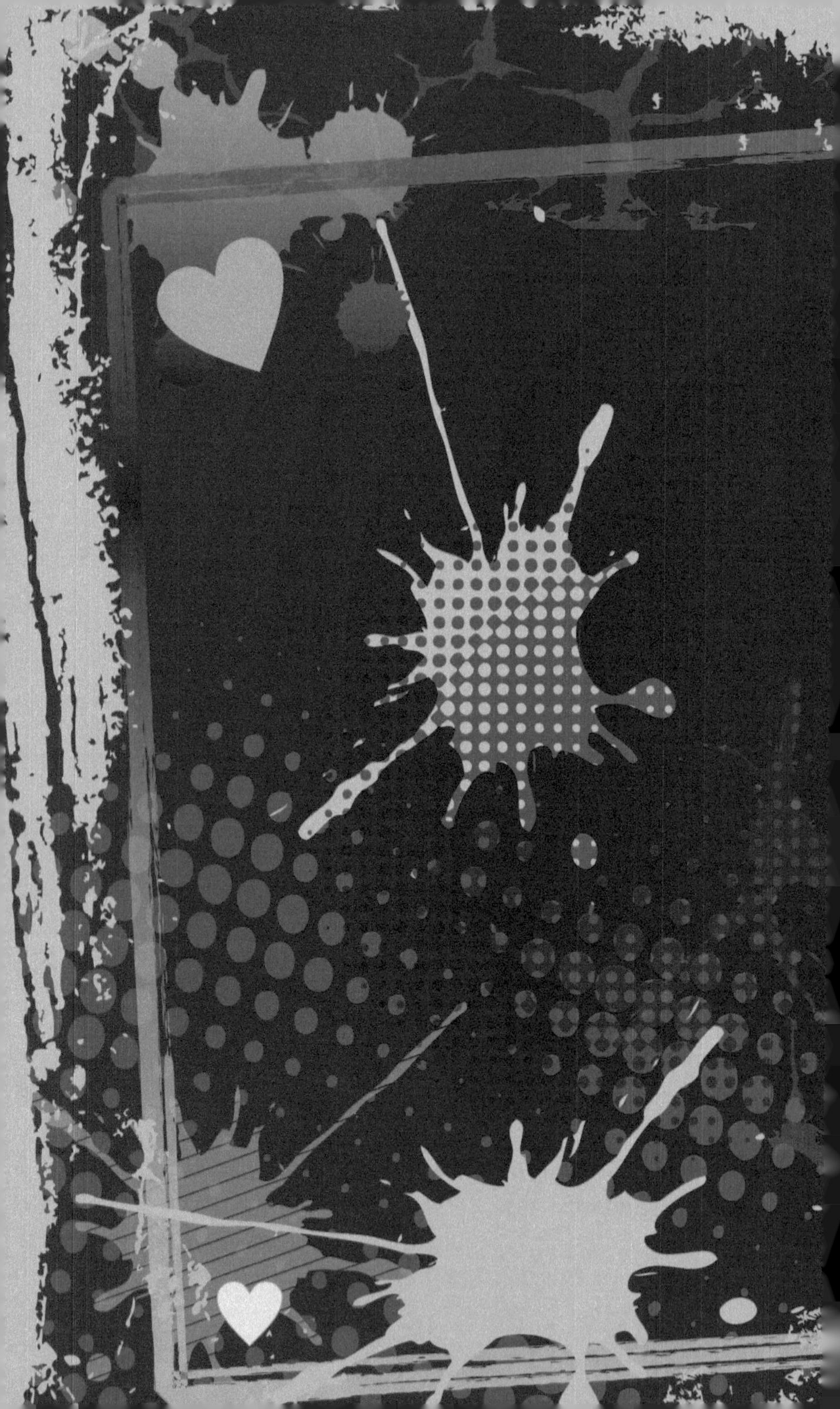

NINE

We were standing at the baggage claim when warm arms wrapped around me from behind. I spun around, ready to punch the creep when I recognized Rob's face. "Rob," I gasped, "I almost punched you."

"That's not a very nice hello," he teased.

I laughed and squirmed out of his hug to grab my bag. "Hello."

He smiled. "Much better."

The others grabbed their bags and walked over to us. "Rob!" Lisa said happily as she dropped her bag to hug him. He hugged and shook hands with everyone and then took my bag and headed towards the exit. "Come on, I've got a limo waiting for us."

"A limo?" Amy asked, eyes wide.

He smiled and draped his arm across her shoulders. "I always get the best for my family." She whispered something to him and he laughed. "That could be part of it, too."

The girls climbed in quickly while the guys put the bags in the trunk, and I opened the fridge and frowned.

"Why the long face?" Amy asked.

"No booze," I whispered.

"Booze is gross," Lisa said, her brows knotting. Emma and Amy nodded in agreement.

I just stared at them like they were crazy, because they obviously were. The guys climbed in, and surprisingly, the girls didn't separate to their respective guys and instead we stayed split, guys and girls. The driver took off, and Tom opened the sunroof, standing up and waving to everyone as we drove by. We all laughed at his craziness and sang along to the music playing.

We stopped in front of a huge hotel, and I whistled. "Wow, this place looks amazing."

"Wait until you get inside," Rob said with a smile. "Come on."

The guys climbed out and grabbed the bags, and the girls and I climbed out and looked at the ocean which was only a few yards away. "I can't wait to go play tomorrow," I said excitedly.

"You like the beach?" Amy asked.

I shrugged. "I've never been before."

Everyone turned, and stared at me.

"You've never been to the beach before?" Rob asked.

I shook my head. "Nope. Not the snow either."

"Oh, we are definitely taking a snow trip this year," Tom said with a wicked smile.

"I don't like the look you're giving me," I said warily.

Tom laughed. "You'll have fun, trust me."

Rob grabbed my hand and tugged on it. "Come on let's get up to the room." I let him hold my hand as we walked inside and then took an elevator that was a little too small for all of us and forced us to cram together. Somehow, I ended up smashed between Dylan and Rob while they talked. It was physically comfortable, but emotionally uncomfortable and awkward. We fell out of the elevator, and Rob led us to the farthest door and pushed it open. "Ladies first."

Amy, Emma, and Lisa grabbed onto me and we all walked inside to find the room was as big as a house with three separate bedrooms, a full kitchen, living room and balcony. I escaped their hands and ran to the first room, taking the bed by the door. "Dibs!"

Amy ran in and hopped on the second bed in the room I'd claimed. "Dibs!"

"You know you have to share," Lisa said.

"Actually, you don't. The couches turn into beds and there are some hidden beds, so I figured all you girls would have your own beds and the guys would use the couchbeds," Rob said with a wide smile.

Lisa hugged him, and she and Emma ran to the second room. I walked out of the room and to the balcony, looking out over the seemingly endless ocean.

"Beautiful, isn't it?" Dylan asked.

I nodded. "Yeah."

"You guys hungry?" Rob asked.

"Starving!" I yelled back and then walked inside to sit on a barstool facing into the kitchen to smile at him.

"What would you like?" he asked as he leaned on the counter so that our faces were inches away from each other.

"Pizza," I suggested.

"What's your favorite?"

"Pepperoni and black olives," I said as I stared into his eyes. He had such intense yet kind eyes that you felt instantly safe, almost like Dylan.

"Do half combination," Tom suggested as he plopped down

on the stool next to me. I leaned back and pretended to gag. He frowned at me. "You're the odd duck out here. Everyone else loves meat and veggies."

"You can just order a combination and I'll pick off the toppings and give them to someone else," I said as I headed towards Amy's bedroom. Amy was changing so I had to quickly shut the door behind me. "Can I have some more medicine?" I asked her. "The other stuff wore off."

She nodded and then tossed me the bottle. "Don't overdose," she teased.

I laughed and poured three more out. "Right. I wouldn't want to prove the guys right, now would I?"

She laughed and shook her head. "Nope. You should change into pajamas," she said.

"It's only three," I said, blinking at her.

"Yeah, but we won't be going anywhere else today."

I shrugged. "I'll just wait." I took the pills and then laid down. "A nap would be nice though."

She shut the door and whispered, "Good night."

I knew I shouldn't sleep and I should go hang out, but at the same time I was really tired. Sleep won, and I took another nap, this time getting fully rested when I woke up to the ding of the bell announcing the pizza had arrived.

I used the restroom and freshened up my hair and makeup before walking back out into the living room and was extremely grateful that I had since the hotel room was now full of other skateboarders. Rob must have seen my confused face because he made his way through the people and linked hands with me, pulling me through everyone. "Come on, the pizza's here."

I let him pull me along and then stared at the massive pile of pizza boxes. "How many did you order?"

He laughed. "I knew my friends would be stopping by so I wanted to make sure I had enough." He reached around the other boxes and grabbed a smaller box. "Here," he said with a smile.

I opened it and asked, "Did you get me my own pizza?"

He shrugged. "I didn't want you to have to pick everything off. Besides, this way no one else can steal a piece."

I kissed his cheek and took out a slice. "Thank you." He walked off to mingle with his friends and I hopped up onto the counter, eating my pizza, which was fabulous.

"I don't think I've had the pleasure of meeting you yet," a guy said from behind me.

I turned around and my eyes widened in shock at Marco, the most famous skateboarder in the past four years. "You're Marco Polo," I said softly.

He smiled. "Well, you know who I am, but I still don't know your name."

"I'm Chloe," I said with a smile.

"And are you taken like the rest of the females here, Chloe?" he asked with a sinfully seductive smile.

"Sadly, she is," Amy said as she walked up to us.

"By who?" Marco asked.

"That is the question we are all waiting for her to answer," Amy said with a wink at me.

"I'm not taken," I said to Amy with a quick glare that Marco didn't see.

"You're not?" Marco asked and then hopped over the counter to sit beside me. "Well, that is the best news I have heard all night."

Amy laughed. "Girl, you better watch it."

I rolled my eyes. "Amy, do we really need to have this talk?

One doesn't care and I've only gone on one date with number two. Therefore, I am available for number three."

She shook her head and walked away. "Just don't say I didn't warn you."

"Three?" Marco asked.

"You are the third boy to show interest in me since I moved," I explained.

"Only the third?" he asked, eyes wide. "Surely you have more boys after you than that?"

I laughed. "Nope."

"Well that makes me happy," he said with a wink. "So, what brings you here?"

"Rob," I answered.

"He is which number?"

I laughed. "Two."

"So you've gone on one date with him? No fireworks?" he asked.

"He behaved like a perfect gentleman," I said defensively.

"But you're used to the bad boys?" he guessed.

"I'm trying to avoid that," I said with a smile.

"Marco, what are you doing here?" Rob asked as he walked over to us.

"The guys told me they were headed over so I came with. And I'm glad I came," he said with a smile at me.

"Chloe," Dylan called as he walked towards us. "Can you come here a minute?"

"Boy one?" Marco guessed in a whisper.

I smiled and hopped off the counter. "It was great to meet you, Marco."

"You as well, Chloe. I can't wait to see you tomorrow."

I smiled at him and then walked over to Dylan who was standing by the balcony. "What's up?"

"What are you doing?" he snapped at me.

"Um, you called me over," I reminded him.

"With Marco," he explained.

"We were just talking, and why do you care?" I asked him.

"Marco isn't a good guy," Dylan said with a frown. "You should stay away from him."

"Are you saying that because you don't want me to hurt your friend?" I glared at him.

"Just trust me, okay?"

I walked away from him, refusing to answer. Why was he such a buzz kill? I didn't feel like being social anymore so I walked out of the room and headed towards the elevator.

"Where you going?" Rob asked.

"Just for a walk," I answered. "There are too many people there for me."

"You shouldn't go out alone," he said seriously.

"Then come with me," I said with a smile.

He looked at his hotel room door and then at me and smiled. "Okay, but just a quick walk."

I nodded and pushed the button for the elevator. The doors opened and we were lucky enough to get an empty elevator. I pushed the button for the ground floor and Rob turned me around and kissed me deeply as the elevator descended. He was a really good kisser and part of me could definitely see a future with him, but now wasn't the time for a huge make-out session.

"Rob, can we slow down?"

"Is this because of Marco?" he complained as he looked at me.

I laughed and shook my head. "No way."

"Dylan?" he asked.

I couldn't really say no to that, but I said, "I want to get to know you first. Plus, I can't do a long-distance relationship so I would like to be friends first. I like you—you're handsome and great—but I know there are girls everywhere throwing themselves at you."

The elevator reached the ground floor, and he pushed the button for his floor, making the elevator move up without opening the doors. "I'm moving back," he said as he stepped forward, pressing me against the side of the elevator and kissed my neck. "And I can tell you want to fool around," he said as he ran his hand from my back down to cup my butt.

I pushed away from him and stared at him in disbelief. "I do not want to fool around. I want you to stop acting like this. What happened to the nice, sweet Rob?" I asked him.

"I thought you liked the bad boys."

The door opened, and I started to get out, but he grabbed me and pulled me against him again. "Come on, Chloe. I know you want me. I can make you forget Dylan. I can make you forget everything. I think you just need a few drinks in you," he said. I inhaled and the scent of alcohol hit my nose, making me realize that he was drunk.

It was still no excuse for his behavior, and I tried to pull away from him again. "I'm not interested in doing anything with you while you're drunk," I said.

"Give me one night, and I guarantee I can change your mind."

"Let me go," I said as I tried to pull away.

He gripped my arm harder, hurting me to the point that I knew I was going to have a nasty bruise. "Is this about him?"

"I haven't chosen anyone!" I said. "Let me go. You're hurting me."

He pinned me against the wall with his fill form, hiding his face from me and ran his hand down the side of my body. "I want you," he whispered in my ear as he started to run his hand towards my midsection.

"Let me go," I said as I tried to get out of his hold. Why wouldn't he look at me? Was this fake? Was he just testing me? What the hell was going on?

"I can smell you," he whispered. "I can smell that this is arousing you. I bet if I—"

"Let her go," Dylan snarled from nearby.

"Leave," Rob said as he whipped his head to look at Dylan. As he turned, I caught a glimpse of his eyes which looked amber in the hallway lighting.

Dylan took a step towards us, and Rob said, "I'm not doing anything wrong."

"She doesn't want you to touch her right now. You are drunk and being rude and hurting her."

"You can smell her just like I can. You can smell that she's aroused," Rob said.

I couldn't argue with him. Even though I didn't want to sleep with him right now, I was. It was a bad side effect from my past. Knowing they could smell it somehow made me really uncomfortable, though. What did they smell? Was it a gross smell?

"She said no," Dylan whispered as he walked closer, even though he had no idea what had transpired.

"She doesn't know, does she?" Rob asked.

Dylan shook his head. "No, now let her go. Right now."

Rob flicked his tongue out to touch my neck and sighed. "She smells so good, but I'm sure you already know that."

"You're drunk," Dylan said again. "In the morning you are going to feel awful about this and that is why you should let her go now so you don't make an even bigger fool of yourself or ruin your relationship with her."

"I want her," he said.

Dylan nodded. "I know."

Rob stepped away from me, and I moved around Dylan towards the room.

"Go inside the hotel room," Dylan said as he walked closer. "I think Rob and I need to talk."

I started to walk by him, and I whispered, "Thank you."

He nodded, but didn't take his eyes from Rob who was squatted down in the center of the hallway.

"I thought she knew. I like her a lot and I don't want her to be mad. I thought she knew."

"I know buddy, but she doesn't know. I'm sure she will forgive you tomorrow."

I walked into the room, and Amy rushed over to me. "Are you alright?"

I shook my head and headed to the room, shutting the door behind us. I told her what had happened and she sighed. "He used to be an alcoholic," she explained. "When he drinks, he turns into this completely different person. We call him Bob when he's drunk. I had thought he was past that, but apparently not. Are you okay?"

I examined my arm, but there was only a slight red mark. "I think so. I think I'm going to go sit on the balcony for some fresh air though."

She nodded, and I made my way through the crowd to sit on the balcony and stare out over the water. I'd had other friends like Rob before. They were sweet people until they drank whiskey or something else and then they turned into complete jerks. It didn't excuse him, but it made me less angry at him, especially since he hadn't meant to hurt my arm.

"Are you alright?" Dylan asked as he sat down next to me.

I nodded, but didn't look at him.

He put his arm around my shoulders and pulled me closer to him, making me shiver from the temperature difference of outside and his body. "He scared you, didn't he?"

I wanted to lie, I wanted to hold on to my tough girl façade, but I couldn't. I nodded and then started to cry.

He turned so that my face was against his chest and he sighed. "I am so sorry he hurt your arm. He isn't normally like this."

"Amy told me," I whispered around my sniffles.

"Why did he get so upset?" he asked.

I turned away from him and wiped my eyes. "Because I told him I wasn't sure I could do long distance and I wanted to take things slow."

"He is going to feel like a complete jerk tomorrow and I'm sure he'll be really embarrassed."

"Yeah," I whispered. "Maybe I should just go."

"Go where?" he asked.

"Go back home."

"No, don't do that," Dylan said as he turned my face back towards his. "If you act like it didn't happen, so will he and we can all hang out and have fun."

"He won't want me there," I whispered.

"He won't remember what happened," Dylan said. "He is beyond blacked out. Besides, it seemed like nothing really bad happened, right? Or did I miss something?"

"No, he just scared me. I just don't want him to feel bad."

"Please don't go," he whispered.

"What's going on out here?" Tom asked as he plopped down between us. He saw my tear-streaked face and turned to Dylan. "You making her cry again?"

"Again?" Dylan blinked at me.

I punched Tom's arm and stood up. "I'm going to bed."

"What did I say?" Tom asked as he rubbed the spot I had punched.

"When have I made her cry?" Dylan asked.

I ignored them and went to the bedroom, this time shutting it and ignoring everyone else. I was not in a partying mood anymore. Hopefully tomorrow would be better.

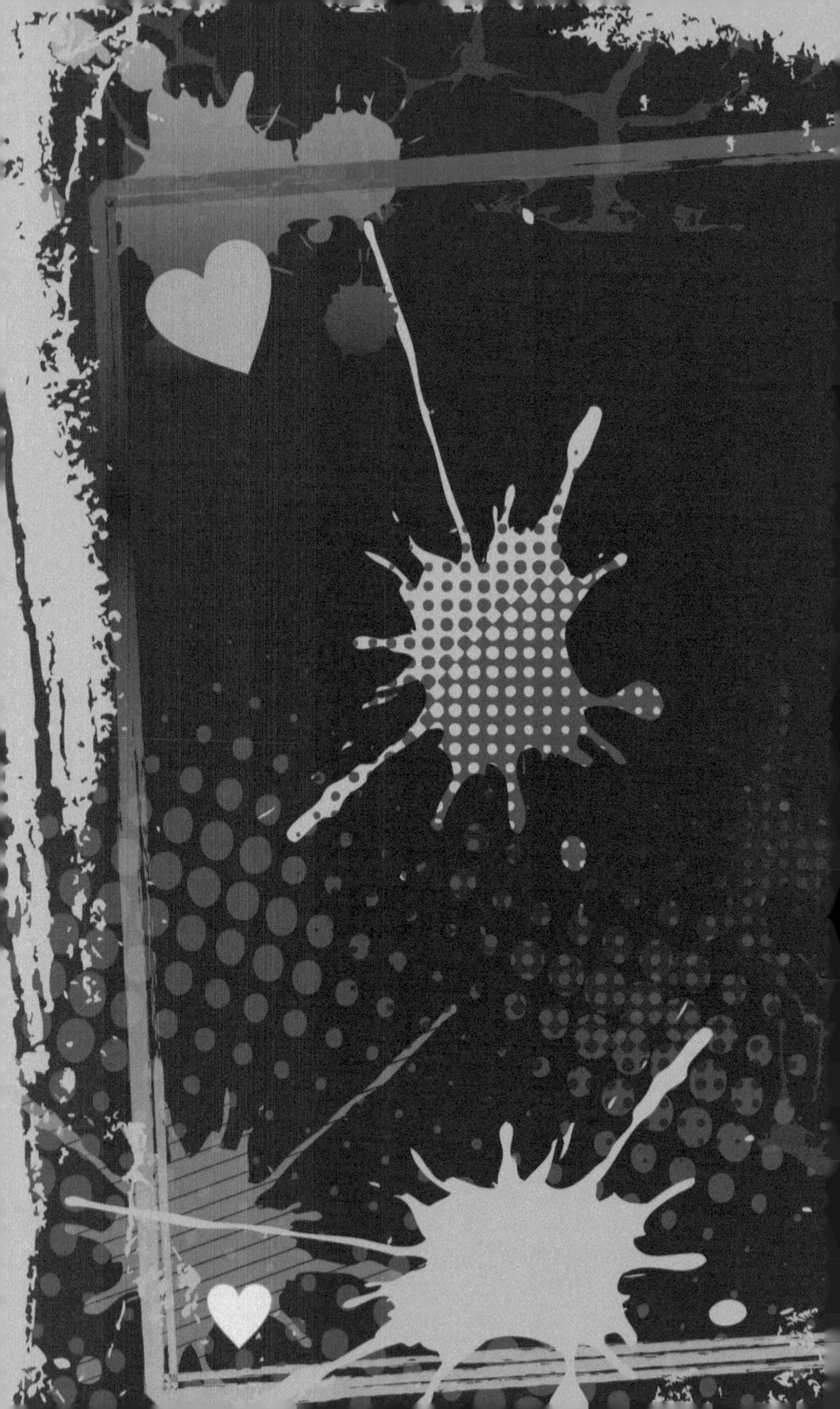

TEN

"Wake up, sleepyhead," Amy said the next morning. "Time for breakfast."

"What time is it?"

"Seven."

"Why are you waking me up so early? It's the weekend," I complained as I pulled my covers up higher.

"We have to get up and eat and then get on the way to the competition. Come on, you're the last one up and you need to get ready."

I sighed and tossed my covers back and grumbled the entire way to the bathroom, ignoring the looks from everyone sitting in the living room. After quickly getting ready in the bathroom and running to the bedroom to change, I was ready and standing by the door as everyone walked out to head to a restaurant for breakfast. I had just taken a step out the door when Rob tapped my shoulder.

I turned around, and he said, "I am really sorry for whatever I did last night."

"You really don't remember anything?" I asked him.

He shook his head. "I remember giving you your pizza and talking with people and then nothing. Dylan said I was really over the line with you and I feel awful. I thought I had only had three drinks, but obviously I must have had more. Will you forgive me?"

"I forgive you, and we can talk more later tonight if you want, but first you need to go rock this competition. Which, by the way, you are totally going to win." I smiled and kissed his cheek. "Also, let's keep you away from the alcohol, okay?"

He laughed bitterly and hugged me. "Okay. Thank you."

"You coming?" Dylan called from the elevator where he had stuck his head out.

I jogged down the hallway to the elevator.

He looked down at my arm where a nasty black and purple bruise was very visible. "You okay?" he asked softly.

I smiled, nodded, and turned away from him, not able to meet his eyes for some reason. At the lobby, we all climbed out of the cramped elevator and Rob led the way to a waffle place two blocks down the street.

"You okay?" Dylan asked me quietly as we straggled behind the rest of the group who were all talking excitedly about the day.

"Yep."

"Chloe, I know he scared you—" Dylan began, but I interrupted him.

"I am trying to get back to having fun, okay? Yes, he scared me, but it isn't the first time a guy has done that. Let's just forget it." I could tell he wanted to say something to me, but I didn't give him the chance. I walked faster so I was caught up to Emma and Amy and I linked arms with them. "Can't we walk faster? I'm starving!"

"Race you to the door!" Emma shouted and then sprinted

down the street towards the restaurant with a big waffle painted on the side of it. I sprinted after her, trying to beat everyone, but Amy and Lisa zipped past me and stood with wide grins at the door.

"I must be getting out of shape," I said as I tried to slow my breathing.

"You should start going for runs with us in the mornings," Lisa said seriously.

I nodded. "We'll start Tuesday."

"Tuesday?" Rob asked. "Why not Monday?"

"Because I hate Mondays and want to sleep in."

Everyone laughed, and we walked into the restaurant. It took half an hour before we were seated and by then, my stomach was growling loud enough for everyone at the table to hear.

"If you had woken up sooner you wouldn't be so hungry," Amy said.

I rolled my eyes at her and then the waiter came to the table and took our orders. The guys ordered double what the girls did and when the food came out, they surprisingly ate all of it. I was having trouble finishing my plate and pushed it towards Emma.

She regarded me. "Why are you pushing it at me?"

"Because you are closest to me," I said, "and I can't eat anymore or I'll explode."

She pushed it to Dylan. "Here, I know you still have room to eat more."

"You sure you don't want it?" Dylan asked me.

I nodded. "I'm about to pop," I whispered as I patted my stomach.

Dylan ate the food and then we all went back to the hotel where the limousine was waiting for us. I climbed inside and groaned as I leaned back against the seat. "I ate too much."

"You should eat more," Lisa said as she looked at me. "You're too thin."

I stared at her. "You are one to talk, beanpole."

She smiled. "I have great genetics."

"So do I."

She gave me the first serious look ever and said, "You can't keep up the charade forever."

I just gaped at her, dumbstruck. "What charade?"

"Now is not the time to discuss that," Dylan said to Lisa.

"Discuss what? I don't get what you guys are trying to say," I said seriously.

Tom laughed. "You're really sticking to this hard."

"Sticking to what?" I asked angrily.

"We know you're bulimic," Ethan said.

I blinked at him a moment and then started laughing uncontrollably. "You guys are crazy. I'm not bulimic."

"We've heard you throwing up after dinner," Tom said.

I shook my head. "Nope. You heard me groaning and wishing I could, but I never threw up."

"What do you mean?" Amy asked.

"I am an overeater. I'm always eating too much and getting stuffed so bad that I end up moaning and groaning and feeling exactly like I do now. I can't make myself throw up even when I try to gag myself. Geez, I can't believe you guys actually thought I was a bulimic. No way."

"Really?" Dylan asked. "You're not lying?"

I shook my head. "Nope. The only time I throw up is when I'm drunk and you took all my alcohol when I first moved in."

"Well, that's a relief," Lisa said with a smile.

The limo stopped at a giant arena where hundreds of

people were outside waiting to get in. "Here are your passes," Rob said as he handed us each a VIP pass on a lanyard. "Don't lose them." We all put them around our necks and then he smiled and said, "Showtime!" He stepped out of the limo and the waiting crowd exploded in cheers.

Tom grabbed Lisa's hand and pulled her out of the limo with, him and I was sad to see everyone pairing off. Dylan smiled and waved me out the door.

I followed everyone as we walked behind Rob up to the side entrance and inside. People waved and cheered at us like we were celebrities too and the others smiled and acted like they were used to it. I felt slightly embarrassed and wished I'd put more makeup on.

Rob led us to the stage, and we were met by all of the skaters that had come over the night before. "Alright, I need to practice a little. Your seats are right down there." He pointed to the front row and everyone started to head that way. He grabbed my hand before I could go and said, "Thank you for coming. It means a lot to me."

I smiled and squeezed his hand. "I wouldn't miss it."

Camera crews were already set up, and as we took our seats, a few came over asking for interviews. Tom and Dylan did the interviews, leaving the rest of us to relax.

"So, I take it you and Rob are a no-go?" Amy asked in a whisper.

"We're good for now."

"Oh. That's good," she said and then whispered to Tom.

"Miss," one of the reporters called out to me. "Who do you think is going to win?"

I smiled for the camera and said, "Well, I know Marco is a favorite, but my money is on Rob."

The reporters moved away from us and I closed my eyes.

"Good thing my dad knows I'm here. The last time I was on TV I was supposed to be sleeping in bed and that's how I got caught."

"You snuck out?" Lisa half-laughed, eyes wide.

I laughed. "You guys have no idea how bad I used to be."

"Your dad told Kelly you were a bit of a wild kid before, but didn't really specify," Ethan said.

"He was probably embarrassed that I managed to be so crazy."

"So, we know you have drunk alcohol and gone to a concert, but what else?" Amy asked.

"Oh please, I've done almost everything. I went to raves. I went to parties. I went out of town for the weekend without him knowing."

"Why?" Dylan asked.

I shrugged. "Because it was fun."

"You're having fun now and aren't doing those things," Amy pointed out.

"Yeah, but that's because I am not hanging out with bad people who like those things," I explained.

"So, if we liked doing that stuff, you would do it again?"

"Most likely," I admitted.

"And here we thought we were being a good influence on you," Amy said with a shake of her head.

"You are, otherwise I would be doing it," I said with a laugh.

The first skater was called out and conversation about anything besides the competition stopped. These skaters were incredible and did some amazing things that I could never dream of being able to do.

Rob was definitely the most amazing, though. We cheered

the loudest at the end of his performance and he winked in our direction, but I felt like it was at me.

All of the VIPs were invited to the after party which was actually right where we were. Once the security had cleared out everyone else, a DJ arrived and everyone started dancing. There were so many people there still that I started to get nervous, but Amy came and danced with me which took my mind off of it.

We danced so long that my legs hurt. I sat down a bit away from the dancing group and drank from a water bottle.

Rob sat down next to me and grinned. "Having fun?"

I nodded with a wide smile. "Yes. Thank you for letting me come."

"Of course."

We sat in silence a moment and I asked, "When will you be back in town?"

"In a month," he admitted, his shoulders drooping. "But we can text each other until then."

I smiled sadly. "I would have been texting you even if you were in town."

He leaned over and kissed my cheek softly. "I really like you, Chloe. I'm so glad I got up the nerve to talk to you in the store."

"You had to get up your nerve to talk to me?" I asked, my mouth agape.

"Duh. You can't just walk up to a beautiful girl and talk to her. I half expected your boyfriend to come over and start a fight with me."

"Well, my imaginary boyfriend would have totally taken you in a fight," I said with a smirk.

"Maybe when I'm not touring and back in town, I can take the place of that imaginary boyfriend."

"I don't know. He's been with me a really long time," I teased.

"But can he do this?" he asked and then kissed my cheek again.

I smiled and said, "Only in my dreams."

He laughed and put his arm around my shoulders. "Well, I better figure out a way to infiltrate your dreams then."

We sat in companionable silence, and I felt relaxed and happy. I couldn't stay mad at him for something that had happened when he was drunk, especially since he didn't remember it now. And I knew it was better for me to let someone who liked me in, than to pine after someone who didn't like me. Then, I rubbed my bruised wrist. He had crossed a line, drunk or not.

"I don't want to ruin the night, but—"

"You aren't sure if we can continue because of my drunken idiocy. Plus, you don't want to be committed to someone who is long distance," Rob finished for me.

My mouth opened and then closed before I finally said, "Uh, yeah."

"I get it. I'm fine with that. Can we still text and chat as friends?"

"I would like that," I said with a nod and smiled. I looked out at the beach beyond the grounds and wondered what the ocean felt like.

"Let's get everyone so we can go change and head to the beach," Rob said as he stood up.

"I think they're all having fun already," I commented.

"Yeah, but they'll have even more fun on the beach where we can play in the sand and still hear the music," he told me as he led me through the crowd, hand-in-hand.

Girls glared at me with jealousy in their eyes, and it made

me smile to know that Rob was interested in me. It made me even happier to know that he understood and respected my wishes not to continue dating.

He grabbed people from our group as we went and then headed towards the waiting limo where Dylan was already standing.

"Grab your suits and let's go to the beach!" Rob ordered them.

Amy grabbed the bag that had all of the girls' suits in it, and we headed to the bathroom to change. Once I had changed, I stood and stared at myself in front of the mirror.

"What's wrong?" Lisa asked.

"Just picking out my flaws," I said with a smile.

"Shut up," Amy said with a roll of her eyes.

"You know you all do it, too," I countered.

"Okay, maybe, but knock it off," Emma said with a laugh.

We shoved all of our clothes in the bag that had held our swimsuits and walked out to find the guys waiting for us. The muscles that were showing on all of them surprised me and made the view much better than I had anticipated.

"Let's go!" Amy yelled and started running towards the beach. Emma and Lisa ran after her and their guys all ran after them. Rob walked to me and I enjoyed the view—he had an incredible chest and set of abs.

"You look amazing," he said with a smirk.

"I believe hot is the word you're looking for," I said with a return smirk.

He nodded. "Yes, hot for sure."

"You're pretty hot yourself," I replied. He tried to put his arms around me for a hug, but I backed up and smiled wide. "Catch me if you can!" I yelled and then ran away from him. The sand was extremely hard to run in and he grabbed me around the waist and spun me around before I had run very far.

"You have to run faster than that to escape me," he whispered and nipped my shoulder.

I laughed and struggled out of his arms. "This sand is hard to run in."

"I forgot you said you haven't been to a beach before," he said with a laugh. "Yeah, sand sucks to run in."

"Are there sharks out there?" I asked as I looked at the ocean in front of us.

"There might be, but don't worry. I'll protect you," he told me and put his arm around my shoulders.

The setting sun cast beautiful orange hues across the water and horizon. With the sound of the waves crashing, the music not too far behind us, and people having fun, I could totally understand why so many tried to live near the beach. However, I still wasn't sure I wanted to chance a shark attack.

I shivered and said, "I don't know if I want to go in the water."

"Just go in a little bit," he said. We walked slowly through the hot sand to the edge of where the waves were rolling up onto the beach.

"It smells so salty," I said and wrinkled my nose.

He laughed. "You have no idea."

"What?"

"Come build a castle with us!" Lisa yelled at me.

"One sec!" I yelled back as I faced the water. "Is it cold?" I asked him.

"Oh yeah."

I stepped forward so the water could roll over my toes and yelped. "Cold. Super cold."

Rob walked down until he was knee deep in the water. "It's not that bad. Come on."

"I've heard that sharks will attack in water that shallow," I told him as I waded closer to him. The water surged around my ankles, and I shivered from the cold. "Burr."

"You're a baby," he teased me.

I stopped, gasped, and looked down when I felt something touch me.

"Don't freak out; it's probably just kelp," he said fast.

"Ew," I groaned when it slid around my ankle and away with the outgoing tide.

"Are you going to come out here with me?" he asked softly.

I shook my head. "I think this is as far as I'm going to go."

He waded back towards me and hugged me against his chest. "That's okay. I'm impressed you made it this far."

"I don't think I would have come in at all if you weren't with me," I told him as I hugged him back.

"Come build a castle," Lisa ordered me.

"We better go before she gets mad," Rob said. "She's small, but fierce."

We walked back towards the group and for a second, I thought Dylan was glaring at Rob. When I looked back, Dylan was smiling at me, though.

Rob dropped down to his knees, grabbed my hand, and pulled me down with him. "Let's build a huge castle, Chloe!"

I laughed at his childlike enthusiasm and taunted, "I bet ours will be better than yours, Lisa."

"Bring it on," she challenged me.

Rob grabbed a bucket that I hadn't seen the guys bring and jogged down the beach to get water to help with the castle. I started digging a moat and trying to make a gate on the outside of the moat, but the sand wouldn't stick.

"There's a science to it," Rob informed me. "You have to put water in the sand to make it stick, but not too much or it'll just slop around."

"And here I thought sand castle building was easy enough for children."

"It is if you dig down deep enough to the sand underneath that hasn't been dried by the sun," Amy informed me.

For over an hour, we built our castles and at the end, I was pretty impressed with them.

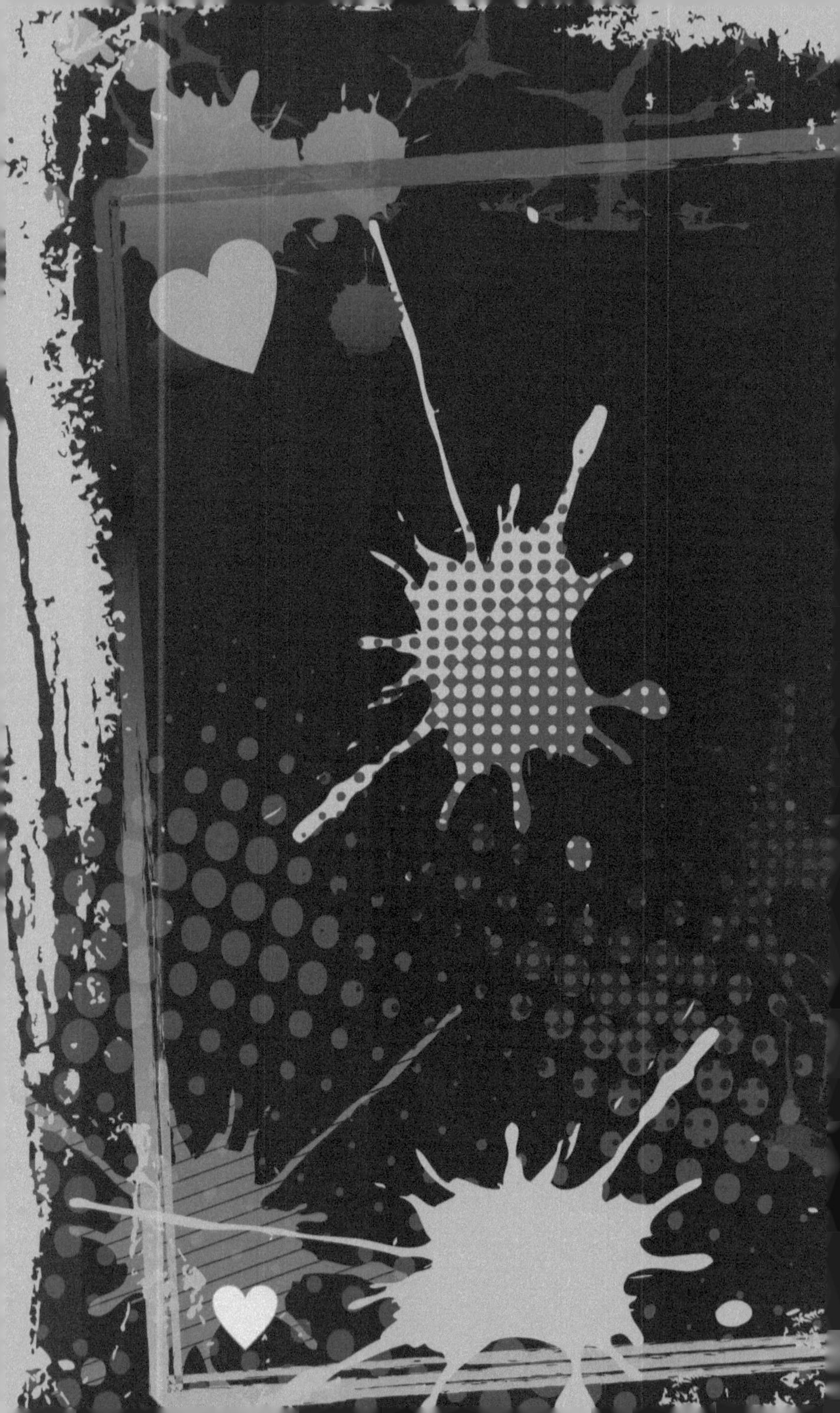

ELEVEN

I t was harder to say goodbye to Rob than I had anticipated, but he promised to text me as much as possible. I promised the same and gave him the biggest hug I could before I left. Sometimes, people were just better off as friends.

The others took a long time to say goodbye as well, but we made it to the airport in just enough time to board our flight.

The flight back was relatively somber. Dylan sat with the boys and I wondered if things between us would ever be okay. Could he ever accept me?

It didn't seem likely.

I sat beside Lisa with Amy and Emma sitting in front of us.

"You okay?" Lisa asked.

I shrugged. "As okay as I can be, I guess."

"We heard you broke it off with Rob," Amy said.

I chuckled. "Of course you guys know. Yeah, I did. I just wasn't sure I could, or should, continue with a guy who acts so different when he's drinking. I'm trying to get away from that lifestyle. We are still going to be friends, but I doubt it will ever go beyond that."

Saying it out loud to them made it so much more final and made me a bit sadder.

"Well, look on the bright side," Amy said with a smile. "Now you can be single and free to date whoever you want."

"Like a certain broody boy we all know," Emma said, leaned up and over the seat, and wiggled her eyebrows.

I rolled my eyes. "I think that just means I'll be single the rest of my life."

All three of them rolled their eyes.

Dad and Kelly were at the airport waiting for us when we landed. They hugged each of us before herding us into the SUV.

"Did you have a good time?" Kelly asked as she looked in the rearview mirror.

"Loads," Amy and Lisa said simultaneously.

"Good," Dad said and turned around to smile at us. "We missed you all, but it was nice to have a quiet house for once."

"Well, vacation is over," I teased him. "The kids are back and your quiet time is gone."

He sighed loudly and dramatically. "You sure we can't send them to a boarding school?" he asked Kelly.

She laughed. "They would pay *us* to take them back."

"That could be a good scam," Emma said.

Everyone laughed and then took turns filling Kelly and Dad in on the events. I noticed Dylan avoided talking about the party, which I was grateful for. Even though I hadn't gotten drunk or anything, I didn't want Dad asking me questions.

"We really are happy to have you all home," Kelly said once we made it back and climbed out of the car. She hugged me tightly. "It's been really depressing."

"They're back!" a male voice yelled and then ten adults ran around the side of the house to hug everyone.

Dad pulled me to the side and draped an arm around my shoulders.

"Dad, you sure we didn't join a cult?" I asked softly.

He chuckled. "They're not a cult."

I wasn't so sure. They lived on the same property. They had weird dating dynamics. They treated Kelly like a leader. It was eerily similar to a cult.

There didn't seem to be any religion that they followed, but maybe I just hadn't found out about it yet.

"Did you have fun?" Dad asked.

I nodded. "It is so beautiful and warm. I understand why people want to live near the beach now."

"Did you go in the ocean?"

"I let my feet get wet and some slimy kelp touched me."

He laughed. "Nice."

"I'm going to go inside and rest. I'm beat," I said, hugged his side, and went into the house.

A few minutes later, someone knocked on my door.

I debated ignoring it, but stood and opened it instead.

Dylan looked at me and asked, "Are you okay?"

"Just resting," I explained. "Did you need something?"

"I just wanted to check on you. You seemed down last night and this morning."

I shrugged. "I ended things with Rob and even though it was my decision, I'm a bit sad about it," I admitted.

His eyes widened. "Why?"

"I don't want to be with someone who is that different when they drink."

There was a tense moment of silence before he said, "I'm sorry."

"Not your fault. Actually, I wanted to thank you for helping me out that night when he was acting so out of character. I really appreciate it. Not everyone will intervene or stop their friend when they think he might get lucky."

He cringed. "You told him no, and he should have respected that. I'm sorry you've had to deal with things like this before. I wish I could have helped you those other times."

I looked down at my feet and whispered, "Me, too."

"Well, I need to go unpack and wind down a bit since we have school tomorrow," he said softly.

I raised my head to look at him. "Thanks again for letting me go and for defending me."

He smiled and said, "Anytime, Chloe."

I watched him leave and wondered if we could be friends after all.

SCHOOL WAS EVEN HARDER to deal with after our vacation. I tried to focus, but by Tuesday afternoon, I just knew it wasn't going to happen this week.

Since I wasn't allowed to walk home alone anymore, I waited until we got to the house to hike out into the woods to find a quiet, empty area, and set up my picnic and studying spot.

Luckily, the couples were off on a joint date somewhere, so I didn't have to worry about losing them. And I had no idea where Dylan was, not that I was looking...or cared.

With headphones in, snacks on the blanket, and my books in front of me, I set myself to studying.

The sun began to lower, but I was on a roll, so I continued

to focus, not only catching up on my math, but for once getting ahead.

I took that super focus next to my science and English classwork, getting ahead on those as well.

It wasn't until I couldn't stop shivering and I realized I was using my cell phone for a light, that it was late and dark.

"Whoops, I got too focused," I whispered to myself and chuckled. I removed my headphones and immediately cringed as I heard several voices calling my name.

These noise cancelling headphones were no joke!

"I'm here!" I called back as I gathered up my stuff and put it in my backpack. "I'm fine!"

They called out to each other and then I heard panting in front of me.

I looked up and my mouth dropped.

Dylan was bent over, hand rested against a tree trunk, panting as he tried to catch his breath. "You're...you're safe?"

"I'm fine," I said. "I had headphones on and didn't hear you guys yelling for me."

He straightened, took a deep breath, and walked forward.

I straightened as well and tensed.

He pulled me into a hug and inhaled deeply. When he exhaled, his entire body sagged against me. "We were so worried."

Dylan was...hugging me?

I returned his hug and said, "I'm sorry I worried you."

He pushed me back and asked, "What were you doing all the way out here?"

"I was studying," I explained. "I couldn't focus in school, so I came out to the forest to work."

"Where is she?" Dad yelled. "Is she okay?"

"I'm here and I'm fine," I said with a sigh.

Dylan quickly backed away from me and brushed his hands off on his jeans.

There he went again, acting like it was disgusting to touch me. What the hell?

Dad gripped my upper arms while Kelly hovered behind him. "You're really okay?"

"I was studying with headphones on and didn't hear you. I'm sorry I worried you," I said and felt tears stinging my eyes.

No, dammit. I would not cry.

Kelly pushed Dad aside and hugged me. "It's okay. We're just glad you're safe."

I sniffled. "Thanks."

"Come on. Let's get to the house so we can eat dinner," she whispered, kept an arm around me, and steered me towards the house.

Dinner was a somber affair and as soon as I could, I beelined for my room.

Why did Dylan act so hot and cold?

I thought we'd made some progress this weekend, but maybe I was wrong.

Maybe I was wrong about a lot of things, but seeing Dad happy was the most important thing.

I could suck it up and deal with a lot if I got to see him smile.

The next day, I shoved all my emotions down into the box I kept them in and put a smile on my face as I went through the school day.

Dylan kept glancing at me while scowling, but didn't try to talk to me, which was probably for the best.

We stopped at the little store to grab snacks before heading home. I wanted to go straight to my room, but the girls asked me to hangout with them instead.

"Okay," I agreed and followed them out into the backyard. With the sun shining, we sat together in a circle on the grass. The guys came out, but formed their own circle a bit away and talked to each other.

"How was your day?" Emma asked me.

"Good," I said with a smile.

"You sure you're okay? You seem...off today," Lisa said softly.

"I'm good," I assured her, but judging by their expressions, they didn't believe me.

Honestly, aside from the Dylan issue, I was good. This group of people felt like family already. I had always assumed I would leave my dad's house as soon as possible, but now leaving sounded awful.

"What are your plans after you graduate?" I asked Lisa.

She looked at Emma and Amy before responding. "We're going to get jobs nearby."

"No plans to leave the nest?" I asked. "Run off with your guy and live alone in the woods somewhere?"

She smirked. "We live in the woods, remember? And we have a house in the woods so we don't need to run off."

Amy elbowed her and gave her a glare.

Lisa's cheeks flushed, and she looked down at her hands.

What was that about?

"I've always wondered where you guys live," I said. I didn't want to invite myself over, though, so I dropped it.

"What are your plans?" Emma asked me.

Looking down at my lap, I said, "I'm not sure anymore. I had planned to leave as soon as I turned eighteen."

"Leave?" Dylan asked, breaking off from his conversation with the other guys. "Where would you go?"

I shrugged. "I was planning to find someplace near the

beach and an easy job like waitressing or being a barista. Just something that would pay the bills. And to go someplace I've never been. To experience what life is like on my own."

He scowled. "Being alone sounds awful to me."

The three girls nodded their agreement.

"What about you, Dylan?" I asked and looked straight into his eyes.

He scowled and then shrugged. "Get a job and see how it goes from there. I don't plan on moving away from this city or my family."

"So, you'll just live in your hidden house in the woods and drive however far to your job?" I asked.

He nodded.

"What if you can't find a job close?" I asked.

"I've still got a year to figure that out," he said. "I'm sure I'll be able to find something."

They didn't make any sense to me. There weren't many towns close by, so how could they all find a job nearby?

My curiosity was also piqued at trying to find their houses. Why were they secret? What were they like? Did they live together?

My head started to throb, and I rubbed my forehead.

"You need to drink more water," Amy chastised me.

Dylan walked into the house and then returned with a bottle of water for me. "Here."

"Thanks," I whispered and chugged it. They were probably right; I was probably just dehydrated.

"So, your plan is to move far away and take a basic job? You don't have any goals aside from that?" Ethan asked.

"I don't really have a specific type of job that I want or any goals like that," I admitted. "Maybe I'll figure out something else or some other goal between now and graduation. Who knows? A lot can change in a year."

"That's for sure," Dylan muttered.

For some reason, I felt like that comment had to do with me and it made my chest hurt.

Emma reached over and smacked Dylan who looked up at her with a scowl.

I dropped my head and peeled the water bottle label. "Is it common for your family members to stay nearby? Is that why there are always so many people around on the weekends?"

They all nodded.

"We don't like being apart for too long," Tom answered. "So, we'll move somewhere that allows us to come visit each weekend."

It sounded really nice to have family that close knit. Would I feel that way about them by the time graduation was here? Or would I want to leave still?

Only time would tell, I supposed.

"Family meeting!" Kelly called from the barn door.

We all filed into the barn, and I froze when I saw at least a hundred people inside.

Amy looped her arm through mine, and Emma walked on my other side as we entered, finding a place near the door to stand.

Kelly smiled, met eyes with me, and said, "I think it's time you learned about us."

Dylan walked forward and took off his shirt.

Kelly looked at my dad, and he came forward to hold hands with her. Kelly said, "What we're about to tell you and show you isn't something you will easily believe, but I promise you that it is the truth. Once you know the truth you will understand more about our family and each of us individually. After you see Dylan, you can ask me any questions you want."

I frowned and looked at Dylan. "Um, okay. What does him being shirtless have to do with whatever you're talking about? I mean I can see he's really muscular, but—"

"Chloe, just wait," my dad interrupted me.

Dylan walked to me, stopping inches away from me and whispered, "Chloe, I'm sorry I've upset you, but I'll explain everything after this. Please, just remember that I would never hurt you. You know that, right? That I'd never hurt you?"

I nodded.

He smiled. "Okay, so please don't scream or freak out. Please. *Please.*"

I nodded again, and he backed up.

Amy and Emma also moved back away from me, leaving me standing in the open alone.

What could he possibly show me that would freak me out or make me scream?

Dylan dropped to the ground on his hands and knees. I watched in shock, horror, and interest as Dylan's body quivered and then began to change. It started with his hands turning into paws, his fingernails elongating into thick black claws, then worked its up way his legs, to his back, head, and then a tail sprouted. The pants he'd had on were gone and fur sprouted all over him. Dylan the boy was gone, replaced by Dylan the wolf.

Dylan panted a moment and then looked up at me. His eyes were still emerald, but a lighter, shinier color. It was the most beautiful pair of eyes I'd ever seen, even if it was attached to an animal that could kill me in two seconds.

"Werewolves. You're...all of you are werewolves?" I asked as I continued to stare at Dylan.

Dad said, "All of them, except you and me."

Dylan took a step towards me, and Dad growled at him, sounding like an animal himself.

Kelly laid her hand on Dad's arm. "He won't hurt her. You know that."

Dad relaxed and sighed. "Sorry, Dylan."

Dylan snorted softly and then walked towards me. The closer he walked, the bigger he became. Dylan stopped in front of me, his eyes level with me and exhaled against my face.

I held my ground, refusing to run away, even though every instinct was telling me that he was the predator and I was prey. I was staring into his eyes when I remembered that staring into dog's eyes was often interpreted as a dominance battle. I dropped my eyes and looked down and to the right, but Dylan whined, making me look back up at him. I held out my palm and approached him. Dylan snorted against my hand and rolled his eyes at me, a gesture so incredibly human that it caught me off guard.

I wasn't certain why I wasn't freaking out or how I knew this wasn't a dream, but I felt calm and just...accepted it. Yes, I'd known a witch or two at my previous school, had a few dealings with vampires, but they'd sworn they were the only magical creatures in existence. That was probably something they had to tell humans that found out, though. They didn't want people to know that there were lots of non-human beings in the world. They didn't want the humans freaking out or trying to capture them. I could just see the number of girls who would trample each other to have a werewolf boyfriend like Dylan.

Like being struck by lightning, understanding hit me.

"I understand now," I said softly and felt tears stinging my eyes.

Dylan tilted his head to the side in a very canine-like move.

"I understand why you act disgusted every time you touch me. You should have just told me that you don't want or can't be with me instead of embarrassing me in front of everyone." I looked at all of the people watching us. "Or maybe that was your point. Maybe you wanted to embarrass the stupid human girl."

I backed away from him, heading towards the loft which had a window on the second story since the main door was blocked by Ethan and Tom.

"Chloe, you don't understand. Just let Dylan explain—" Kelly started saying.

I shook my head and jumped up, catching the bottom floor of the loft and pulled myself up. "I understand perfectly well. Now, if you'll excuse me, I'm going to go die of embarrassment."

I jumped out the window and tried to roll as I landed, but ended up landing more on my left arm. I screamed in pain as I heard the bone crunch, but pushed myself up and started running.

I had to get away. I needed to get away from them all even for a little bit.

I headed towards the forest and almost turned away when I remembered that I'd promised Dylan I wouldn't go in there alone, but then the stab of betrayal pushed me forward.

This explained so much.

"Chloe!" Dylan called after me.

I ignored him and continued on my path, tears streaming down my face as I ran. I'd never been so embarrassed and so hurt at the same time. I collapsed on the bench by the lake and the sobs broke through. He could have just told me. He could have just said that he didn't want to be with me because I was human. Or that he couldn't be with me because I was human. Whatever his reason, he didn't have to make a public mockery of my feelings for him.

"Look what we found here, a weeping mortal."

I sat up and looked around for the speaker, but the forest was too dark.

"I was just planning on killing one of the young wolves, but stealing their pet human is an even better idea."

"I agree."

"Who's there?" I yelled as I stood up and searched for the speakers.

"We'd better grab her before boy wonder shows up."

Grab me?

I turned to run, but Steve appeared in front of me. "Going somewhere?"

"Steve? What the hell are you doing here?" I gasped, walking slowly backwards.

He followed me with a smile on his face. "I'm here to help push the war to a more drastic level."

I'd heard his plan to kill one of the younger kids, and I was actually glad that me being captured could save someone's life. If only I could think of a way to stop Kelly's family—or pack—from coming after me.

Steve reached for me and grabbed my broken arm. I screamed in pain and he released his hold. "Oh, sorry. I didn't know it was broken."

Another man, a much larger and scarier man, stepped out of the trees and jabbed something into my arm. "Let's get out of here before the pack comes after us."

My eyelids grew heavy, and my tongue started going limp. He must have given me a tranquilizer. I opened my mouth and yelled, "Don't come after me, Dylan!"

Steve glared at me and said, "He'll come. You're not going to stop this war, Chloe."

I wanted to argue with him or yell to Dylan again, but the tranquilizer took effect and I fell asleep.

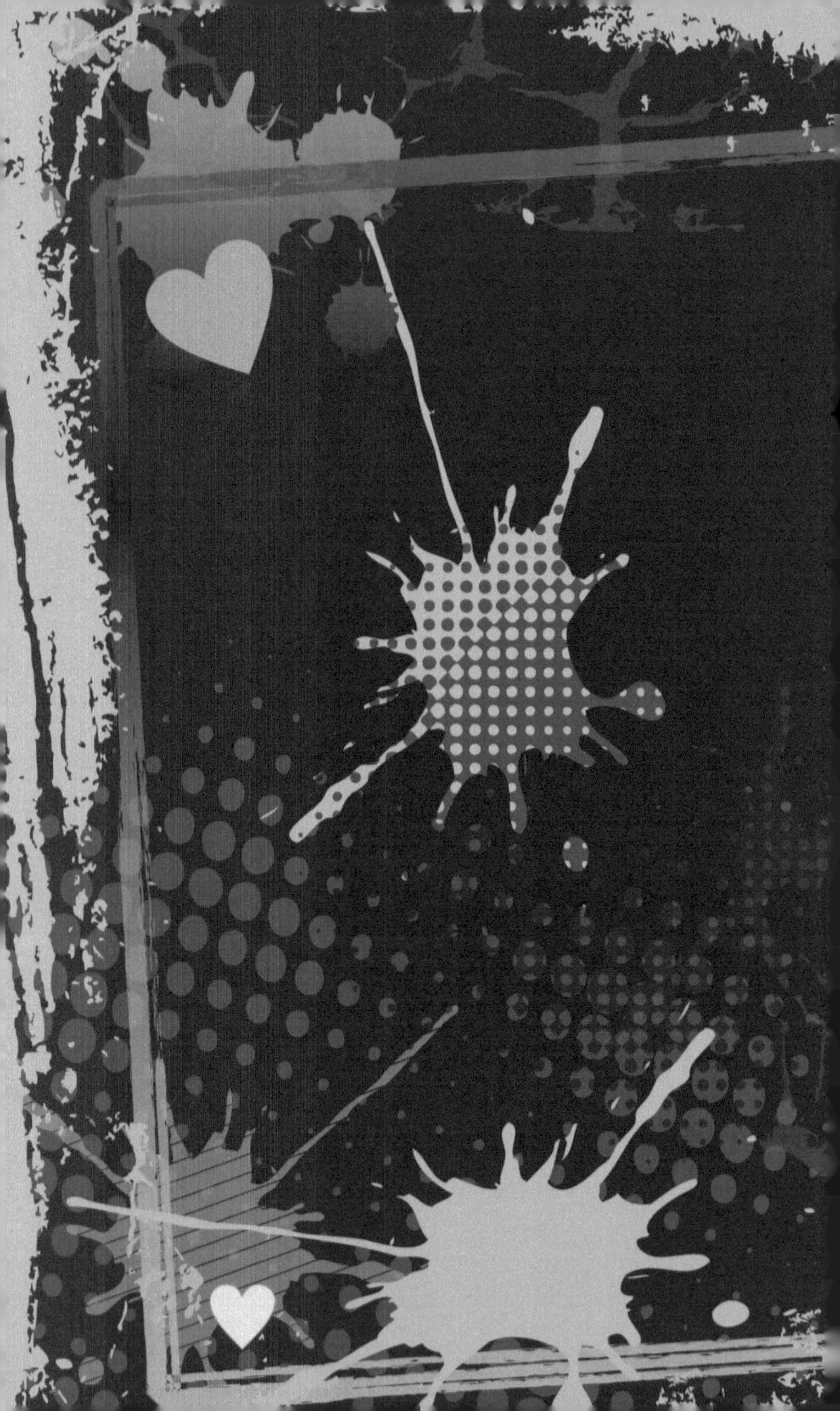

TWELVE

A light turned on behind my closed eyelids. I groaned and opened them. Steel bars surrounded me and people circled the cage, staring at me.

I sat up and then looked down at my heavy left arm. A purple cast covered it now. "Who?" I asked with wide eyes and looked up at the faces of the people around me.

A man in his thirties approached front of the cage door and smiled at me. "Our doctor put the cast on. We figured it was best to do it while you were still sedated."

"Where am I?"

"In the holding cell in the center of our pack's territory."

"What are you going to do with me?"

"You, my dear, are bait." He smiled wide, and it made me shudder in revulsion. This guy was a creep, it was clear with just one look at him.

"They won't come for me. I told Dylan not to come. Besides, he showed me why we can't be together in front of the entire pack." I picked at the cotton coming out of the cast by my thumb and sniffed. I wasn't usually so open with strangers, but I didn't care anymore. They were probably going to kill me anyways. "I would have understood if he had just told me that because he was a werewolf he couldn't or didn't want to be with me. I didn't need to be humiliated."

"They'll come because we sent them your clothes," the man said.

I looked down and my jaw dropped. I was dressed in a pair of sweatpants and a loose t-shirt. Crap.

"Wait, what do you mean he can't be with you because he's a werewolf?" asked a man in his early twenties who came to stand beside the first man.

I looked up and sniffed. "Every time he got near me, he acted disgusted, and before he changed, he told me it would explain everything. I get it. Humans must disgust you guys. He could have just told me in private."

The younger man shook his head. "He wasn't disgusted with you because you're human. He was disgusted with himself for not being human. Wolves don't exhibit standard human protocols when they like someone and want to touch them."

"I don't understand what you're saying," I admitted.

The older man shook his head. "I need to get outside. If you need to use the restroom just shout and one of the guards will escort you to the facilities over there." He pointed to a door a few feet away from the cage. "If you try to escape though, you'll have to use a less clean alternative which forces you to stay in the cage to use the restroom."

Crap. There went my hopes of escaping.

"Are you going to kill me?" I asked softly.

Every man laughed.

The older man shook his head again. "No. We are just

going to keep you here until the war is over. We'll discuss your options after that point."

"What's your name?" I asked.

"I'm John, the alpha." He turned and started up a set of stairs with everyone except the twenty-something man, who sat down in a chair facing my cage.

I turned and studied my surroundings again to try to catalog everything. The cage was three sided, with the fourth side being the brick wall of what I guessed to be the basement. A small window sat over my head, but out of reach even if I were to jump. I could fit through it though if I figured out a way to climb up high enough to reach it.

"I can open that for you, if you want," said my guard.

"No, I'm sure it's too cold right now, but thank you." I sat down on the mattress and faced him. "What's your name?"

"Jesse."

"Hi, Jesse. I'm Chloe."

Jesse smiled. "Nice to meet you."

"Can I ask you a favor?"

Jesse's smile disappeared and suspicion filled his eyes. "You can ask."

"Will you give me a rundown on werewolves? I only just found out about what everyone was before I was taken by Steve. I'd like to find out as much as I can."

He frowned and asked, "Why?"

"If I want to live among them, I need to know more about them. I don't want to make a mistake and hurt their feelings that could have been avoided if I just asked questions. If I just took the time to learn about them. Plus, what else are we going to do down here?"

Jesse nodded and chuckled. "Sure." I adjusted myself into a more comfortable position on the mattress and then he began. "To become a werewolf, you have to be bitten while a werewolf is in wolf form. The change is very difficult and not everyone makes it."

"Do you have female werewolves in your pack?"

Jesse said, "We have some, but most of the female werewolves choose to go to Kelly's pack. No male would ever hurt a female, but they feel more comfortable with a female alpha."

"Why aren't there very many kids?"

Jesse sighed. "Werewolves cannot have children with each other. In order to have a child, a werewolf must mate with a human."

I blinked at him. "What?"

He smiled. "That's why Dylan was so worried about showing you what he was. You are his one chance at a family and it all depends on how you feel about him being a werewolf."

I noticed that a few men had made their way down the stairs and were sitting around the basement, listening to us.

I tried to ignore them and looked at Jesse. "It doesn't matter to me what he is. I mean, as long as he isn't going to go crazy and rip me apart or anything, it's not his fault he was bitten or born or however he was turned into a werewolf."

The room was eerily silent. I looked at the men around and found looks of shock, appreciation, and curiosity all directed at me.

"That is a very uncommon response," Jesse said softly.

Now I understood completely why Dylan had acted like he had. I had to escape so I could get back and warn them.

"I need to use the restroom," I said softly.

Jesse stood up and opened the cage door with a key he had in his front pocket. "There are five of us so you have no chance of escape, honestly you wouldn't have a chance of escape if there were only one of us."

I rolled my eyes. "Like I'm going to try to run from a werewolf. I may be human and only recently learned your kind was real, but I do know a little about wolves and I know better than to run."

I walked to the bathroom and closed the door then looked up and sighed. No window. I'd been hoping I could at least escape through the window in the bathroom.

After doing my business, I walked back inside my cage and sat on the ground. Jesse and the other men stared at me, wide-eyed. Did they really expect me to try to escape?

"Can you teach me greetings and gestures?" I asked as Jesse finally recovered from his surprise and locked the cage door again.

Jesse sat down and frowned. "Greetings?"

I nodded. "Yeah, I mean, if someone comes up to me in wolf form what's the proper way to greet them? Do I pet them on the head? Do I look them in the eyes and then drop my gaze? What do I do?"

Jesse smiled. "Oh, I see. Tony, will you help me?"

Tony, a short bulky man with a shaved head and piercing blue eyes, walked to stand next to Jesse. "Yeah, what you want me to do?"

"Change," Jesse said.

I looked down at my lap as Tony started stripping his clothes to change.

"You can look now," Jesse said with a hint of a smile in his voice.

I looked up and my heart rate increased as I saw the massive grey wolf. Jesse cleared his throat, making me look back at him, now standing in front of Tony the wolf. "Now, if you're greeting a dominant wolf—"

"What do you mean dominant wolf? How do I know if they're dominant or not?"

Jesse sighed. "I'll teach you that another day, but today, just watch and learn. Now, if Tony is, say, the alpha then when he walks up to you, you make eye contact and then look at the ground and tilt your head to the right."

I watched as Jesse made eye contact with Tony and then averted his gaze and tiled his head to the side, exposing his neck. "This is a sign of submission, where you give your neck to the alpha."

I swallowed. "Does the alpha grab your neck?"

Jesse shook his head and smiled at me. "Not in this instance." Tony whined at Jesse who nodded. "Good point."

"You understood what he was saying?" I blinked.

Jesse tapped his temple. "Telepathy. We can communicate mind to mind in human or wolf form once a pack bond has been established."

"Oh." Well that was useful information.

"Tony suggested that I show you how a couple, such as you and a male wolf you are interested in, would greet each other. This is how you would show affection towards the wolf without admitting to being only with him. So, in your situation, if you wanted to show Dylan you liked him, you would do this." Tony walked up to Jesse and then rubbed his nose against Tom's.

I gaped at them. "Dylan did that, but then he freaked out and acted all upset and embarrassed."

"He must have been worried you would think that was a weird gesture," suggested one of the other men watching us.

"Well, it is *different*, but I thought it was cute. I thought he was disgusted at having done it," I said.

Tony sighed, and Jesse shook his head. "You have a lot to learn about boys," said Jesse.

I laughed. "I have a lot to learn about werewolf boys apparently."

"Now, let's say you are already mated, or are planning on being mated soon. This is how you would greet him." Jesse walked up to Tony, making eye contact the whole way, and then rubbed his left cheek against Tony's furry left cheek. Jesse then repeated the cheek rubbing on the other side. Jesse stepped back and rubbed at his face with his hands. "Doing that greeting marks you with the wolf's scent so that the others will smell him on you. You can also do this to simply calm a male down when he is worried about your well being."

"Okay. How do I greet my friends while in wolf form? The girls, I mean."

Jesse shrugged. "You could just wave at them, or, if they are comfortable enough with you, you can run your hand through the fur on their scruff, but don't make eye contact until you're right beside them and about to touch them."

"What about a random wolf in the pack?" I was getting a lot of valuable information. I just hoped I'd get out before the packs went to war and get to use it.

"Since you're human, you are technically the lowest ranking in the pack. So, when you greet any of the wolves, except your friends, mate and alpha, you avert your eyes and hold your hand out, palm up. If they sniff and lick your hand, then you're allowed then to touch their front shoulder. If they sniff your hand and walk away, that's the only greeting you will get."

I watched as Jesse and Tony demonstrated them both.

Jesse wiggled his finger around in a circular motion at Tony. Tony nodded and then his body started changing. I looked back down at my hands and waited until I heard him zip up his pants.

"You're going to have to learn to be less modest about nudity. Nudity is a common occurrence with werewolves," said Tony.

"Okay."

"There's also a bond that is formed when you become mates. You *can* make the bond before being mated, but it's not recommended because you can't break the bond." He looked upstairs and frowned. "Are you hungry, Chloe?"

I nodded. "Yes."

He nodded and then looked back at me.

"Um, aren't you going to get me food?" I asked Jesse.

Jesse tapped his temple again. "Telepathy. I told one of the boys in the kitchen to make you something since he was already in there."

"Can I have something to drink too?" My throat felt dry, but I was sure that was partly from the tranquilizer.

Jesse stared off into space a moment and then smiled. "Done."

"So, what's going to happen to me after they take the bait?" I asked softly.

"You'll have to live here until the war is over and once it is, you'll be allowed to either leave or choose one of our males."

I stared at him. Did he really think I'd choose to stay with their pack after they'd kidnapped me and presumably killed Kelly's pack? Not a chance in hell. "That's not the best set of options."

He shrugged. "I don't make the rules. The alpha is the one who decides."

The alpha sounded like a real jerk.

Jesse said, "Just another piece of information, werewolves are really big on touching. We get comfort from the touch of a packmate."

"So, if someone's afraid or mad, if I touch them, I'll make it better?" I asked even though it sounded strange. I knew touch made humans feel better, but an angry or fearful werewolf seemed less likely to want to be touched.

Jesse nodded. "Even just a hand on an arm is immensely calming."

I couldn't think of anything else to ask so I relaxed on the mattress and dozed until a teenage boy brought my food. He smiled at me and opened his mouth, but Jesse growled and the boy hurriedly walked up the stairs.

I frowned at Jesse. "Why'd you growl at him?"

Jesse shook his head. "Like I said, you have a lot to learn about boys."

I had no idea what that meant, but I decided to leave it alone and eat my bacon, lettuce, and tomato sandwich. I guzzled down the first bottle of water and then half of the second Tony brought down.

"So, what now?" I asked as I lay down on the mattress and looked up at the ceiling.

Jesse sighed. "Now we wait for them to try to rescue you."

"It's not going to happen. I don't care if you sent my clothes to them or not, they are not going to come. I'm just a human girl who ended up living with them because of my dad and they have no reason to—" My tirade was ended when someone upstairs yelled for everyone downstairs.

The other men in the basement charged up the steps. Jesse looked at the steps then back at me. "I've got to see what's going on. Your cage is locked so don't get any ideas."

I rolled my eyes. "Like I could get past you guys even if I somehow managed to get the lock off."

Jesse smiled. "True. Okay, stay put and stay away from the edges of the cage in case some random member comes down here."

I nodded and sat on the mattress in the center of the cage. Jesse looked at me one more time and then darted up the stairs. As soon as the door shut at the top of the stairs, I faced the wall and looked up at the window. I jumped up as high as I could, but barely touched the bottom of the window with my fingertips.

"I hate being short," I mumbled angrily, turning away from the window.

"I think it's cute that you're short," said a familiar male voice.

I turned and looked around the basement, but couldn't see him. Something touched my shoulder, making me squeal and spin around.

Dylan was leaning through the window, holding out his arms. "Come on, we don't have much time."

"You came for me?" I asked with wide eyes.

Dylan smiled and wiggled his fingers. "Of course I did. Now come on so we can get you out of here."

I grabbed his forearm with my good arm and held on tightly as he dragged me up and out the window. I slid through the window and across damp grass.

We were in the backyard. I heard growling and yelling around the front of the house, but before I could ask what was going on, Dylan tugged me to a standing position. Our eyes met, and I leaned forward and rubbed my nose against his.

Dylan stared at me in silent shock before finally smiling.

He grabbed my good arm, and we started running towards woods behind the house.

"Do you all have forests behind your houses?" I asked curiously.

Dylan nodded. "We pick houses that back up to the forests so we can run in them. Now stay quiet or someone will—"

"Find you," Jesse finished, standing in the center of the path we were headed down.

Dylan snarled, dropped my hand, and lunged at Jesse who met him halfway with his fist raised. Dylan was a good fighter, but Jesse obviously had more training. After a few minutes of fighting, Jesse wrapped his hand around Dylan's throat and held him up off the ground, choking him.

I ran forward and grabbed Jesse's arm. "Please, Jesse. Please let him go." Jesse growled and continued to glare at Dylan. "Jesse, I'm begging you, please, as a favor to me, let him go."

Jesse released Dylan and stepped back. "I'll hold you to your debt, Chloe."

I jumped up and hugged Jesse in both disbelief that he actually did it and that he took it so seriously.

"Thank you," I whispered into his ear.

Dylan growled and pulled me away from him. "Come on," Dylan said, his brows furrowed in anger.

Jesse watched us a moment and then ran towards the house.

Dylan tugged my hand. "Chloe, we have to go." I nodded and followed Dylan, but after a moment he sighed in frustration. "Let me carry you."

"Carry me?"

He scooped me up into his arms and smiled at me. "Yes, carry you." He leaned closer to my face, but then someone shouted behind us and he started running. I'd never experienced anything in my life like being carried by a werewolf running in human form. The wind pressed against my body and the trees passed by in blurs. I hoped Dylan could see the trees because I couldn't tell where anything was.

Dylan slowed down after what felt like an hour and I realized we were back on Kelly's property. Dylan walked into the barn, closed the doors, and set me down. I laid down and tried to stop the spinning.

"Are you alright? Did they hurt you? Why do you have a cast? Did they…touch you?" he asked as he inspected my cast and bare feet.

The spinning stopped so I could sit up. I smiled. "I'm fine. They were very nice and didn't touch me or hurt me. I broke my arm jumping out of the barn and they had their doctor put it in a cast."

Dylan exhaled and sat down beside me. "I'm sorry, about yesterday."

I shook my head. "No, I'm sorry. I should have listened to you instead of just assuming I knew what you were trying to show me."

"What did they tell you?" he asked suspiciously. "Why are you so calm?"

I really shouldn't have been so calm, but I was and I didn't want to question it too much. "Just some basic werewolf 101, but how about you tell me what you wanted to say yesterday." I said the last part looking down at my hands, unable to meet his eyes.

Dylan asked, "How do you feel about me being a werewolf?"

I looked up at him and saw the worry in his eyes. "I don't feel anyway about it. It's a shock you exist, but besides that…

as long as you don't try to tear me apart, then I'm fine with it. I know I have a lot to learn about you guys, but I'm willing to try."

Dylan looked like I'd told him I was a mermaid. "You're serious?"

I nodded.

Dylan inhaled then leaned over me and kissed me on the lips. I wrapped my arms around his body and he wrapped his around mine, pressing us closer together. When he pulled back from the kiss, I rubbed each cheek against his and whispered, "Does this mean you don't think I'm disgusting?"

Dylan laughed and hugged me tighter. "I think you're beautiful."

We sat in each other's arms in silence for a moment and then I asked, "Where is everyone?"

Dylan groaned and pulled a cell phone from his pocket and dialed. "It's Dylan. We're at the ranch." He listened a moment and then said, "She's perfectly fine. No harm done."

"Who was that?" I asked.

Dylan shut the phone and put it back in his pocket. "Kelly. She and the rest of the group were creating a distraction out front so we could sneak away and I was supposed to call them when we got here. I kind of forgot though."

I blushed and looked down at my hands. "So, what does this mean?"

Dylan tilted my head up and asked, "Would you go out to dinner with me tomorrow?"

I blinked, at a loss for words, and then nodded. "I'd like that."

"Chloe!" Dad called from outside the barn. He threw open the doors and ran to me, picking me up in a bruising hug.

"Oh, thank God. I was worried sick." He set me down. "Are you alright? Did they hurt you? What happened?"

I smiled and hugged him one-armed. "I'm fine. They took me, but were very nice and other than being locked in a cage, nothing happened. Dylan got me out."

Dad turned to Dylan and held out his hand. Dylan shook it, and Dad said, "Thank you and you have my blessing now."

Dylan exhaled and smiled wide. "Thank you."

"Blessing? For what?" I asked.

Dad smiled. "For him to date you."

I looked at Dylan. "What if he had said no?"

Dylan shrugged. "Then I would have tried to change his mind."

Wolves ran into the barn and surrounded us. I turned to each wolf and averted my eyes and then raised my palm up. Each wolf sniffed and licked my palm and then I ran a hand down each of their shoulders. One wolf bounced up to me and rubbed her body against mine and then licked my face happily, her tail wagging wildly the whole time. It reminded me of Lisa, though I couldn't be certain. After everyone came to touch me, they all started changing.

Kelly walked to me and wrapped me in a hug. "Are you alright?"

I relaxed into her hug, suddenly feeling the fear I'd been holding back. I sniffed and then pulled back from her. "I'm fine. They were extremely nice to me, considering I was their prisoner."

"What happened?" asked Amy.

I looked out at all of the pack's faces. "I'm sorry about how I reacted yesterday. I misunderstood what was happening. I panicked and ran out into the forest where Steve and another man from his pack were waiting. They told me that they had planned to come and kill one of your young wolves, but thought stealing me was better. I went with them willingly because I'd rather be taken than have someone die. They used a tranquilizer on me and when I woke up, I was inside a cage in their basement with this cast." I held up my arm. "They told me that I was just bait to start the war between you guys and no harm would come to me. They let me use a bathroom and fed me and one of my guards even talked with me about your kind. Then you guys came and they left me in the basement since they knew I couldn't escape alone. Dylan pulled me out the basement window and we escaped."

I left out the part with Jesse because I didn't want to embarrass Dylan and I figured that was a bit of information they didn't need to know.

"Did they say what they were going to do with you?" Kelly asked softly.

I nodded. "They said that I would have to live in the cage until the war was over and once it was, that I could either leave or choose one of their males as a mate."

Dylan growled behind me, which made me smile in spite of the topic. I felt him move closer to me and reached back to touch his arm. His muscles were taut, but after a moment I felt them relax.

Kelly and the other adults were staring at me in shock. "How did you...?" she asked suspiciously.

I laughed. "I just asked, Jesse, err, one of my guards, about werewolf etiquette. He told me a lot of useful information."

Kelly hugged me again. "I'm so glad they didn't hurt you. I wouldn't have been able to stand it if you'd been hurt."

"Well, I'm fine," I said with a smile, "but very hungry."

Dylan grabbed my hand and tugged on it. "I'll take you to the house to get something to eat."

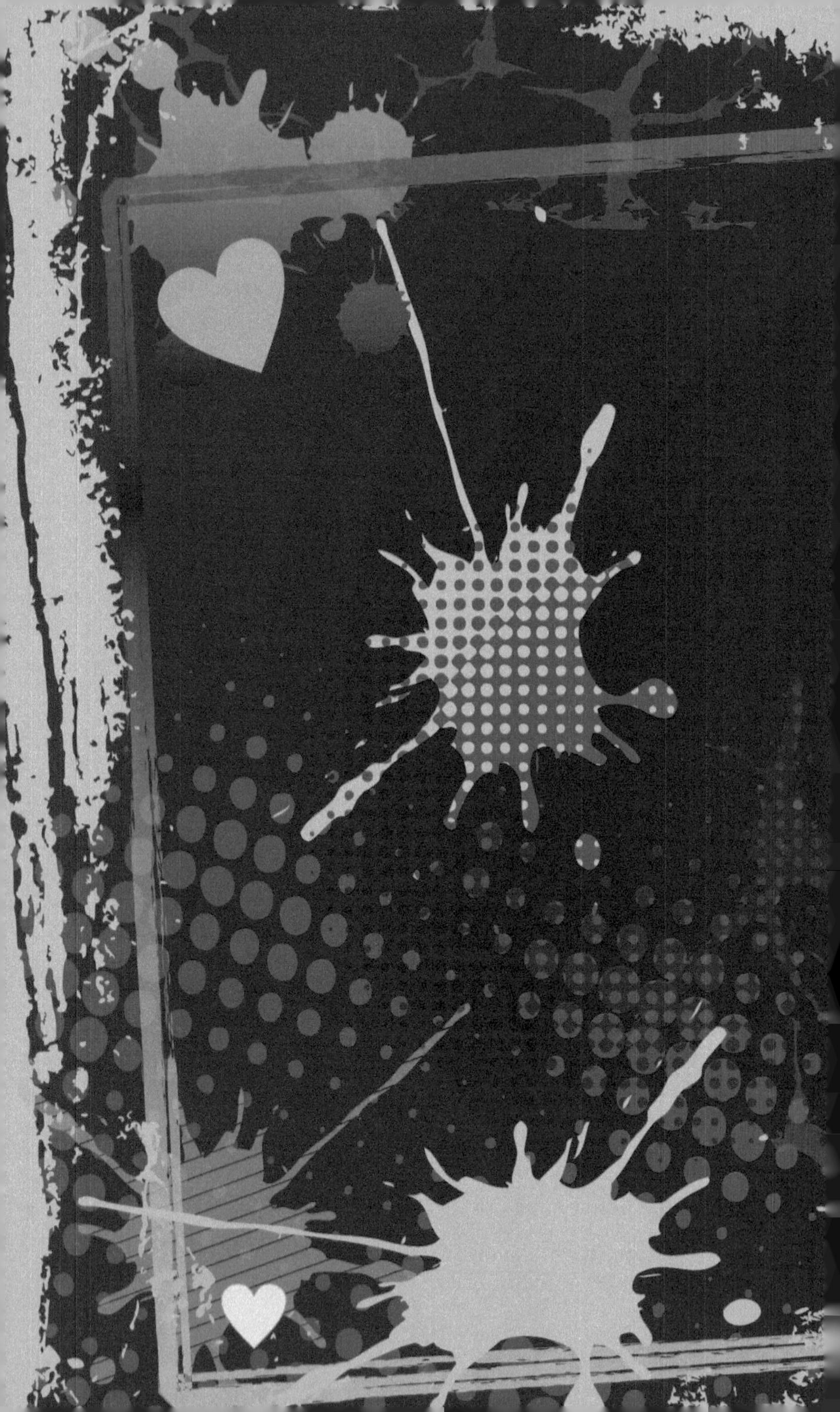

THIRTEEN

"Wait!" Cynthia yelled as she walked towards us.

"What?" I asked. "What do you want?"

She growled at me, grabbed my wrist, and pulled on it so that my hand was jerked out of Dylan's. "I will not allow this."

"You don't have a choice," I said as I jerked my arm away from her.

She snarled, and I could see her canines lengthening. "Yes, I do."

"You harm her and I'll kill you," Dylan said menacingly.

She turned and stared at him with wide eyes. "What?"

"You heard me. She is part of our pack and she is under my protection since I'm courting her. If you harm her, I will kill you. And yes, that is a threat," Dylan said as he came to stand between her and me.

"She's *human*!" Cynthia yelled. "She isn't right for you. You need a wolf. You need someone who can help you lead."

"Even if that were true, I wouldn't pick you," Dylan said.

Cynthia lunged around Dylan and reached for my throat,

but I was prepared for her to try something. I ducked her grab, punched her in the stomach, and stepped back.

Dylan grabbed her and threw her, sending her over fifty feet across the barn.

"Kelly?" Cynthia begged as she stood. "Are you going to let him do this?"

"If he hadn't said it, I would have. Honestly, I've been considering kicking you out of the pack for a while; you don't seem to be settling in well here no matter what we do to help you and your inability to accept our newest pack member is getting on my last nerve," Kelly said with a straight face.

"Why are you all picking her, a human, over me?" Cynthia yelled.

"No one is picking anyone," Amy said. "You are pushing us all away because you can't accept that Dylan doesn't want you and you can't accept that Chloe is part of our pack now. You are the only one. You are outing yourself."

"Shut up, Amy."

Amy ran forward and punched Cynthia in the face and then kicked her in the stomach. I was surprised at Amy's brutality, but she had obviously been holding in her anger for a while now. She continued to fight her until Cynthia finally whined in pain and stopped trying to fight back. "I am higher in the pack than you. You would do well to remember that."

Adam picked up Cynthia and headed out of the barn. "Come on, girl, let's get you home."

Dylan grabbed my hand again, and we walked out of the barn, this time without any interruptions. I was surprised that he was holding my hand especially since he had been so standoffish and freaked out each time he touched me before, but it was nice. Definitely not something I was used to.

He dropped my hand as soon as we stepped into the house

and spun around, pinning me to the door, and kissed me deeply. He pulled back and inhaled with his nose buried in my hair. "Don't ever try to sacrifice yourself again, you understand?"

I nodded and kissed his cheek. "Thank you for rescuing me."

"I will always come for you," he whispered.

"Why didn't you tell me sooner?" I asked. "Why did you push away from me?"

"I was afraid that you would reject me once you found out what we are. I was afraid that you wouldn't want to be with a half-human."

A tear formed in the corner of my eye, and I wiped it away. "This whole time I believed you were disgusted by me and only being nice because you had to be."

He kissed my lips and then my forehead before pulling me against him in a hug. "I'm sorry, Chloe. I am so sorry I hurt you."

"Do you only want to be with me because you can't mate with a werewolf?" I asked him before he could pull back and look at my face. I was too afraid to ask him while looking at him.

He jerked back anyways and forced me to meet his eyes. "Of course not."

"You swear?" I asked him. It wouldn't be the first time a guy only wanted me to sleep with me, but it would definitely be the first time they only wanted to have a kid with me.

"Chloe, I want to be with you because you are beautiful, smart, and tough. You are all I think about, and I want to be able to touch you and kiss you and keep you by my side as long as I can. You are the only girl I want."

I had no words to reply so I just kissed his lips and then

walked into the kitchen. "What are you making me?" I asked as I hopped up onto the counter.

"What would you like?" he asked as he stood between my legs and smiled at me.

"Breakfast," I said with a smile.

"Breakfast?" he asked in shock. "Like a bowl of cereal?"

"No. I want eggs, bacon, and pancakes."

"That sounds great! Make some for me, too," Tom said as he and the rest of our group walked into the kitchen.

"I'm not cooking for all of you," Dylan said.

"Oh, I see, Chloe gets special treatment," Tom complained.

Dylan nodded. "Yes, she does. If you want food, make it for you and your girl."

"I'm not hungry," Lisa said with a smile.

"I am," Amy said. "Dylan, please make food. You make the best pancakes ever and your bacon is perfectly crisp."

"Come on," I urged him. "Just make enough for everyone."

"Bribe him with a kiss," Lisa suggested. "That always works for me."

"You bribe me?" Tom asked, blinking in feigned surprise.

"So, how did you all become werewolves?" I asked.

"That is a very personal question," Dylan whispered.

"For most of us, when our human parent figured out what we were, they dropped us off on Kelly's doorstep," Amy answered.

"Well, except for me," Alex said. "I was bitten by a were-wolf and changed."

"So, you can be changed then?" I asked.

Dylan's head whipped around and he stared into my eyes with his serious face. "No," he said in his no-nonsense tone.

"What do you mean 'no'?" I asked.

"You are not being changed," he said.

"I didn't ask to be changed or say I wanted to be. However, let's get one thing straight, I can do whatever I want," I said sternly. I was not about to get pushed around by a guy, even one I cared about.

He sucked in a breath and then wiped a hand down his face. "Sorry. You're right. It's not my decision to make for you, but I won't do it or stand by and watch someone do it to you. Besides, there's plenty of time to think about this decision since we're still young. Just...don't rush into it since you can't take it back."

He was right, but my anger was still high. I turned back to the rest of the group and asked, "Is it painful when you change?"

Everyone shook their head.

"Just the first time," Alex said.

"Obviously you guys aren't controlled by the moon so why the myth?" I asked.

"So the humans wouldn't be able to find us," Kelly answered. "If they believed we only changed on full moons they looked for people who go missing around then. And of course, we are always visible around town on the full moon."

"Why is there a war between the two packs?" I asked.

"Because that pack is mostly old and dying out. The younger wolves come to this pack instead, which pisses them off. They think we're a bit odd, too, in how we run our pack. So, they want to combine our packs," Dylan said.

"How does fighting you end with you joining them? Wouldn't you always fight them?" I asked.

"If they defeat Kelly and are able to show their dominance over us, we would be forced to join them. Or, we would have to leave," Alex said.

"Which is hard to do when we're only teenagers and have no money," Amy added.

"They have some younger people," I whispered, thinking about Jesse and Steve.

"Yes, but most are here. They're an old school type of pack and it bothers their alpha that our pack of outcasts has managed to continue for so long," Dylan explained.

"The alpha is also pissed because I refused to become his mate," Kelly added and shrugged. "I don't like assholes."

"Can't fault you there," I said and chuckled.

Dylan started cooking and it was quickly obvious that he was making food for more than just me. He really was a good person.

"So, will this war ever be over?" I asked softly.

Kelly sighed and dropped her head. "I'm not sure." She raised it and met my eyes. "They've definitely crossed a line by taking you, though. It may be time to go on the offensive."

"Don't they have more seasoned fighters, though?" I asked with a squeak of fear.

Dylan put the pan of bacon in the oven and then stood between my legs. He set a hand on my cheek and said, "We won't let them take you ever again."

"I'm not worried about me," I explained. "I'm worried about you guys getting hurt." About *him* getting hurt.

"It is true that they have more seasoned fighters," Kelly said. "We could win, but there would be loss. Probably too much loss for it to truly count as a win."

"So, what are we going to do then?" Amy asked. "We can't just give up."

"What if we try to barter a truce?" I asked. "There has to be something they want that we could barter, right? Aside from combining the packs or Kelly becoming the leader's mate?"

"I don't think so," Kelly said, "but it is worth looking into. I could send a message and see what he sends back." She shrugged. "I can always tell him to pound sand if what he wants is ridiculous."

"It wouldn't hurt to try," Dylan said and went back to cooking.

Amy leaned against the counter beside me, pushing gently on my leg with her side. "You're really okay?" she asked softly.

I set my hand on her shoulder and nodded while smiling. "Yes."

She wrapped her arms around my waist and exhaled. "I'm so glad."

"Me, too," I teased despite knowing she was serious.

We ate the food together and then I went to my room and immediately collapsed and fell asleep.

When I woke, it was to find several wolves on the floor of my room.

Fear clawed at my throat, but I quickly shoved it down and after a bit, my heart slowed.

I couldn't tell the difference between them yet, so I just tiptoed around them all to get to the bathroom for my morning ritual. When I came back, they were all in the same spots, so I moved around them and got back into bed.

I started to fall asleep again, but my door was opened and Kelly peeked inside. She smiled and said, "They all felt worried about you still and wanted to sleep in your room. I figured you wouldn't mind, especially if they were all in wolf form."

"It's a little scary to wake up to a bunch of predators in my room, but since I know they won't hurt me, it's okay," I said with a smile.

"Why don't you come downstairs and get some breakfast? They'll likely be asleep for a while longer," she said.

I hopped out of bed and maneuvered out of the room and followed her to the dining room.

As soon as I stepped inside, Adam stood out of his chair and wrapped me in a tight hug.

I tensed a moment and then hugged him back. "I'm okay," I reassured him.

He released me and sat down quickly, resuming eating his breakfast.

"What are your plans for the day?" Kelly asked.

Dad wasn't there, which meant he was likely sleeping still. It was rare for him to sleep in, so it made me happy.

"Nothing," I answered as I sat. "I want to just lie around and be as lazy as possible. The couch is calling to me and I'm going to answer it." There were a ton of TV shows I'd missed out on, so I wanted to spend some time getting caught up on my favorites.

"Sounds like a good day," she said and nodded while eating.

A few minutes later, Dylan stumbled in, hair rumpled and eyes half closed. Yet, he still looked gorgeous. He stopped behind my chair, inhaled from the top of my head, and then sat beside me. "Morning," he said in a grumbly voice.

"Morning," I replied and tried to hide my face so no one saw my blush.

Dylan made his plate and then slid a buttered biscuit onto mine before buttering another for himself.

I hadn't grabbed one because I was trying to watch my diet, but didn't want to say anything to him or refuse it. I was pretty sure that food was a big thing with dating werewolf couples.

"So, why don't you tell me how you know about supernaturals already," Kelly said while she buttered a biscuit on her plate.

I swallowed the bite of food I'd had in my mouth and said, "Huh?"

She gave me a look. "Come on."

"I knew a witch at my previous school," I admitted. "She told me that they were the only supernatural race, though."

Dylan looked at me and his eyebrows rose. "Kelly."

Everything seemed to go slow motion.

Dylan stood up, knocking his chair over in his hurry, and reached out towards me.

Kelly was up out of her chair and running towards me, as was Adam.

Arms wrapped around my body and then a high-pitched voice I hadn't heard in over a year said, "She's mine."

"No!" Dylan yelled, his hand inches from me.

Kelly yelled, but the sound faded.

A tunnel of light and swirling colors appeared before me and I fainted.

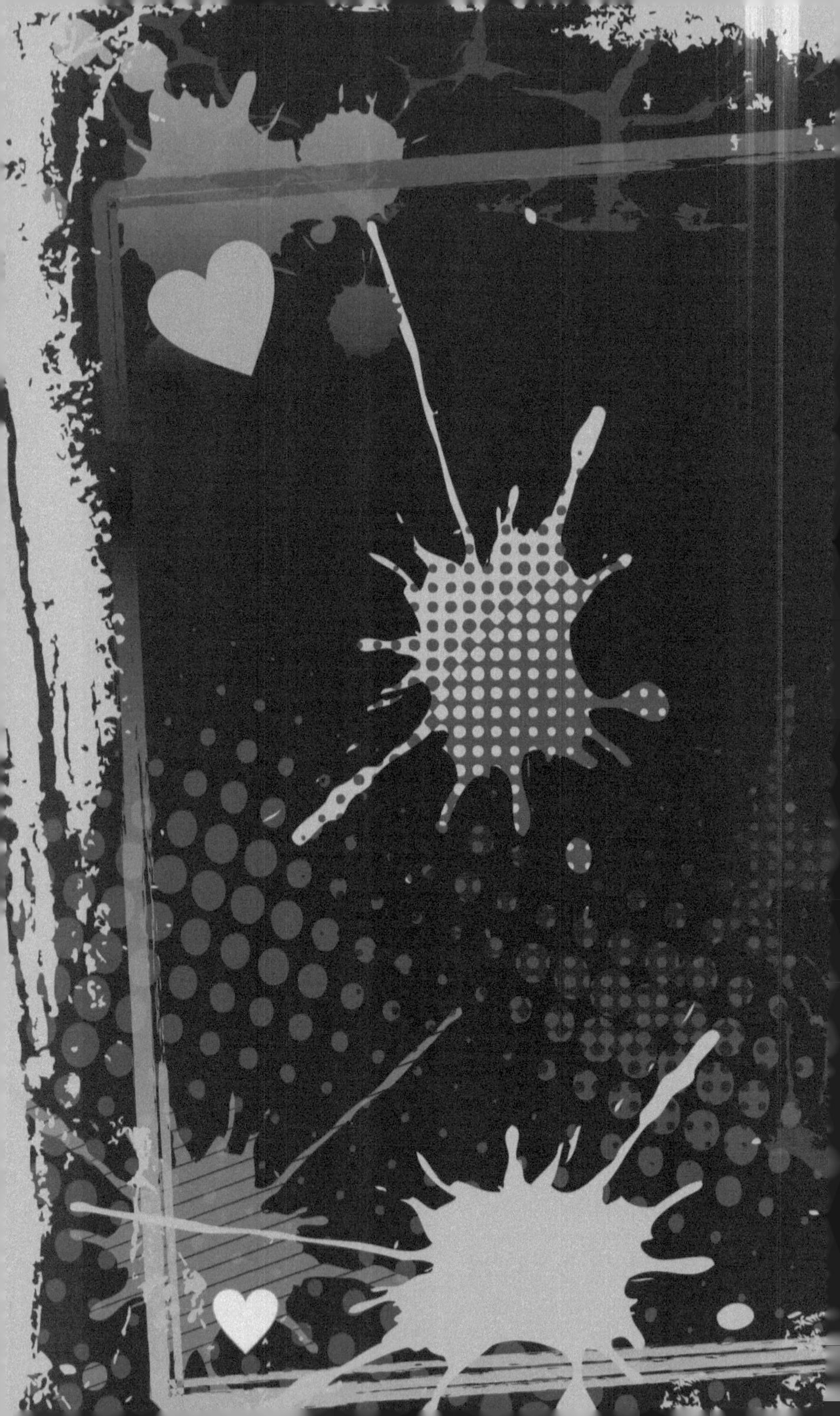

FOURTEEN

"Please explain to me why you thought you could ignore me?" Jacqueline asked. "And why haven't you been answering my summons? I've been trying to contact you for weeks!"

"Where are we?" I asked her instead of answering.

The room we were in looked like her bedroom, but that was across the state, so that didn't make any sense. We couldn't have crossed the state in just seconds.

Jacqueline squatted down beside the bed I lay on; her dark brown hair was wind-tousled and her jaw was clenched. Her piercing blue eyes bore into mine as she set his hand on my cheek. "Chloe, I told you that I wasn't going to give up on our friendship just because you had to move far away."

"Wh-what?"

She sighed and rubbed her thumb over my cheek bone. "Your disorientation should wear off in a moment. I forgot that it effects humans in this way."

"Jacqueline, did you just kidnap me from my stepmom's house?" I asked softly.

She chuckled. "Maybe. In my defense, I've been trying to contact you and you keep ignoring my summons. I got worried you were in danger."

"What summons?"

"The pains in your head, remember? Those are indications to go to a mirror or bowl of water so I can communicate with you," she explained.

"Oh," I whispered. "I kept thinking they were just headaches."

She groaned and dropped her head forward. "You forgot." I sat up and she moved so that she could lay across my lap. "You forgot me," she whispered and there was no mistaking the pain in her voice.

"I never forgot you," I whispered and pet her hair. "I just didn't realize the headaches were you since I couldn't hear your voice at all in my head and I could at least hear whispers before."

"It's probably because you were around those werewolves," she whispered. "They have telepathy and being around so many of them likely blocked my voice."

"Why did you steal me?" I asked.

She sat up quickly and asked, "Haven't you missed me?"

"Yes," I admitted, "but I thought you'd given up on our friendship since you hadn't mentally contacted me. I'm sorry, I should have sent a letter or something, but I got overwhelmed making this new life, finding out they were werewolves, and all of that."

"Are you telling me that you aren't interested in being friends anymore?"

Of course I was.

"I thought it would be too hard to stay friends since it would be long distance," I whispered.

She stared into my eyes and said, "I'm a witch, remember? I can teleport to you like I just did."

"Right. Speaking of that, you should really return me before they all freak out. My dad is probably worrying out of his mind."

"Not until you agree to stay friends," she whispered.

"Let me fill you in on everything that's happened and then let you decide what you want to do," I suggested.

She nodded and sat cross-legged in front of me. "Please, I want to hear what has happened with you since we last talked."

It took me half an hour to tell her everything that had happened.

She sighed once I'd finished. "I'm sorry I couldn't tell you about the others. It's against our laws."

"It's okay, I understand," I said. And I did because it couldn't be easy to keep secrets like that from people you loved.

"I think the best option here is for me to talk to this were-wolf boy, Dylan, and his pack," she said. "We can hash things out to ensure we can stay friends."

She stood and held her hand out. I let her pull me up and she hugged me while looking down at me. "Do you want to stay friends with me?"

I nodded.

"Then I will work it out with them. Besides, I really want to talk to this Dylan guy."

"You should teleport us outside of the house so I can protect you."

She arched a brow. "You protect me?"

"I don't want them to hurt you," I said.

She nodded. "Fine."

Jacqueline wrapped an arm around my waist, pulled me against her side, and then cast the spell.

We teleported to the front lawn of Kelly's house and the disorientation wore off a lot quicker this time.

Kelly, Dad, Adam, and Dylan rushed outside almost immediately.

I stepped in front of Jacqueline and held my hands up. "She's a friend. Don't attack her. She didn't realize this was my house and thought I might be in danger."

Dad sighed. "Jacqueline, you're not human?"

Jacqueline smiled. "Sorry, sir, I'm not, but I couldn't tell you that."

"You knew?" Dad asked me.

I nodded. "Yeah."

"Chloe, who is this?" Dylan demanded.

Jacqueline draped an arm around my shoulders and smiled. "Hey, wolf boy. I'm Jacqueline, Chloe's best friend."

Dylan's face completely shut down.

"She didn't understand that when I said we weren't ending our friendship, I was serious because I could still teleport to her," Jacqueline explained. "Total misunderstanding. So, Dylan, I think you and I need to have a talk."

"Okay," Dylan said through clenched teeth and walked towards the driveway.

"Witch?" Kelly asked me.

I nodded. "Yes, she is."

"She a good kid?" she asked Dad.

Dad nodded. "One of the best. I was actually really sad we had to move away from her."

"Well, looks like that issue is fixed now," I said and smiled wide.

I looked over at Jacqueline and Dylan who were talking

with serious scowls on their faces. What was she saying to him? Why had she wanted to talk to him so badly?

"Why don't we go inside and finish breakfast?" Dad suggested. "They can come inside when they're done talking."

"No maiming!" I yelled to Jacqueline who gave me a wide smile that made me feel really uneasy.

Dylan gave me a smile also, but his made me smile in return.

Dad pulled me into the house and sat beside me at the breakfast table.

I ate my food, but constantly worried about the two outside. A few minutes later, they entered, Jacqueline smiling and Dylan scowling.

Jacqueline sat beside me, taking what had been Dylan's spot and immediately filled up the plate in front of her with food.

"Everyone, this is Jacqueline or Jacqui," I introduced.

Jacqueline raised a hand and smiled with food in her mouth. "Hi."

"Welcome to our home," Kelly said, smiling wide. "It's great to meet one of Chloe's friends."

"Best friend," Jacqueline countered.

Kelly smiled wider. "So, you're able to teleport?"

Jacqueline nodded while eating. "Makes me super hungry after."

"She has manners, but forgets them sometimes," I said, nudging her, and she rolled her eyes at me.

"Your stepmom is neat," Jacqueline said. "And this house is pretty dope."

The rest of the teens came into the house, and Jacqueline perked up.

"The view ain't so bad either."

I pinched her leg under the table. "You will behave or I will beat you."

She winked. "Don't threaten me with a good time."

Dylan growled softly, which I ignored.

"Who is this?" Emma asked, her eyes narrowed as she looked at Jacqueline.

"Hey, I'm Jacqui, and I'm Chloe's best friend, but you can call me whatever you like, gorgeous," she said and winked at her.

I dropped my head forward and sighed. She was incorrigible.

"Oh, incorrigible. That's a good word. Have you been studying?" Jacqui asked.

"She didn't say anything out loud," Dylan said, his voice menacing.

I raised my head and said, "She can hear my thoughts when she wants to."

"When I open the door," she corrected.

"Why do you have the ability to do that?" Emma asked.

"Blood bond or pact," I answered before Jacqueline could say something to get me in trouble.

I, however, miscalculated what their response would be to my statement.

"You have a blood bond with her?" Dylan asked.

"Non-sexual, wolfie," Jacqueline said with a bright smile. "It's so I can ensure she's safe and teleport to her if anyone steals her."

"That would have been convenient to have before," Amy whispered.

Jacqueline scowled and nodded. "Had she not forgotten everything I taught her, she could have called me and I could have teleported her out of that cell."

"Wait, how do you know about that?" Emma asked, her eyes wide.

"We talked after she kidnapped me," I said with a smile.

"I didn't kidnap you," Jacqueline grumbled and stabbed her piece of egg harder than necessary. "I thought you were in danger and I was rescuing you."

"I appreciate it," I said and bumped her shoulder with mine.

"Okay, I'm lost," Tom said.

"I can show you a thing or two if you want," Jacqueline said, her innuendo obvious.

Amy growled loudly. "No."

Jacqueline stuck her lip out in a pout and looked at me. "They're all taken?"

I nodded and patted the back of her hand on the table. "Sorry, boo."

She muttered to herself while she continued eating.

"Can I talk to you?" Dylan asked me.

Jacqueline whispered in a sing-song voice, "Someone's in trouble."

I stuck my tongue out at her and walked out of the dining room and out of the house into the backyard with Dylan following closely behind.

"Can you make sure she's not listening?" he asked.

After closing my eyes, I imagined locking the door in my mind and heard a double tap that let me know Jacqueline had felt it and was not happy about it.

"Okay," I said and opened my eyes. "She can't hear now."

"Why didn't you tell me about her?" he demanded. "Why didn't you tell me you had a blood bond?"

"I thought I wasn't ever going to see her again," I answered. "And the blood bond doesn't matter. I'm not sexually or romantically interested in her and she's not in me either. We are just friends. Platonic friends. The bond is to ensure that if another witch finds out that I know, she can rescue me."

"If you have a blood bond, I can't form one with you," he said softly and I realized that there was pain in his voice. He was upset about that.

"Actually, you are wrong," Jacqueline said from the back porch.

I sighed. "Why are you eavesdropping?"

"Because wolfie here looked like he might bite you," she said and walked towards us.

"I would never hurt her," Dylan snapped.

"She can have a blood bond with a wolf at the same time as a witch," she informed him. "I checked on all of that before we made the bond—not that she knew I checked, but I did because I am a great friend. She can have a blood bond with every type of creature, but only one of each creature."

"So, if I made a blood bond with him right now, I wouldn't be able to make one with any other werewolf?" I asked.

She nodded. "Which is why you should *not* make one with him until you've been together at least 3 years. Seriously, don't make one with him until you're an adult and well into your relationship. He may seem like he's *the one*, but a lot changes in your late teens and early twenties."

"So, you can have one with her, but I can't?" Dylan asked.

She put her hands on her hips. "I'm not going to break her heart or make her cry because I'm an asshole and saw a pretty girl walk by who made the blood rush from my brain elsewhere. I am her friend and nothing will change that. Besides, there are no witch boys and she's not interested in women."

I couldn't help the smile that formed. I'd missed my bestie

more than I realized. Wrapping my arms around her shoulders, I hugged her tightly.

She patted my back. "I missed you, too, brat."

"Can we please talk in private now?" Dylan asked. "I won't hurt her."

Jacqueline released me and gave him a warm smile. "If you do, I'll kill you."

With that threat, she skipped back into the house, the door shutting behind her with the use of her magic.

I looked back at Dylan and said, "There's your answer to that. Also, if you turned me into a werewolf, I wouldn't need a blood bond with you for you to be able to communicate telepathically with me and find me."

"If you're turned, you won't be able to have kids," he said softly.

"What if I don't want to have kids?" I asked.

"You're a bit young to decide that," he said, but quickly added, "I just think you should take the time to consider it for a while first. Just like she said not to make a bond with me so quickly, you shouldn't decide to be turned so quickly."

He was right, and I knew that.

"What else did you talk about?" I asked.

"She threatened me with vivid descriptions of how she would torture and kill me if I ever let you get taken again and she wasn't notified," he said and then looked at the ground. "And she told me about the things I had done that had upset you."

Meddling jerk!

He looked up to meet my eyes and said, "I'm sorry that I made you feel unwanted. I'm sorry that I made you feel ugly or like I didn't want to be around you. I've only ever wanted to be close to you."

"I accept your apology," I said with a smile.

He pulled me into a tight hug and buried his face in the crook of my neck. "I really am sorry. I think you're hot and all I've thought about doing is holding you like this and kissing you."

I slid my arms around his sides and up his back to pull myself closer to him. "Same."

"So, are we still on for dinner?" he asked.

"You still want to date me?" I asked back, hiding my face against his shoulder.

"Yes," he replied instantly.

I smiled against his shoulder then pulled back to look up at him. "I'd love to have dinner with you."

Dylan asked, "So, do I get to call you my girlfriend or are we still just dating?"

I arched a brow. "Moving a little fast, aren't you?"

He opened his mouth, but I interrupted him.

"I'd love to be your girlfriend."

He closed his mouth, smiled wide, picked me up, and spun us in a circle before kissing me. "Thank you. I can't wait to see Steve's face when he realizes you're dating me."

"I'm not looking forward to all those girls giving me death stares for dating you," I admitted.

"They never leave me alone, so hopefully now they will," he muttered.

I rolled my eyes. "You really don't understand girls, do you? They're just going to become even more flirtatious."

"Well, you can beat them off with a stick," he said. "Wait, no don't do that. You'll get suspended."

"Spoilsport," I teased with a pouty lip.

He chuckled, and we headed back inside. He took his spot back at the table, but I stayed standing.

"Show me your room," Jacqueline ordered me as she stood.

I saluted her. "Yes, ma'am. This way to my cave."

She followed me up the stairs, shut my door, and fake gagged. "It's so...boring in here."

"I know!" I agreed. "I need to brighten things up. Make it really my own."

She sat on the end of my bed and asked, "Are you really okay?"

After raising my cast I said, "Aside from this. Yes."

"This war...I'm worried about you getting caught up in it. I don't like the idea of you getting killed by some werewolf prick," she whispered.

"There's really not much I can do about it," I reminded her. "I just have to stay out of the woods from now on so they can't steal me."

"You need to keep your eyes open at school, too," she said softly. "With that jerk attending the same school as you, he might try to steal you during or after school."

"I'm sure Dylan will keep close to me at school," I said, already imagining him just following me everywhere.

"I wish we lived closer and I could provide you with some type of spell or something to protect yourself, but I haven't learned that magic yet," she whispered as she stared off into space, her mind off on the path of her train of though.

"Do you really think they'll try to kidnap me again?" I asked softly.

She sighed and shrugged. "Adults are strange in general, but werewolf adults are even weirder. The alphas have incredibly odd instincts and habits. If they could just work their crap out, you would be safe." Again, she stared off into space.

This time, I let her, flopping down onto my bed to relax. It had been an intense month to say the least.

"What are your plans for your birthday?" she asked.

"Is that soon?" I asked.

She turned so I could see her roll her eyes. "You're never going to pay attention to dates. You'll end up missing your own funeral."

I chuckled and the smile stayed on my lips the rest of the evening as we hung out and talked.

A couple of hours later, Jacqueline stood and brushed her clothes down. "I have to get home. First, I'm going to talk to your dad and stepmom. I'll come find you to say bye afterwards."

I narrowed my eyes. "Why do you want to meet with them privately?"

She gave me a peck on the cheek and then skipped out of my room without answering.

Such a brat!

Sneaking down and spying sounded fun, but knowing Jacqueline she would be standing right by the stairs or the doorway to detect me sneaking around.

Jacqueline had my best intentions at heart, so I trusted her and didn't spy.

About an hour later, she came up rubbing her temples.

"Meeting go that well?" I asked with a smile.

She shook her head. "Yeah. Anyway, give me a hug and stop ignoring my summons."

I stood and hugged her as tight as I could. "Thank you for coming to me. I'm glad I won't lose you as my bestie."

She pulled back to look down at me, a radiant smile on her face. "You're stuck with me to death, baby." Stepping farther back so we weren't touching at all, she winked once and then disappeared.

"How come you never talked about her?" Dylan asked from my doorway.

I turned around to face him, swallowing hard because I hadn't heard him approach and he'd scared me. "It was a really sore subject. I thought I'd basically lost my best friend and I didn't want to talk about it."

"She's something else," he said.

A bark of laughter burst from me. "That's one way to say it. How many times did she threaten you?"

He put his hands in his pockets, which made his biceps flex in the short-sleeved shirt. "Only about a dozen times."

"Really? Well, she must have believed you if it was only one dozen," I said with a chuckle.

"So, in addition to our dinner, I was thinking we could watch a movie," he said.

"I'd love that," I said.

"Only issue is that the others will likely crash it and it won't be a private viewing," he added.

"Am I correct in assuming that you guys crave the nearness of others in your pack? If so, then it makes sense that they would want to join us and spend time with us."

He blinked a couple of times. "Yeah, you are correct."

I stepped closer to him and asked, "So, when do I get to see the rest of the property now that I know your big secret?"

"How about now?" Lisa asked in a chipper voice.

Dylan stepped out of the doorway to reveal Amy, Emma, and Lisa.

"Yes!" I exclaimed. "I especially want to see where you guys live. If that's okay?"

"We would love to show you our houses," Emma said with a soft smile. "We really hated not being able to invite you over, but since a lot of us run around in wolf form by the houses we couldn't risk it."

Somehow, I could feel her distress. Quickly, I stepped forward and hugged her.

"I don't blame you guys at all. I'm just happy you can finally share your true selves with me," I whispered.

She patted my back.

Lisa grabbed my hand and practically dragged me down the stairs. "I want to show you my house first!" she exclaimed. "You're totally going to love it."

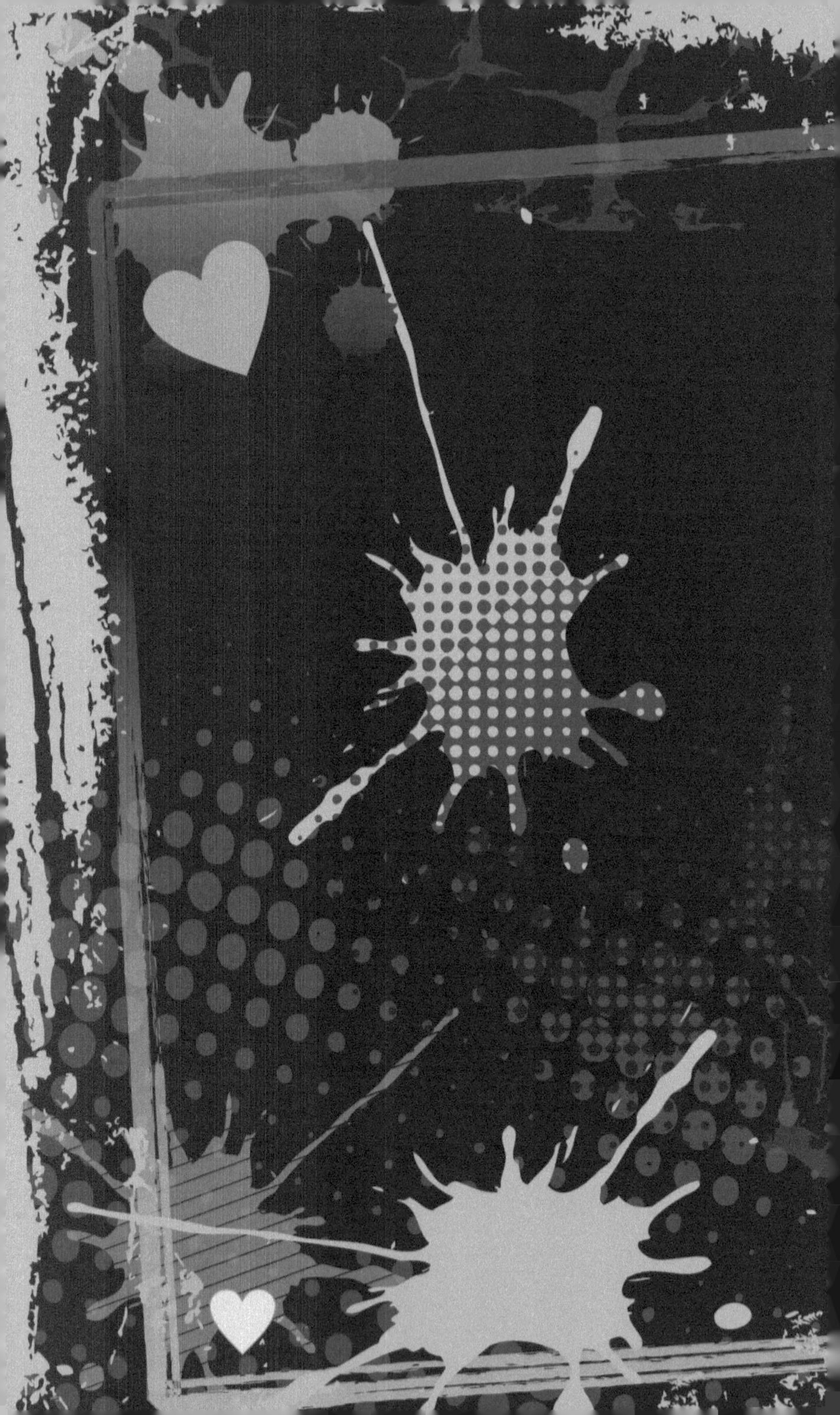

FIFTEEN

The trek to their houses was a lot farther than I expected. They were nestled deep within the woods, and I passed at least a dozen wolves on the way.

Lisa's was a single-story house painted a soft gray with white eaves. She had a small porch that had a porch swing and a few chairs.

"This is so cute," I told her.

She beamed as she skipped up the three steps to her porch and then to her front door. "Wait until you see inside!"

I stepped into the house, and my jaw dropped. The living room was painted a bright fuchsia. Large purple and green flowers were painted on the walls, obviously done by someone who wasn't a professional artist, but it added such a homey feel that I loved it.

"So, you live here alone?" I asked.

She shook her head. "Amy lives here, too."

"I let her pick the paint without thinking it through first," Amy mumbled and sat on a black sofa.

"It totally fits you, Lisa," I said.

"I'd show you the bedroom, but Tom's sleeping right now," she said and then flushed bright red.

"Let's go to my house. It's a lot less…bright," Emma said.

"How come you guys didn't just move into Kelly's house?" I asked.

"Females like to have their own spaces. We don't usually get along well with each other," Emma explained. "We are a lot more territorial than the males."

"Wait, I swear Dad said there were two people who lived in Kelly's house?"

"Me and Dylan, but I moved out when you moved in. Too much estrogen in one place," Amy explained. "Lisa is one of the few non-territorial females so sharing a space with her isn't an issue."

That seemed strange to me considering the girls were so close and spent so much time together. Maybe it was about what you actually owned or considered your space?

"How many acres are there? Does everyone in the pack have their own houses?"

"Over one hundred and no. Several live away from our territory," Dylan answered. "We have some houses that are basically like bed and breakfasts where they can stay when they visit."

"That's really cool," I commented. "Why don't you live in your own place?"

He shrugged. "Haven't really felt a need to yet. Though I have to admit that having your dad in the house has been setting my hackles up."

"What happens when you need to build a new house?" I asked.

"You are so full of questions," Tom muttered as he walked out, rubbing the sleep from his eyes.

"Can you blame me?" I asked with an arched brow.

He chuckled and then yawned as he answered, "I suppose not."

We walked out of Lisa's house and followed Emma towards hers, which was conveniently just two houses down.

"Did you pick a house that wasn't right next to hers because of the territorial thing?" I asked.

Emma smiled down at me. "You're learning quick."

"She has to if she's going to stay with the pack," Amy said and bumped her shoulder into mine. "I really hope you don't end up leaving after you graduate."

I forced myself not to look back at Dylan. "We will see what happens in the future. Nothing has been decided yet."

Amy chuckled. "I suppose there are things in motion still."

"Shut up," I muttered.

Emma pushed open the door to her house, which looked exactly like Lisa's, but inside the walls were a dark grey and the furniture was all black.

Once I stepped inside, I felt something within me settle a bit. I'd never felt that type of reaction before. "This is...relaxing," I admitted.

Emma smiled wide. "Right? I love the colors. It just settles something in my spirit whenever I come in."

I nodded. "That's what it felt like for me, too."

She plopped down on a couch and patted the seat next to her. "You're welcome to come over anytime you want. Just no canoodling with Dylan."

My face burned as I glared at her. "I wouldn't do that."

"You won't canoodle with Dylan? That's sad," Amy teased me.

"I meant I wouldn't go into a friend's house and do something like that. You two are...are..."

"Incorrigible," Tom suggested as he walked in.

Ethan beamed. "You really have been using my word a day calendar. I'm so proud."

Tom growled at Ethan and jumped at him. The two toppled to the ground, wrestling and play fighting.

Dylan sat on the couch on the other side of Emma and sighed. "Those two will never learn."

"Oh, please. You're just as bad as them," Emma scoffed.

"Am not," he shot back.

"He's just scared and knows we'll kick his butt," Tom taunted while trying to wrap Ethan in a chokehold.

Dylan's eyes narrowed and his nostrils flared. "I am *not* scared."

"Chicken!" Ethan yelled as well as he could with Tom's arm around his throat.

Dylan leapt from the couch over the other one and landed on top of Ethan and Tom.

"So easy to manipulate," Emma said and shook her head.

Lisa sat beside me and turned the TV on. "We can watch some shows while they work out their excess energy."

Amy plopped down with a sigh. "Sounds good to me. Got any popcorn?"

Emma stood and walked around the couch towards the kitchen behind us. "Do you know who I am? Of course I have popcorn."

"It's her favorite snack," Lisa whispered. "She always drenches it in butter until it's almost impossible to eat with your hands."

"It tastes best that way," Emma yelled.

"Can you add more salt this time?" Amy requested. "It wasn't salty enough last time."

"Maybe if you weren't such a salty bitch you wouldn't need to eat so much salt," Emma teased.

Amy rolled her eyes. "Look who's trying to goad people into a fight now."

Emma muttered something under her breath that I couldn't hear that had Amy storming into the kitchen.

I laughed as I watched all of the friends interacting and felt so comfortable for the first time in a long time. Most of the friends I'd had wouldn't have been able to tease each other like this or just hang out without getting inebriated in some way.

Jacqueline had saved me from enduring it as often as I had been, but my stupid self decided I didn't want to give them up. Those people hadn't cared if I was there or not.

Something I found out right before I left.

This pack was definitely a better fit for me. Somewhere I could definitely see myself staying.

Then again, that depended on how things went with Dylan.

Would it have been better not to try a relationship with someone in the pack? So I could ensure that I always had a place here?

Knowing myself, that wasn't really an option anyways. I had to see if things could work between Dylan and I. My obsession with him wouldn't fade anytime soon and there was only one way to handle it.

Dylan sat down beside me and leaned over to push his shoulder against mine. "What's going on in that head?"

I turned and smiled. "Just worrying like I always do."

He gently pushed his finger against the center of my eyebrows above my nose. "You scrunch this part up when you're worrying."

I rubbed the spot when he pulled his finger away. "I know. I can't control it, though. Dad always points it out."

Emma dropped down onto the couch, forcing herself between Dylan and me, a big bucket of popcorn in her lap. "Popcorn has arrived."

I dug in without hesitation and moaned at the buttery, salty deliciousness. "This is amazing."

"Right!" Emma yelled. "It's the best."

"You're going to need a drink with that," Dylan said. "I know from experience. I'll grab you one."

"Thanks," Emma said with a smile full of popcorn.

He rolled his eyes. "Sure, I'll get you one, too."

"He's so considerate," Amy teased and sat on my other side. "So, what are we going to watch?"

"What do you guys normally watch? Nature documentaries?"

All of them turned and looked at me, their eyes wide.

I burst into laughter, doubling over. "I'm totally teasing."

Amy started tickling me. "You brat."

I squirmed to get away from her, but Emma was beside me. "Hey, watch the popcorn!"

Standing, I tried to get away from her, but Lisa jumped up to join the tickle fight.

"No," I said and pointed at her.

She wiggled her fingers. "Oh, you're so getting tickled."

"I bet she snorts when she laughs," Emma teased.

Amy, Lisa, and I all turned towards Emma. The three of us turned back towards each other, evil smiles spreading as we unanimously agreed to form a truce to go after Emma instead.

Dylan seemed to sense what was happening as he set the drinks on the table and took the popcorn bucket from Emma despite her protest.

I leaned over and tickled her side.

She grabbed me by the shoulders and pulled me over the back of the couch to end up in her lap. Her finger pointed in my face, she chastised me. "No tickling."

Amy and Lisa leapt to my rescue, tickling Emma who was now somewhat pinned with me on her lap.

"No!" she yelled and struggled against their hold. With strength I forgot they possessed, she bucked me off of her.

I would have fallen directly onto the coffee table if Dylan hadn't miraculously caught me.

Immediately, Amy, Lisa, and Emma stopped horsing around, dropped their heads and mumbled, "Sorry."

Dylan righted me and set me on the couch. "You okay?"

I nodded. "Thanks."

"Sorry," Emma whispered again.

I waved off her apology. "It's okay. I just forgot how strong you guys are."

Her frown remained unchanged.

"All is well," I assured them with a wide smile and nudged her shoulder with mine.

"Let's watch a movie," Tom suggested.

"Stop fidgeting," Amy ordered me as she worked on my makeup. "You're going to make me screw ,up and I know you don't want to go out looking like a clown."

"Clowns are creepy," Emma whispered and shuddered.

"Are you sure this outfit is the right one? I mean I have this other—"

"No!" Emma, Amy, and Lisa yelled at the same time.

"You already spent way too much time going over your

outfit choices. No more. This is the one you are wearing. Dylan wouldn't care what you wore anyways," Amy assured me.

"Fine," I muttered.

She made her final strokes and stepped back to look at me. "Perfect."

"You did a great job," Lisa praised.

"Even I like it," Emma admitted.

I swiveled on the bathroom counter to look in the mirror and gasped. "You're a magician." My makeup was magazine ready. I couldn't believe it was me under there.

"Well, it's time, so get your shoes on and go meet him out front," Amy urged me.

Instead of wearing jeans and a blouse, the girls had convinced me to wear one of the few dresses I owned. It was a dark blue and was super cute.

I had some sandals that were classy enough to wear with the dress so I could avoid wearing high heels. Skipping down the steps, I gave dad a peck on the cheek as I hurried out the front door, ignoring whatever warning he gave me.

Dylan leaned against the car, black pants, a button-up shirt with the sleeves rolled up to his elbows, and black chucks.

"Ready?" I asked after swallowing my drool over the sexy boy.

He looked up, a smile on his lips, that quickly morphed as his eyes widened. He walked slowly up to me and whispered, "You look gorgeous."

"You look pretty good yourself," I replied, feeling unsure how to respond to his compliment, something I'd never had an issue with before.

He pulled open the passenger door for me and inhaled as I walked by.

I was slowly getting used to him smelling me when he was near me. He did it more and more.

He drove us to a nice little Italian restaurant that was owned by a local family.

It was about half full, so we were given a table immediately.

"This place is nice," I said with a smile.

He nodded. "They have the best beef lasagna."

"I'll take your word for it," I said and tried not to scrunch my nose up. I had never been a fan of lasagna.

"What type of pasta dishes do you like?" he asked, his menu folded and on the table.

"Chicken alfredo, chicken parmigiana, or just alfredo by itself."

He chuckled. "So, you like alfredo sauce and chicken?"

I nodded vigorously. "It's the best."

"What are your least favorite food items?" he asked.

"Mushrooms and onions," I said and felt my nose scrunch up immediately.

"Really? I love onions," he said.

"What are your favorite foods?" I asked, wanting to get to know him better.

"I like pretty much everything," he said with a shrug. "Though, chocolate chip cookies and fish tacos are some of my favorites."

"Oh, I haven't had fish tacos in a long time," I said. "We should make some for dinner later this week."

"Tom makes the best fish tacos," he commented.

We lapsed into silence a moment and I blurted out my next question, one I'd been curious about.

"So, why don't you have your own house?" I asked.

He smirked. "I do have my own house."

"Then why are you living in Kelly's house?"

"She asked me to stay there to keep an eye on you for a bit. I'll likely move back out now that you've settled in and know about us," he explained.

"Does that mean I'll see less of you?" I asked softly, looking down at the menu to give myself a reason not to look at him.

He reached across the table and slid his hand beneath mine. "No," he said and squeezed my hand. "I'll still drive you to and from school and come eat meals with you. That won't change."

It felt like a big change, though. One I was positive I wasn't going to like. Would it help our new relationship grow to be apart a bit? People said that distance makes the heart grow fonder, but was that true?

He squeezed my hand, forcing me to look back up at him. He smiled softly and said, "Don't worry. I won't abandon you."

His statement eased the pressure that had been building in my chest and I relaxed a bit.

"I hope not," I said and squeezed his hand back.

The waitress came and took our order, forcing Dylan to release my hand and sit back in his seat.

When the bread and butter came out, he buttered a piece and gave it to me. It was the dark bread that I had no idea the name for, but was absolutely delicious, so I took it without hesitation and ripped a large piece off to eat while we waited for our food.

"How's school going?" he asked while he buttered a piece for himself.

I shrugged. "School is school. I neither love nor hate it and just try to get by each day. I'll be glad when I graduate, but also know life isn't easy after school either. Dad showed me that when he let me help him with the bills one month. Bills suck"

Dylan chuckled. "Yeah, you should see the pack's bills sometime. If it weren't for all the adults chipping in and some lucrative investments, we would be in a world of hurt."

"I didn't know everyone chipped in," I commented.

He nodded. "You know how some human churches have tithing? We sort of have that, too. Except in our situation people do live on the land and use the electricity and water so it makes more sense for them to give some to the pack finances."

"It's almost like you have your own town," I said with a chuckle.

He smiled and nodded again. "Basically. It's better that way since we don't really get to be ourselves when we're around those who don't know about us."

"That must be hard," I said softly as I looked at him and set my bread on the plate before me. "I hope now that I know about you, you'll be able to act naturally. I want to get to know the real you."

He looked at me silently a moment before saying, "I will try my hardest to let you see the real me when we're on our pack lands. At school and in public like this are a little different, though."

I thought back to school and how he'd ignored me at times. "Are you...are we going to be public at school about us...dating? I know we aren't exclusive yet, but I wasn't sure if we would be public about the fact we had started to date." I'd almost said our relationship, but I wasn't sure he really considered us as being in a relationship yet. Yes, we'd both been interested in each other for a while, but this was our first date and I didn't want to come off as super clingy or anything.

He scowled. "Are you saying you don't want to be exclusive?"

"I…" Crap, how did I respond to that? Honesty was probably the best option. "I would like to be exclusive, but I wasn't sure what you preferred."

His scowl slipped away and his shoulders dropped slightly. "Okay, I would like us to be exclusive as well."

"And public?" I asked to be sure.

He smiled and nodded. "Yes."

I returned his smile and said, "Okay."

Our food came out, and we ate in silence. After eating with the pack for so long, I had learned that they preferred to focus on eating first and then talking once they'd finished eating. Some might have found it weird, but I actually liked it.

Trying to talk while eating stressed me out when I was with people I didn't know well because I didn't want to come off as rude.

Sure, I knew Dylan and the others pretty well by now, but that didn't mean I wanted to worry about talking with food in my mouth if I didn't have to.

I finished first, which wasn't surprising since I ate significantly less than him. While he finished eating, I looked around the restaurant at the other customers and wasn't surprised to find it mostly older couples enjoying a nice quiet meal.

What would my life be like in thirty years? Would I be married? Have kids? Would I become a werewolf?

The waitress came back, and Dylan whispered something to her that had her smiling wide and nodding before she left.

I wanted to ask what that was about, but it seemed like it was a surprise or something, so I bit my tongue and didn't ask.

The waitress took my leftovers in the back to box up and when she returned, she handed the bag to Dylan.

"Ready?" he asked.

I took one last drink of my water before nodding.

"So, what's your favorite movie genre?" he asked as we drove home.

"Action," I answered immediately. "The bigger the explosions, the better."

"Great," he said with a wide smile. "I have the perfect movie for us to watch."

Somehow, we ended up with the house to ourselves and I took advantage of the chance to snuggle close to Dylan on the couch.

The surprise from the restaurant was cake, which I gladly dug into as we watched the movie.

My eyes grew heavier and heavier as the movie continued. No matter how hard I tried, I couldn't keep them open long enough to finish the movie.

Fortunately, it seemed Dylan had the same issue, and we ended up asleep on the couch sitting up together.

"Oh, you two are so lucky I found you instead of your dad and Kelly," Tom whispered as he shook Dylan's shoulder.

"Huh?" I asked as I sat up, wiping my mouth to make sure there wasn't any drool.

"Time for bed," Tom whispered. "Kelly and your dad are asleep. Somehow, they didn't notice you two were in here, probably since the television turned off on its own and it's pretty dark in here."

"Why are you here?" Dylan asked as he stood and stretched.

"The girls were worried because Chloe hadn't returned their calls or texts and begged me to come check on you two,"

Tom answered with a smug smirk. "They'll be excited when I tell them that you two were sleeping together."

I smacked his arm. "Don't you dare start rumors like that."

"He's just teasing you," Dylan said. "We should go to sleep, though."

"See you two later," Tom called over his shoulder as he walked away.

"I had fun tonight," I said as I stood and faced Dylan.

"Me, too," he replied and gave me a soft smile.

I kissed his cheek. "Thank you."

As I started to walk away, he grabbed my hand, pulled me back towards him, and kissed me hard on the lips.

I set my hands on his chest and kissed him back.

He pulled back first and despite it being incredibly dark, his eyes seemed to be glowing. "I'll see you in the morning."

I nodded and bit my lip, resisting the urge to continue kissing him.

He turned and walked out of the room, pausing in the entryway to look back at me once more before leaving.

I quickly, and quietly, made my way upstairs to my room where I responded to the dozens of text messages to let them know I was alive and fine and going to sleep.

Tomorrow was the first day that we would be public about our relationship. What would happen? Would it change anything?

Despite all of the negative things I'd experienced so far, I looked forward to this next step in my life.

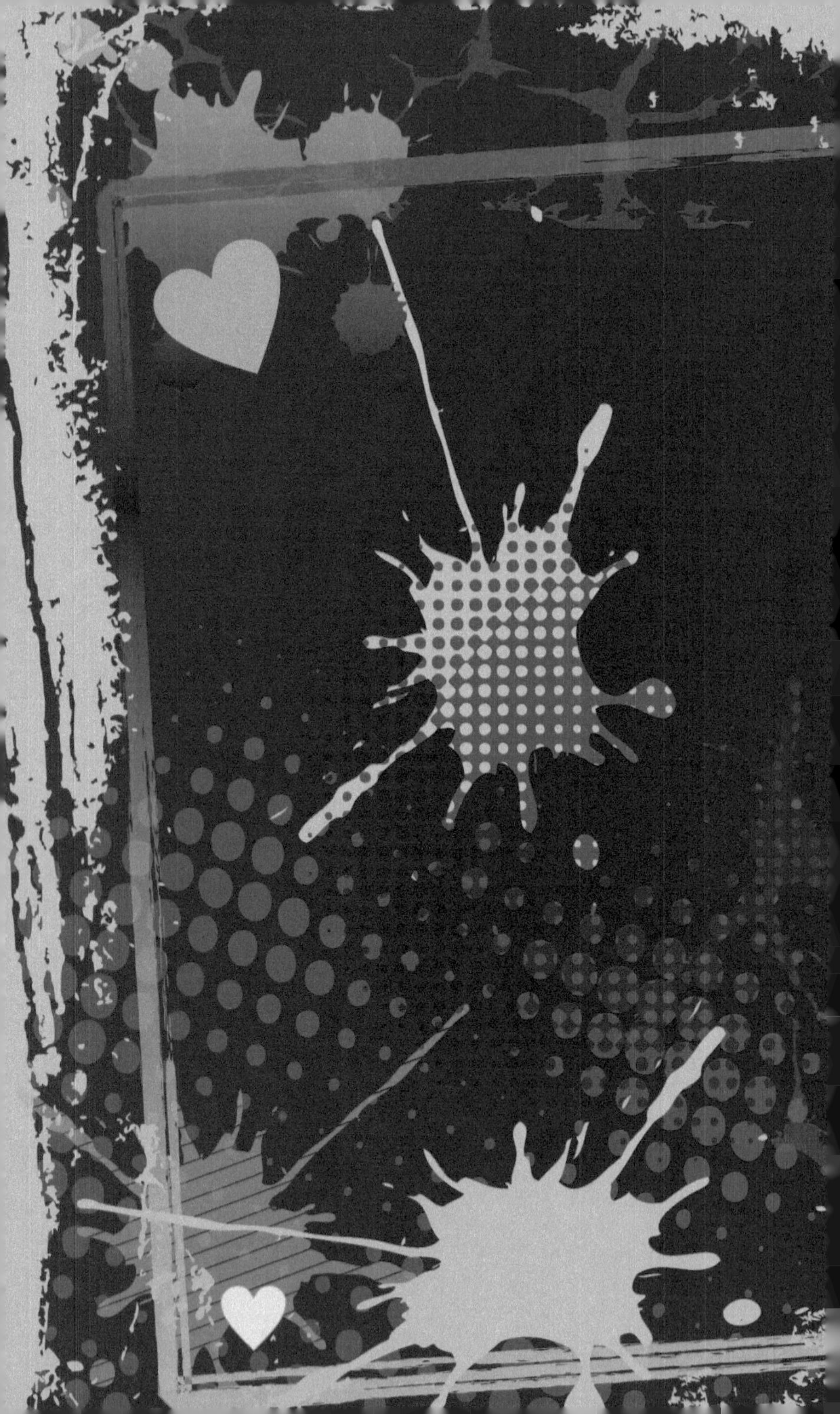

SIXTEEN

"Finally!" Lisa yelled and threw her arms around me, forcing me to let go of Dylan's hand.

"Can't breathe," I whispered as she tightened her grip more.

Immediately, she released me and took a step back. "Sorry. I'm just so excited."

"We can see that," Tom teased.

She stuck her tongue out at him and climbed into the SUV.

"We're going on a girl's trip after school," Emma informed me with a smile.

"Sounds great," I replied and got into the SUV, taking the front passenger seat while Dylan took the driver's seat.

"Everyone ready?" Dylan asked, turning to look back at everyone.

"Yep," Ethan replied.

I could hear the girls whispering behind me, but ignored them. I already knew they wanted all the details from our date and would tell them during our trip after school.

After parking, we got out and I started walking into the school beside Emma, like usual.

Dylan came to my other side and held out his hand.

There was no hesitation as I took the invitation and laced our fingers together.

He smiled wide, kissed my cheek, and continued walking.

The stares and whispers started as soon as the first person saw us. The one good thing about it being a small school was that everyone would know by lunch that we were an item now.

"And here I thought you actually had taste," Steve said from where he stood, leaned against the side of the building.

"You'd do well to remember your place," Dylan growled. "Don't speak to her or anyone else in my pack."

Steve pushed off the wall and smirked. "You can't do shit to me while we're at school." He turned to me, scowled, and asked, "I know your dating options are limited here, but him, really?"

I flipped him off. "Go eat a cat."

Steve smiled. "I'll eat your pu—"

The vulgar comment he was about to make was cut off when Dylan punched his jaw.

Steve stumbled sideways and pressed a hand to his chin. "Ouch, Dylan."

"Hey! No fighting!" Mr. Armstrong yelled, just happening to step out of a classroom nearby to see the punch.

Dylan tugged me away from Steve and into the school.

"See you later, Chloe," Steve said in an incredibly creepy tone.

"I should kill him," Dylan whispered.

"You good, man?" Tom asked from behind us.

Dylan turned past the next building, pulling us out of the

eye of most other students, and pulled me against his chest, hugging me tightly. "I'm sorry."

"It's alright. He's an ass and totally deserved that punch," I said as I stroked his back slowly.

"If he touches you—"

"He won't," I said adamantly.

Dylan growled softly and pressed his nose against the side of my throat.

"Teacher's coming," Tom whispered.

I turned and realized that everyone had stayed with us and had formed a wall with their bodies to give us more privacy.

"You okay to go to class?" I asked Dylan.

He kissed my neck as light as a feather's touch. "Yes." When he pulled back, he closed his eyes, took a deep breath, and then took my hand again. "Okay."

Tom turned around, looked at Dylan's face, and nodded. "Okay."

The rest of our day was rather uneventful, but Steve was right that we couldn't really do anything while at school. Would their pack try to steal me again? Would they actually kill me this time to start the war?

"You sure I can't come?" Dylan asked.

Emma and Amy stepped between us and crossed their arms.

"Fine!" Dylan said and threw his hands up in the air. "Call me immediately if anything happens."

Amy patted his shoulder. "We'll take care of your girl."

Heat bloomed on my cheeks, and I quickly turned away only to come face to face with Lisa who was smiling like an idiot.

The four of us headed to the store, and the girls let us get some distance for privacy before interrogating me.

"Spill!" Lisa yelled.

After laughing at her enthusiasm, I recapped the night for them.

Lisa squealed while the other two just smiled.

"We're happy for you," Amy said.

"Thank you."

"Just don't hurt him so we don't have to hurt you, okay?" Emma said.

Shaking my head I said, "I'm pretty sure I'm the one who has to protect their heart."

"Chloe!" Jacqueline yelled behind me.

I spun around, but the others had already turned and taken defensive positions around me.

Jacqueline lay on the ground, blood soaked through her shirt on the side of her stomach and her right leg. "Chloe!" she called out again.

I pushed past Lisa, dropped my backpack, and ran to her. Lowering myself to my knees in front of her I asked, "What happened?"

"Vampires and werewolves united and attacked," she whispered. "My coven...the entire coven..."

Oh, no.

"Let's take her back to the house," Emma said.

Jacqueline seemed to finally see them and scowled. "No."

"It's okay, you met them, remember? They're friends," I said as I pushed sweaty hair off her face.

Jacqueline whispered, "I need you, Chloe. Please."

I swallowed hard, fear making my heart pound. The fact that she was asking meant things really were dire. Plus, I'd made a promise.

She discreetly put an invisible magical shield around us, sealing me in with her and the girls outside.

"Tell Dylan I'll come back," I said while staring into Jacqueline's eyes. "I've got a promise to keep."

"What are you talking about?" Emma asked, coming closer, but stopped when she ran into the shield Jacqueline had put up. Emma punched it and growled. "No! Let us in!"

"You sure you're strong enough?" I asked Jacqueline.

She whimpered. "I have to be. Close your eyes."

Emma, Amy, and Lisa yelled at us and punched the shield.

I couldn't look at them. Couldn't bring myself to see their faces as Jacqueline teleported us back to her house.

Her room was destroyed. The bedding was shredded, claw marks were across almost every surface, and splashes of red were all over the ground.

"What happened?" I asked as I looked around. "Are you sure it's safe to be here?"

"Share first," she whispered.

I nodded and pressed my palm against Jacqueline's where we'd made the pact.

She whispered words in the witch's language and our hands began to glow.

Slowly my energy began to seep away, making me feel like I desperately needed a nap.

She jerked her hand away from mine, and I was glad to see her face was no longer pale. "They attacked here first and then went to the coven," she explained, going to her closet to grab a change of clothes. "Vampires and werewolves were working together. I never thought I'd see the day."

"Why did they attack you?" I asked, sitting on her bed despite the claw marks.

"They wanted one of our spell books. My father had found it years ago, so they thought we still had it, but he'd put it in the archives for safekeeping."

"What kind of spell is it they're after?" I asked.

She sat down beside me and sighed. "I can't tell you. I want to, but I'm sworn not to."

"Did you reach out to the coven?" I asked.

She nodded and clenched her hands together in her lap. "I went there after my parents were killed." Her breath hitched and tears built in her eyes.

I wrapped my arms around her shoulders and hugged her.

"When I got there, everyone was already dead."

"Does that mean they have the book?" I asked, sitting back from her.

"Yes, and I need your help to get it back," she said, her brows furrowing as she turned serious.

"How am I supposed to help you? I'm just human and even if I lend you my power through our bond, it won't be enough to take on someone strong enough to slaughter your coven."

She set her hand on my shoulder and said, "I need you to trust me, okay? I have a plan and I'm certain it will work."

"And you're not going to tell me the plan?" I asked.

"Bait never gets to hear the plan," she said with a smirk.

I groaned. "Wonderful." A thought occurred to me. "Why didn't you go back to Kelly's and ask the pack for help?"

"They're werewolves, Chloe. They'll want this book, too. I can't even let them know it exists."

"The spell is that serious?" I asked.

She nodded. "It is."

"Well, tell me what you need me to do," I said. "And let's get an energy drink on the way."

All she told me was that I had to trust her and I would be bait for them. Since she wouldn't give me more specifics than that, it likely meant she needed my reactions to be genuine.

I chugged an energy drink as we headed to a park on the

far side of the city. "It's still daylight," I reminded her. "You sure they'll show?"

She nodded. "Definitely."

"How did you contact them?"

"I haven't. I'm going to use magic so they sense it and come to finish the job," she answered.

"And that's where I come in?" I guessed.

She nodded. "Remember, I love you and no matter what, will protect you."

"You are not instilling a lot of confidence with that statement," I muttered.

She patted my shoulder and then pointed to a concrete bench. "Sit there, please."

I obeyed.

"Here we go," she whispered and shook her hands at her sides. After taking a deep breath, she sent out a burst of magic that felt like a gust of wind.

"That enough?" I asked.

"Shush. No more talking," she ordered.

I mimed zipping my lips and crossed my legs as we waited.

We waited all of two minutes before John, Jesse, and a tall, thin man I'd never seen before showed up.

My surprise was evident as was John and Jesse's.

"What's this?" John asked.

"A peace offering," Jacqueline said behind me. "You take her and let me live."

"Why would we care about some human girl?" the tall man asked. As he spoke, I saw fangs peeking out.

He must be the vampire.

"We let you live and you'll come after us," John said.

"Nope. I just want to live. Take her and you can have the war you've always wanted," Jacqueline said confidently.

"You're seriously considering this?" the vampire asked.

"We could use her," John whispered and stroked his chin as he considered.

"We tried that once before and they just rescued her," Jesse said, looking between me and John. "She sent you an offer of peace. I thought we were going to take it?"

"Now that we have the spell, we'll be able to demolish that pack once and for all. However, we need a trump card and she's the perfect fit," John said. He smiled wide and looked over my head at Jacqueline. "You've got a deal. We'll let you live in exchange for this human."

She couldn't really be giving me to them, right? This was all part of the ruse?

My heart hammered in my chest, and I desperately wanted to run.

"Great. Have a good one, boys!" Jacqueline said.

I spun around just to see her teleport away.

Wh-what had just happened?

"She looks tasty and I'm starving. Let me have a drink for the road," the vampire said.

Jesse growled and grabbed my arm. "Back off. You're not drinking from her."

"She…she sold me out," I whispered, tears brimming in my eyes.

Jesse's grip on my arm loosened. "Come on, Chloe. Let's go."

"Yes, come with us to your new home. After we find you some more secure accommodations, we'll reach out to your family and let them know you're safe and sound," John said with an evil smile.

The vampire set his hand on John and Jesse's shoulders while Jesse kept his hold on my arm. "She's probably going to throw up, so just make sure she's not facing me when it happens."

Within minutes, they'd teleported me back to John's pack and locked me up in a cell that was deep underground in a tunnel system I was certain they had to have created recently.

Jesse stood beside the cage I was in, scowling at the ground.

I sat in the back corner, resting against the bars, tucked my legs up, and rested my chin on my knees.

The vampire and John returned, standing beside Jesse.

"Now that she's secure, we need to return," the vampire said. "We still have a lot to do."

"Jesse, I'm leaving you here to guard her. Do *not* fail me again. You understand? If you do, your punishment will be severe," John said and growled a bit on the last words.

Jesse nodded. "I understand."

John winked at me and then the vampire teleported them away.

"Are they going to kill me this time?" I asked Jesse.

He looked over at me and his eyes flashed red a moment. "I don't know."

"I started dating a werewolf," I said sadly. "I took your advice to heart, and he seemed to appreciate that I understood his need for touch and connection with his packmates. So, I guess, thank you for teaching me enough to enjoy the brief time I had with him."

For some reason, I didn't feel terrified like I should've. I was just...sad.

He stared at me in stunned silence for a few moments before asking, "Are you hungry?"

I shrugged one shoulder. "I could use some water."

He whistled, and a male I'd never seen before came into the room. "Get water and food."

The male's eyes lingered on me a moment before he nodded and left.

"You know, I figured out a great nickname for you," Jesse said as he looked at me.

"Yeah?" I asked flatly.

"Clover."

"Clover?"

He nodded with a small, sad smile. "Clover gets trampled on, but just springs back up. You've been through a lot this year and you keep moving forward. So, yeah, Clover."

"I like it," I admitted and felt a little better. "Do you know what they're planning to do with that book?" I asked. "The witch who gave me to you just said it had a spell werewolves wanted."

"How do you know that witch?" he asked instead of answering me.

"We went to school together before I came here." I turned my face away and added, "I'd thought we were best friends."

"It's not a spell we're after, but a curse," he answered. He sighed and I turned back to see him run a hand through his hair while snarling. "They're going to curse Kelly's pack."

"Is it to kill them?" I asked.

He laughed mirthlessly. "No. It's to turn them into wolves."

I scowled. "They're already wolves."

He shook his head. "Permanently."

My eyes widened, and my heart began to pound. Permanently become wolves? That would mean I would lose them all. I'd never joke around with them or anything ever again.

"That's awful," I whispered.

He shrugged. "It would make it easier for John to bring them into our pack."

"What?" I gaped.

"Since we are still part wolves, they would view us as pack and would be able to join us. Their human memories would disappear and they would just view us as wolves that turn hairless sometimes. John could rule over them and he'd finally take Kelly's lands."

No. No, this couldn't happen.

"Why involve me at all? If he has that curse, why would he need to kill me? He wouldn't need to start a war or involve me at all."

"I think he wants to still have his war and if we start to lose, then he'd turn to the curse as the card up his sleeve." He sighed and sat down close to my cage. "I'm sorry. I wish you weren't involved, but Kelly screwed you over the moment she started dating your dad."

We lapsed into silence and our shared despair was only interrupted when the guy returned with food and water for us.

Part of me was still holding out hope that Jacqueline hadn't betrayed me and this was all just a piece to the puzzle that was her plan. She'd told me I had to trust her.

Trust was so easily broken, though.

After eating, I dozed in the cell while Jesse sat outside my cage, keeping guard.

Occasionally one of the other pack members would try to come near my cell, to look at me, but Jesse growled and ordered them all to leave.

Despite him being one of the enemies and preventing me from escaping, I at least felt safe with Jesse guarding me from his other pack members.

Being underground meant I had no concept of time. I wished I'd had my phone on me when Jacqueline had taken me, but I'd dumbly left it in my backpack and set it down before going to her.

I was fairly certain more than two days had passed since I'd consumed around seven meals so far.

Jesse had even made one of the guys bring down more blankets and a futon mattress for me to sleep with. He'd probably heard my teeth chattering the first night and didn't want me to keep him awake constantly.

He tried to engage in small talk with me a few times, but I wasn't up for it.

Each time I refused, he pulled out his cell phone and scrolled through various social media sites.

Three meals later, I groaned and sat up. "Okay, let's play a card game or something."

His lips tilted up in a smirk, but he quickly squashed it and picked up the deck of cards beside him. "What do you want to play?"

I shrugged. "I don't know many card games."

"I'll teach you my favorite one then," he said and started shuffling the deck.

I scooted forward until my crossed knees were touching the bars of my cell, allowing me to reach through them to get the cards.

The game he taught me was simple enough and it wasn't long until we were both so focused on the game and having fun that we didn't realize people had slowly moved into the room with us.

"You seem pretty comfortable with him despite knowing he could bite your arm off at any moment," one of the men said.

He startled me out of my focus, and I almost dropped my cards. "What?" I asked and looked around.

Six men, varying in age from eighteen to forty, stood around the room, watching.

"Why are you in here?" Jesse growled, but didn't stand.

"We heard you laughing and wanted to see what was going on," one of the younger guys answered.

"You going to answer my question?" the first guy asked.

I looked at him and swallowed. He had a thick scar down his right eye and stubble along his jaw dotted with grey. "Jesse hasn't shown himself to be a danger to me. Yes, he could kill me if he wanted to, but then again so could most human men. Should I just be terrified of anyone who is stronger than me?"

The man's eyebrows rose up into his hairline. "You really aren't scared of him being a werewolf?"

"I'm dating a werewolf," I answered, shrugged, and dropped my head as I frowned. "Or, I was anyway." Would he still want to date me after this? He'd not wanted me to go off with the girls alone and now I was in the cell of their rival pack.

"You ever see him wolf out?" one of the other younger guys asked.

"Once, when they revealed to me that they were werewolves. But we just started dating a day before I was kidnapped. I've seen all my friends in wolf forms before, though."

"And you're okay with it?" one of the middle-aged ones asked.

"Why wouldn't I be? It's not like they became werewolves because they wanted to. Even if they had, I don't think it would bother me, honestly. They're just my friends who occasionally grow fur." I chuckled as I said it and slapped down a card on top of the pile which beat Jesse's last played card. "Boom!"

Jesse growled softly and started sorting through his cards, trying to find one that beat mine.

"You're an interesting girl," the older man said. "It's not often we find humans who accept us so readily."

"I think you give humans too little credit. Sure, there will be some idiots who just freak out, but there are humans that freak out because someone's gay. Obviously, those morons won't be able to accept anything outside of their 'norm,' but screw them. There are plenty of people who will accept you. Maybe you just need to wait for the younger generations to grow up a bit and then you could reveal yourselves."

Several growled.

"Or not," I said under my breath.

Jesse sighed. "Pass."

"Hah!" I yelled victoriously and set down my next card.

The others sat down around the room, just silently watching us.

I thought it would bother me, to have strange men watch me play a game, but it didn't.

Jesse and I played until it was the next meal time and then he put the cards away.

"How long have I been here?" I asked softly and lay back on the mattress.

"Three days," he answered.

"What's happening out there?" I asked.

He sighed. "Nothing good."

Despite not wanting to truly know, I asked, "Are they dead?"

"No," he replied immediately. "No one has died...yet."

"Why haven't they turned you?" one of the men, I wasn't sure who, asked.

"Because it's a huge decision that I need time to thoroughly consider," I answered. "It's hard for you guys to integrate back into human society and there's the part where I won't be able to have children. I don't know for sure if I want kids or not yet."

"So, they're letting you decide your future. That's...considerate," the guy with the scar, I recognized his voice, said.

"They're a really nice pack," I whispered. "They treated me like one of them, even before I knew they were werewolves. They're my friends."

"Well, they'll join us if they're smart," someone with a really deep voice said.

I scoffed. "Right. Join the dick bags who think they're better because...why? Why are you better?" I sat up, feeling emboldened since I was inside a cell, and glared at them. "What makes this pack better? From what I've seen, you're more military-like than family. I'd much rather be with Kelly and her family than John and his asshole ways."

A few growled.

"Don't talk bad about our alpha," one of the oldest said.

I scoffed. "Or what? You'll kill me? He's already planning to kill me. What do I have to lose?"

"Kill you?" one of the younger guys asked. "Why would you think that Alpha wants to kill you?"

"Because he said he was going to. He'll probably do it right in front of Kelly to try to break her. Unfortunately, she's not that easily broken so my death will be for nothing." The words came out of my mouth easily and nonchalantly. Was this really what my life had come to? Me accepting my death so easily?

There was so much I wanted to do. So many places I wanted to visit. I hadn't gotten a tattoo, gone to a bar, nightclub, or sailed on a ship yet. I hadn't even had sex!

I wanted to see how things progressed with Dylan. Wanted to see if he could be my true love, or soulmate, or if we could be like one of those best friend couples.

Could we ever be best friends while I was human and he was a werewolf though?

Did he want kids? Was that part of why he was interested in me? I'd thought before he hadn't liked me because I was human, but maybe he wanted to find a woman who he could have kids with.

Was that the only reason he wasn't interested in Cynthia? She was a total bitch, so it had to be more than just her not being able to have kids. Plus, what teenage guy was focused on kids?

I almost laughed out loud at my inner thoughts, but squashed it down and refocused on the men staring at me.

"I'm tired," I whispered to no one in particular, scooted across the cell floor on my butt, and lay on the mattress. Once I wrapped the blankets tight around me, I closed my eyes and willed myself to sleep.

There was no point in trying to figure out the answers to all of those things when I needed to talk to the people I had the questions for first.

If, I survived.

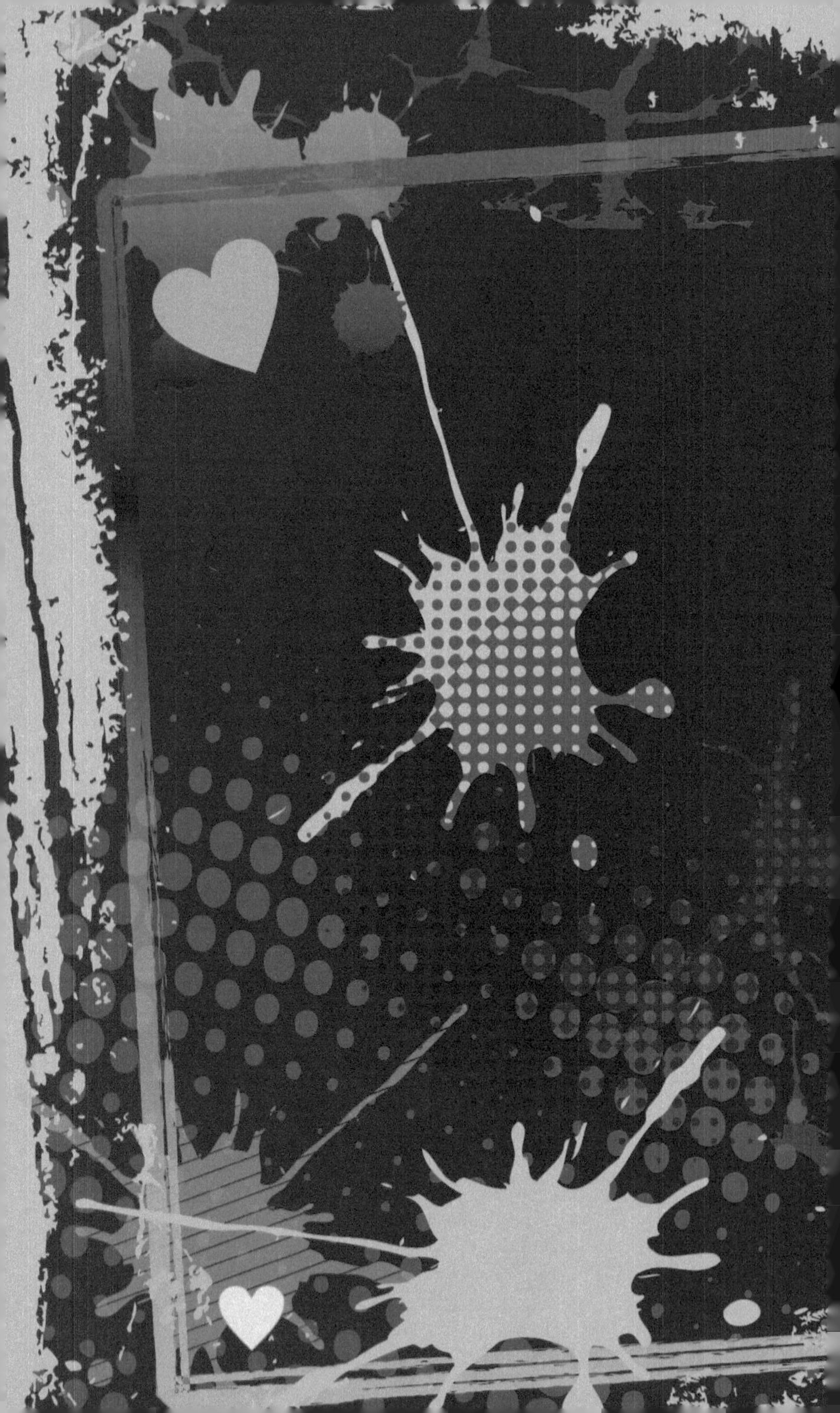

SEVENTEEN

"Open the cell," John snarled as he stomped into the room.

Jesse stood immediately; his brows furrowed. "What?"

"What's going on?" one of the other guys asked.

There were still at least five guys who had decided to start sleeping in their wolf forms in the room with my cell. They wouldn't answer why they were doing it and nothing Jesse said would convince them to leave.

I just accepted it and tried to observe them to learn more about werewolves.

"Decided to keep backup here?" John asked and nodded once. "Smart. They're here and it's time we bring her out."

"What are you going to do with her?" one of the younger guys asked.

Jesse unlocked my cell, and John grabbed my arm, hauling me to my feet.

I clenched my teeth together to keep from making a pained noise, but I would no doubt have a bruise from his grip tomorrow.

"Let's go, girl. If you do as I say, I'll make sure you don't suffer," he growled. His eyes were glowing and the tips of his ears were becoming pointed.

"Yes, sir," I whispered and dropped my head.

He was clearly on the verge of losing control and even if it was a small hope, I wanted to try to survive this.

Jesse started to follow, but John spun and shook his head. "No. You stay here."

Jesse scowled. "If we're fighting, shouldn't everyone be out there?"

John growled, but quickly sighed. "Fine, but don't make me regret letting you out."

Jesse's scowl deepened, but instead of replying, he nodded and walked behind us. The others who had been in the room with us followed as well, all looking as disturbed as Jesse by John's actions.

Once out of the house, I was surprised to see an all-out werewolf war happening. Wolves were attacking each other, killing each other, left and right.

In the middle, stood Kelly and Dylan in their wolf forms. Both of their heads whipped towards me at the same time.

"Submit to me or she dies!" John yelled.

Kelly shifted into her human form. "Let the girl go. She's human and has nothing to do with this."

Dylan growled and took a step forward, but Kelly held out her arm to stop him. More of the pack moved forward, flanking them, including all of my friends and Adam.

"She has everything to do with this!" John bellowed. "You've allowed humans to weaken you, to infiltrate your pack. This bitch was working with a witch and they were planning on destroying us all!"

Several of John's wolves murmured, and many of Kelly's whined in confusion.

Dylan growled.

I wanted to yell he was lying, to explain what had really happened, but I knew the second I made a noise, he would kill me.

Kelly shook her head. "She didn't infiltrate my pack. I invited her in. This *child* has done nothing but try to learn about us and find her place in our world."

John pulled out a thick leather-bound book with the symbol of the witch on the cover and showed it to everyone. "Proof! I took this from her witch friend right before I killed her. This book has a spell that would erase werewolves forever, curse our kind!"

That was the spell book! I had to get it from him, but how? How could I get it from him and get away before he killed me?

Dylan's eyes stayed fixed on mine, and I felt mine tearing up.

"I'm sorry," I mouthed to him. "I'm so sorry."

His eyes seemed to glow as he stared at me, but I looked away from him as I heard John move.

John opened the book, and I remembered what Jesse had said. John was going to curse the pack and all of Kelly's main members were right in front!

He started to read from it and just as he finished and pointed with his fingers, I stepped in front of him and pressed my chest straight into his fingers.

His eyes widened, obviously having forgotten I was there, but it was too late.

The spell coursed from his fingers into me, and I screamed

as I felt the curse beginning to reshape my body, my bones breaking and muscles tearing.

"Chloe!" Kelly screamed.

With one last burst of strength, I slapped the book out of John's hand, sending it flying right at Kelly.

She smacked the book away from her as she continued to run to me. "Chloe!" she cried again.

John finally returned to his senses and swung a closed fist towards Kelly, but she easily blocked his strike and with a roar that would have made a dinosaur proud, she shifted into the largest wolf I had ever seen, her back easily twenty-feet tall.

Judging by the shocked faces of everyone around, it was the first time they'd seen it happen as well.

Kelly tried to bite John, but he was fast and darted around her, heading for the trees and escape.

"Don't let him escape!" someone yelled.

"Chloe, can you hear me?"

The voice sounded familiar and it hurt to ask, "Jesse?"

"It's going to be okay, your body is trying to shift into a wolf. Stop fighting it and let the shift happen."

"Get away from her!" Dylan screamed and slammed into Jesse, knocking him away from me.

Adam stepped over me in his wolf form, growling and snarling at the rest of Jesse's pack who had come out with us.

"We aren't going to hurt her," one of them said and held up his hands. "We didn't agree with the alpha using her as bait or wanting to kill her in the first place."

"Dylan," I whimpered.

He turned towards me, eyes wide when he saw how far gone I was, and ran over. "Shush, it's okay. Don't talk."

"I'm...I'm going to become a wolf...a real one," I cried. "I'm so sorry I…" My legs snapped, and I screamed, but the scream ended as a howl as the change fully finished.

Panting, on my side, I took a few moments to try to reorient myself. I definitely wasn't human anymore, but I still felt like I had most of my human memories and thinking.

Dylan stroked my head between the ears gently. "It's okay. You're okay."

John screamed, and we all turned to see Kelly bite him in half.

She spat him out, tilted her head back, and howled.

Everyone, including me, joined her in howling.

Suddenly, everyone turned and stared at me.

Kelly walked over, her size shrinking until she was her normal wolf size. She bumped her snout against mine and a zip of static electricity snapped mine.

I yelped and staggered to my feet, struggling to gain balance now that I had *four* feet.

"Is she…?" Dylan asked Kelly.

Kelly shifted into her human form and scowled down at me. "I…I think so?"

What was going on?

Adam whined and bumped his nose against my side.

I licked his snout to try to ease his worry since I felt okay. Were normal wolves this intelligent?

Jacqueline appeared in a puff of smoke and put her hands on her hips. "Did you really think I hung you out to dry?"

"What?" Dylan asked.

Jacqueline knelt in front of me so she could look me in the eyes and winked. "You'll thank me later. For now, just relax." She looked up at Dylan and Kelly and smiled.

"What are you going to do with them?" Dylan asked and looked at Jesse and the others of his pack.

Kelly sighed and rubbed her temples. "This could have been resolved so much sooner if that bastard had just been reasonable."

"We urged him to accept your peace," Jesse said.

"I'll give you two options," Kelly said, projecting her voice so everyone around could hear. "One, you join my pack, under my rule, and never challenge me or Dylan."

A few of the older wolves growled, but quickly shut up.

"Two, you leave and never return to this state. You have twenty-four hours to decide." She looked down at me and said, "Let's go home."

Jacqueline skipped as she walked beside me. "Did you know that you're prettier as a wolf than as a human?"

I huffed.

Adam walked beside me, constantly looking over at me.

Was he worried about me trying to run off? Did he think I might just run away?

Back on our own property, the others swarmed me, bumping their noses against my sides and rubbing along me.

I growled in annoyance, but they could tell I didn't really care that much.

Dad ran out and hugged Kelly. "You're safe. I was so worried when I heard the howling. I thought...I thought they were mourning you."

She hugged him and patted his back. "I'm sorry you were so worried. The bastard is finally dead and yet I don't feel any peace. Just sadness that so many of ours died fighting a battle that didn't need to happen."

"Will many of their pack join yours?" Jacqueline asked.

"At least one third will likely join us, one third will leave, and the final third are up in the air," Dylan answered.

"The land is yours now, which will definitely help with

expanding your pack and securing your rights as the official pack here," Dad said. He looked around all of the people returning and scowled. "Where's Chloe?"

Kelly sighed and pointed at me.

I wagged my tail and yipped.

He started to reach out towards me, but hesitated. "Is...she..."

"Do you have a spell to turn her back?" Dylan asked.

Jacqueline scowled at him. "You want me to turn her back? I thought you'd be happy?"

"Happy?" Dylan asked. "Why would I be happy?"

"Because she's a werewolf now," Jacqueline said and scoffed.

As if all of us had known that.

I yapped at her and growled.

She looked down at me with a frown and then sighed dramatically, groaning at the end. "I'll help you turn back this one time, but after this you have to learn how to do it yourself. Okay?"

With a snap of her fingers, my body snapped back into my human form and thanks to her magic fully clothed.

I screamed, but quickly cut it off as the pain dissipated. "Whoa," I whispered and patted myself. "That transition was much easier. My arms not broken anymore!"

"She's...a werewolf?" Dylan asked as he stared at me.

"You're okay," Adam said and hugged me. "I thought you were a full wolf and were going to run off. You looked so...confused."

I patted his back and chuckled. "I was confused. I didn't realize that I was a werewolf and wondered why my mind was so humanlike still."

Dad hugged me. "I was so worried when they took you again."

"I told you I had her protected," Jacqueline said and sighed softly. "So unappreciated."

"I really thought you'd sold me out for a day or two," I admitted to her.

She flicked the tip of my nose. "Rude!"

"Ouch!" I yelled and rubbed the tip.

Kelly hugged me and sniffled. "I was so scared when you took that curse on to save us. I thought it was a death curse. Then when I saw you, I thought you were going to just be a wolf and had no idea how I was going to tell your father. I was certain he was going to end up divorcing me."

"I would have bitten him if he'd done that," I assured her.

She chuckled and pushed me back. "You know, you'll have to officially join my pack now."

"What if I don't want to?" I asked and folded my arms across my chest.

Everyone tensed and stared at me.

I bent over as I burst into laughter and Jacqueline followed.

"Brat," Dad huffed.

Straightening, I wiped my eyes and shook my head. "Sorry, I couldn't help it."

Dylan hadn't touched me since we'd gotten back and as I glanced at him, a sense of dread filled my stomach.

"I need to go check on everyone," Kelly said and pulled my dad away. "We'll get you added to the pack later."

"I'm going to go clean this book off. Adam, come help me," Jacqueline ordered.

They should have just shouted that they wanted to give us time to talk alone, but whatever.

"You going to say anything?" I asked, feeling more confident than I used to. Was this a werewolf side effect? Was this why they seemed so cool?

"I don't know what to say," he admitted.

"Were you worried when I was gone?" I asked.

He scowled. "Of course! Kelly locked me up so I wouldn't run over and try to rescue you by myself."

I sighed. "Are you breaking up with me now that I'm a werewolf?"

"What?"

"I'm not human so I can't have kids anymore, which is something you wanted. So, you don't want to date me anymore, right? Now that I was turned, you're going to want to try to find someone else to date."

His scowl deepened.

"Look, I get it, you don't have to apologize or anything, but I'd just appreciate a confirmation or—"

"Chloe!" Lisa yelled and tripped over her feet as she ran to me and crushed me in her arms in a hug.

Amy and Emma surrounded me in a group hug and I was pretty sure all three were crying.

"I'm fine, guys," I assured them.

"We thought you died!" Lisa cried.

"Girls, give her some space," Tom ordered and pulled Lisa off me. As soon as they stepped back, he hugged me. "Don't ever do that again." He growled in my ear.

Ethan pulled me from Tom's arms and hugged me tighter than the others. "You scared ten years off my life."

Alex patted my back. "Glad you're safe."

"Come on, let's get inside and catch up on what happened," Amy said and draped an arm around my shoulders. She sniffed my hair and scowled. "You smell different."

My brows furrowed as I looked up at her. "Do I smell bad?"

She scrunched her nose. "A little."

Oh, no. What if she couldn't be friends with me anymore because of the alpha female thing?

"Is it because I'm a werewolf now?" I asked softly.

Everyone spun, mouths dropped, and Amy took a step away from me.

"You're a what?" Tom demanded.

"I'm a werewolf," I said. "The curse turned me into a werewolf."

"Puppy kibble!" Lisa shouted.

"You're...you're one of us now?" Emma asked.

I nodded and felt nervous. Were they going to stop being my friends, too?

"This is awesome!" Emma yelled and enveloped me in a warm hug.

Tears sprang to my eyes, and I sniffled.

"Why are you crying?" Emma asked.

"I thought you guys were breaking up with me, too," I admitted and realized that Dylan had disappeared at some point after the others arrived.

"Too?" Lisa and Amy asked, looked at each other, and then at me.

I nodded. "Pretty sure Dylan and I aren't together anymore."

Even the guys scowled.

"I can't believe that," Lisa whispered. "Dylan really cares about you."

I shrugged a shoulder "Well, not being able to have kids sort of puts a damper on his end goal for our relationship. I get it. I don't hold it against him." Even if my heart was shattering the more I said it and the stronger that reality came to be.

"Let's go inside and talk," Emma whispered.

"And eat ice cream," I suggested.

"Ice cream!" Lisa yelled and fist pumped.

Despite my heart breaking, I laughed at my friend and smiled as we entered the house.

Tom and Ethan scooped ice cream into bowls, and we all hopped up onto the countertops to eat and catch up.

I told them everything that happened and just as I finished, Jacqueline came inside.

She took my bowl of ice cream, and I growled at her.

With the spoon, she tapped the tip of my nose. "Bad bestie. No growling."

"Get your own bowl," I mumbled as I rubbed my nose.

"So, I saw your boy toy pouting as he ran towards his house. Did you have a fight?" she asked.

"We...broke up," I whispered and looked down at my hands in my lap.

The spoon hit the bowl, breaking the silence in the kitchen.

"What!" she screeched. "That dumb mother—"

"It's fine!" I shouted, stopping her. "Just...drop it."

"Want me to turn him into a toad?" she offered and wrapped an arm around my waist.

"You can do that?" Tom asked.

She wiggled her fingers. "Want to find out?"

We all laughed and despite everything, I felt lighter.

Things were not perfect, but I could get through this. I'd survived this long without a boyfriend and I could do it again.

Rob suddenly burst into the kitchen, his eyes and hair wild. "Where is she?"

Tom and Ethan pointed at me.

Rob ran over, grabbed my hands, pulled me off of the counter, and hugged me tightly. "I just found out they kidnapped you again." He pushed me back to arm's length. "Are you okay?" he looked me over. "You don't look hurt."

I smiled and patted his arm. "I'm fine."

His pupils dilated, his nostrils flared and he leaned down, pressing his nose against my hair. "You're...you're...you're a werewolf?"

I nodded. "Yeah."

"She saved the pack from being cursed to become wolves permanently. I might have tampered with the spell a bit, knowing my girl would sacrifice herself," Jacqueline said with a shrug of her shoulder. "She's always been meant to be a werewolf."

"You saw it?" I asked. It was super rare, but she could see the future randomly.

"Yep," she said, making the 'P' sound pop.

Rob's eyes widened, and he looked around like he was looking for something or someone. "Oh, this changes everything."

"You mean because that moron dumped her?" Jacqueline asked.

Rob flinched. "I didn't think he would do it so soon. I mean, the same day? That's fucked up."

"We're going to beat him up later," Tom said and punched his fist into his other palm.

"Just leave him alone," I said. "He's not done anything wrong.

"The hell he hasn't!" Rob yelled. "You saved our entire pack, and he can't give up on his stupid desire to have kids?

We should all be groveling at your feet and begging you to let us be your friends."

There was a knock at the door as Jesse stepped in. "Chloe?"

Everyone stepped between us, growling.

"Back off!" I ordered them all and pushed my way through them to stand before him. "Sorry, they are still on edge."

He smirked. "I don't blame them." He rubbed the back of his neck and his cheeks turned slightly pink. "Can I talk to you outside?"

"Sure," I replied before Jacqueline could say whatever she had opened her mouth to respond with.

Once outside, he huffed and faced me. "If it's okay with you, I'd like to join this pack?"

My surprise must have been written on my face, because he laughed softly despite me not replying.

"What you do isn't up to me," I whispered.

"This was your pack first and I...well I didn't stop John despite wanting to and knowing better. I didn't want to join if my presence would just remind you of being kidnapped and—"

I smiled and took his hand. "I think it would be amazing if you joined the pack." My cheeks flushed and I said, "Maybe you could even help me adjust to being a werewolf now."

He squeezed my hand and bent to kiss my cheek. "I'd like that."

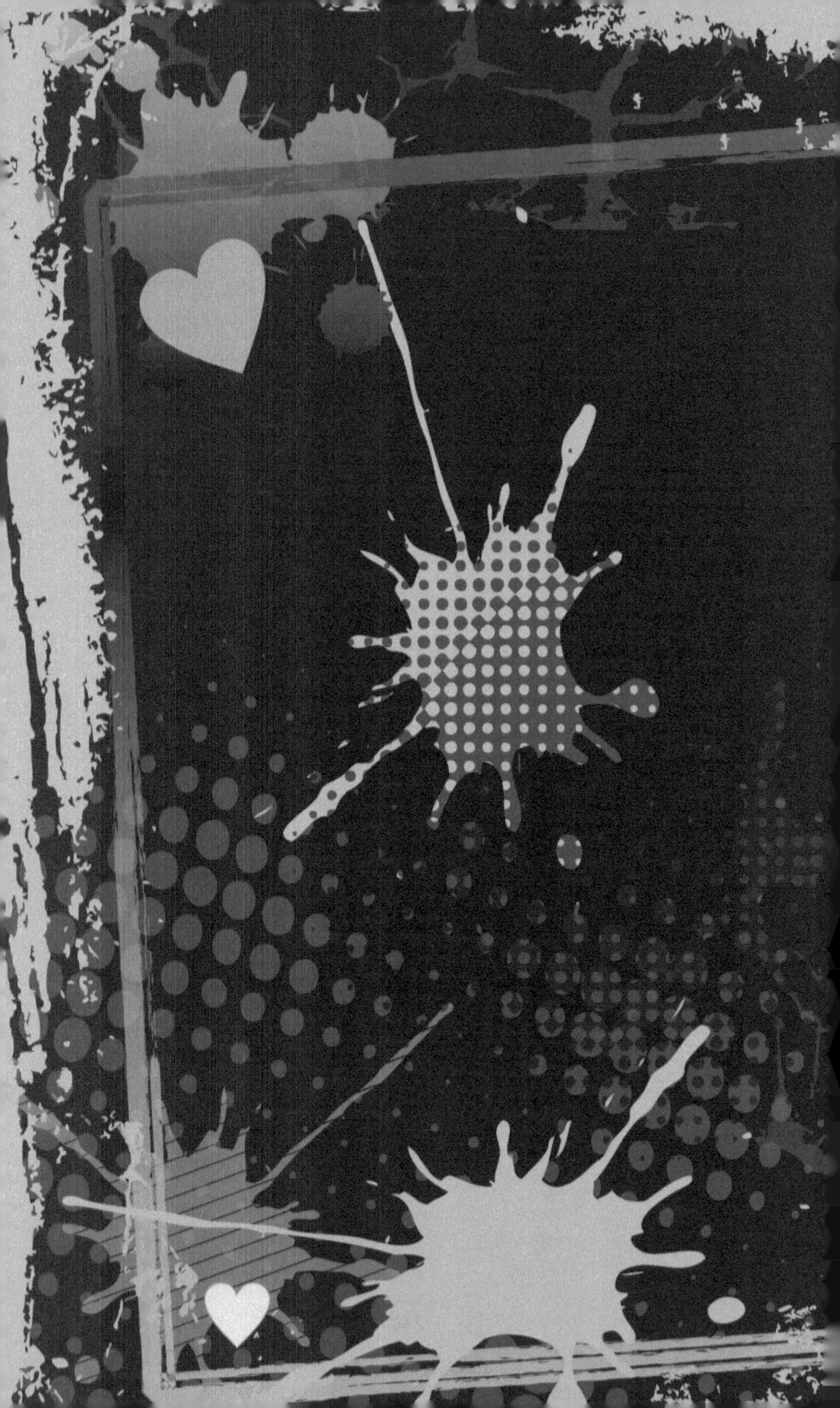

EIGHTEEN

Over two dozen of John's pack joined ours, and I was officially welcomed as a werewolf.

Kelly welcomed Jacqueline as an unofficial member of the pack as well.

There were four human girls, around my age, we'd found in a locked room, hidden from the pack, in John's house. Since they knew about werewolves, Kelly didn't want to just let them go, but didn't want to kill them or hold them hostage either.

Turned out the girls were homeless wanted to stay with our pack. They'd listened to everything going on and said they wanted to be part of Kelly's pack, and pick werewolf mates in the future. Kelly had given them a house near hers so they could assimilate and I knew there were male werewolves constantly approaching them to try to take them out on dates.

I didn't doubt that Dylan would be to see them eventually.

"So, what are your plans for today?" Jacqueline asked as we walked towards a house that was now mine. It had belonged to a member who moved out of state.

"Jesse is working with me on shifting today," I answered and sighed. "It is not nearly as easy as I had hoped." I kept getting halfway there and then reverting back to human. I was worried I might never shift fully.

She bumped her elbow against my arm. "Things heating up between you two?"

My face and ears grew hot. "No."

"Pity," she said with a sigh. "He's hot."

That fact was definitely something I was well aware of. However, my heart still belonged to Dylan, even if that bastard didn't deserve it.

He actually disappeared the day after the joining ceremony and no one had been able to contact him in over a week.

"Tomorrow, let's have a girls' day and get our nails done," Jacqueline suggested.

"Oh! Include me!" Lisa said, waving her arm as she jogged over to us.

Jacqueline smiled. "You and the other two are always welcome with us."

"'Other two?' We have names, you know?" Amy said, flipped her hair over her shoulder and scoffed.

Jesse walked towards us, hands in his pockets, and nodded once. "Hey."

"Hey," I replied a bit too chipper.

Jacqueline snickered, but quickly stopped after I elbowed her gut.

"Ready?" I asked.

"Ready for what?" Dylan asked from behind me.

My heart nearly jumped out of my chest. He'd snuck up on me again. I swallowed hard, closed my eyes, and refused to turn around.

"For our lesson," Jesse answered. "Not that it's any of your business."

Jesse took my hand, and I opened my eyes to meet his. "Let's go," I whispered.

He started to lead me away, but Dylan stepped in front of us, growling.

Amy shoved his shoulder so hard that he flew sideways and slid on the ground. "You have no right!" she snapped. "You dumped her and then disappeared for over a week!"

"I didn't—"

"Save it!" Emma yelled and stepped up next to Amy. "You don't get to say shit."

Lisa waved her hand at me, telling us to leave.

I gnawed on my lower lip, wanting to stay, but also wanting to run as far and fast away from him as I could.

Jesse shifted into his wolf form, and I hopped onto his back, laying flat and holding the fur around his shoulders as he ran the rest of the way to my house.

Once there, I slid off of him and to my butt on the ground. "I'm sorry," I whispered and wiped at the tears falling down my face. "I'm so sorry. This isn't fair to you."

He took my hands gently and whispered, "Do you want me to fight him? To keep him away from you?"

My eyes snapped up to his. "Wh-what?"

"I know we haven't really talked about this, but I can tell it really upsets you, and as your friend, I—"

"She is my girlfriend," Dylan yelled as he stepped out from the tree line.

"No, I'm not!" I yelled back immediately and stood, fury coursing through my body in a red-hot fire.

"Look, I know I got tongue-tied and—"

I marched towards him, my fists clenched at my sides and

my approach made him stumble backwards. "You didn't get tongue-tied. You just accepted it! I was willing to sacrifice myself for you and you wanted to dump me just because I couldn't give you kids anymore."

"I know you don't understand, but having kids was a huge—"

"There are girls here who you can court now," I said. "Human girls that had been held at John's. They can have your babies. Go talk to them."

He blinked. "What?"

"Leave her alone," Jesse snarled. "She's dealt with your crap enough."

"Chloe, please listen to me," Dylan whispered and grabbed my arm.

I snapped my teeth at him. "Don't touch me! You don't get to touch me!"

His eyes darkened and fur rippled along his jaw. "Do not give me orders."

Before I realized what was happening, my body shifted, and Dylan and I were fighting each other in wolf form. Teeth snapping, claws flying, and blood dripping on the floor.

Jesse pulled me off Dylan, and my breaths came in loud puffs.

Dylan shifted and ran a hand across his face, smearing blood down his handsome features. "I'm sorry. I don't want to fight. I came to apologize and to tell you I never wanted to break up."

"What?" I gaped.

"I am a moron."

"Obviously," Jesse scoffed.

Dylan snarled, but looked back at me. "I love you, Chloe. It doesn't matter if you are human, werewolf, or witch. I love you—your soul."

"You…you said you wanted kids. I can't give you kids," I whispered, trying not to let my hopes get too high.

"Don't give her hope if you're just going to dump her after finding a human to birth your pups," Jesse threatened.

"I know!" Dylan yelled. "Why do you think I've been gone for so long?"

Despite knowing he meant it as a way to explain, it felt like a punch to my stomach.

"I'm looking for someone who loves me for me, not because of what my body can offer them. I am not a broodmare."

Jesse set a hand on my upper back, giving me a bit of comfort.

"Apologizing won't fix this, I know, but I am sorry. I really do love you and want to be with you," Dylan whispered.

"If only you had said that two weeks ago," I whispered back, turned, and walked up the steps to my front door.

Jesse followed at my heels and stepped around me to open the door.

"Chloe," Dylan whispered. "Please."

"You had your time to come to a decision and now I need my time," I said without turning around to face him, afraid if I saw him, saw his stupidly handsome face, that I might give in. "Don't come see me again. If I want to, I will come see you."

"Chloe," Dylan whispered, "don't you feel it? In your soul?"

I knew what he meant, but I was ignoring it. "I feel pain," I answered and stepped into the house.

Jesse shut the door behind me, but stood outside of it. He and Dylan were talking in hushed tones that I couldn't hear, but I didn't want to hear. Instead, I walked to the kitchen and washed the dirt and blood from my hands and from beneath my fingernails. My front door opened and closed.

Jesse hugged me from behind, and I broke apart, sobbing in his embrace. I spun and gripped his shirt as I continued to cry. He rubbed my back gently. "It's going to be okay, Clover. Just let it out and I'll be right here." I loved his nickname for me. No one else called me that.

"Why are you so nice to me?" I whispered.

"Because you're the type of friend I always wanted," he admitted. "If only you were a few years older."

I chuckled and the pain ebbed a little. "Or you were a few years younger," I countered.

He pet my hair, and I stepped back to wipe my face. "Seriously, I want you to know that I'll always be your friend. So, if you want me to beat him up for hurting you? Consider it done."

"I shifted," I whispered.

He nodded and smiled. "I saw. You were also winning that fight."

I rolled my eyes. "We both know that's not true. If he had wanted to hurt me, he could have."

"Want to watch a movie?" he asked. "We can watch something absolutely stupid and full of action."

"Sounds awesome!" I agreed. "I'll get some snacks."

"I love snacks!" Tom yelled as he, Ethan, Amy, Lisa, and Emma came inside.

"Who invited you?" I teased.

"You, duh!" Lisa said and skipped into the kitchen to help me grab snacks.

"It was an open invitation, if I recall," Tom said and helped Amy grab drinks.

"What movie are we watching?" Ethan asked.

"This one?" Alex suggested and held up a movie that I had never seen.

"Is it good?" I asked.

"So many explosions," Alex said with a smile and a vigorous nod.

"Perfect," I agreed.

Jesse sat on the left corner of the couch, me on his right, and Lisa, Emma, and Amy squished on my other side.

The other three guys sat on the floor, leaned back against their girl's legs.

It wasn't long before we were all cheering and laughing at the ridiculous hero. The perfect ending to an otherwise not great day. Well, it would have been absolutely perfect if Jacqueline were here, but she was dealing with some witch issues.

When the movie ended, I walked everyone out, and Jesse patted my shoulder. "Things will work out. You just have to wait and see."

I gave him a tight smile and headed back inside.

Despite needing to clean up, I flopped down onto my bed instead with a sigh.

Should I give Dylan another chance? I didn't want anyone else, but was that just me settling?

There were more guys in the pack now, some my age that were definitely interested in me. Not that I'd paid them any attention since I had been heartbroken over Dylan.

Dylan had mentioned the connection I felt. While he'd been gone, I hadn't wanted to admit it, but we definitely had a connection, small and distant as it was.

What could that connection mean?

"Not going to solve that puzzle tonight," I told myself. "Best to go to sleep and try again tomorrow."

"Do you always talk to yourself when you are alone? That's sort of concerning," the vampire who had helped John said.

I yelped and jumped up, but he was faster and had his hand wrapped around my throat.

"Easy. Don't freak out. I don't want to kill you… yet," he said and squeezed until I couldn't breathe. "That moron ruined everything for me, but I can still use you as a bargaining chip with the witch to get that book back."

Jacqueline? He was going to use me against Jacqueline? I couldn't let that happen.

I tried to shift, focusing on the hot feeling in my core that I was beginning to associate with my wolf form.

If I could just shift, I could stand a chance against this jerk.

He flicked the tip of my nose, forcing my eyes open as tears formed. "Tut-tut. No shifting." With one arm, he picked me up by the throat and carried me out of the house. "Summon your friend. I know you have a connection."

"No," I managed to gasp out.

"Kids these days," he huffed. With his free hand, he grabbed one of my fingers and snapped it sideways, breaking it.

I tried to scream, but he tightened his hold on my throat.

Twin connections in my heart lit up as my pain surfaced.

As quick as I could, I snuffed those connections, silencing them.

"Almost," the vampire said. He set me on my feet, but before I could run away, shift, or attack him, he grabbed my arm, the one I'd broken before, and snapped it in two.

I screamed as I crumpled to the ground, cradling my broken arm in my lap.

"Chloe!" Dylan yelled as he ran towards me.

The vampire sighed. "Boyfriend? Really? You already made

a bond with your boyfriend? You young kids are so damn impulsive. Do you have any idea how hard it is to break bonds like that?"

"What do you want, vamp?" Jacqueline asked from behind me.

The vampire grabbed my uninjured arm and turned to face her, giving his back to Dylan, showing that he didn't view him as a threat. "There you are, witch. I am here to make a trade: your friend for the book."

"I don't have it. The book is with the elders," she said.

"Lie," the vampire said and sighed dramatically. "You are so young and dumb, the lot of you. One last time or I bite her and you watch as she disintegrates." He looked down at me and smiled. "Werewolves don't take to the vampire venom well."

Noted.

Dylan shifted into his wolf form and stalked forward.

The vampire didn't even look, just raised a hand towards Dylan and said, "One more step, wolf, and I kill her."

Dylan froze, crouched down, and growled in frustration.

"One last time, witch. The book or your friend?"

"Chloe, deep breath," Jacqueline whispered.

I inhaled as deep as I could, and then let it out in a whoosh.

Jacqueline flipped the vampire off and then sunlight exploded out of her middle finger.

He released me, screamed, and then burst into dust.

I dropped to my knees and gasped.

Dylan ran to me and set his hands on my cheeks. "Anything broken besides your arm?"

"Finger," I whispered, but couldn't lift my arm to show him since it was the same one as the broken arm.

"Clover!" Jesse yelled as he ran to us. He slid on his knees to me and scowled. "What happened?" he looked at Dylan and snarled. Grabbing Dylan by the shirt, he lifted him up to his feet as he stood and yelled, "Did you do this? Did you hurt her!"

Dylan grabbed Jesse's wrist. "I would nev—"

"You hurt her when you left. You making that physical now? I'll kill you before I let you—"

"Enough!" Jacqueline yelled, a force of power exploding out of her to knock them down. She knelt by me and rested her hand against our mark. "It's time for me to reciprocate."

"No," I said quickly. "I just need to go to the doctor and—"

"Too late," she said and poured some of her energy into me. Her power forced my now advanced healing to work double-time and immediately healed the broken finger and broken arm.

I yelped as it healed and let my head drop to her shoulder. "Bitch."

She snickered. "Love you, too."

"What happened?" Jesse asked.

"The vampire who was helping John showed up and tried to use Chloe to get me to give him the spell book," Jacqueline answered.

"I wouldn't hurt her," Dylan said.

Jesse stepped around to face me. "Did he bite you?" He pushed my hair to the side to look at my neck.

Dylan growled. "Stop acting so comfortable with her. She's not yours."

"She's my friend," Jesse said, unperturbed. "Her safety is important to me."

"I'm fine," I assured him. "No bites."

He nodded and hugged me once. "You want me to stay the night? So you aren't alone?"

"No, she does not!" Dylan snapped.

I huffed, turned to face Dylan, and calmly said, "Shut up."

His mouth snapped closed and eyes widened.

"I don't care what we are; you don't get to talk for me."

"Go, girl," Jacqueline whispered.

"If you want us to work, you need to accept that I'm not defenseless. No, I can't shift on command yet, but I am capable of defending myself and I don't need a *man* to speak for me. I don't care if you are the alpha or whatever. You need to respect me as an equal or we aren't going to work."

He opened his mouth, closed it, opened it, and closed it again.

I turned to Jesse. "And you, stop antagonizing him. I'm fine. Go home. I appreciate you coming to check on me—I really do—but I am safe now and you can go home."

He smiled wide, hugged me tight, and waved as he jogged away.

"You going to yell at me, too?" Jacqueline asked with a smile.

"No."

She pouted. "Why not?"

"Go wait inside," I ordered her.

She mimicked me silently as she walked into my house.

Facing Dylan again, I smiled. "So, what's it going to be?"

His brows furrowed. "Huh?"

"Are you going to treat me as your equal and become my mate? Or, are you going to stay stuck in the stone age and find a new girlfriend?"

Wide-eyed, he immediately stepped forward, wrapped his arms around me, and nodded vigorously. "Yes, please. Please, be my mate."

"If you insist," I said with a sigh as though he were making me do something boring with the request.

He crushed his mouth against mine and I wrapped my arms around his back, pulling him closer to me.

The bond between us strengthened and then sealed.

"Don't make me regret this," I whispered as I looked up at him through my lashes.

He smiled, the one that stole my breath and heart. "I'll never make you regret this decision. Ever. I love you."

"I love you, too," I whispered and knew that this love was forever.

THANK YOU

Thank you for reading my book. If you enjoyed it, please consider leaving a review.

Check out the Artemis Lupine Series, a complete young adult paranormal romance series featuring werewolves, fated mates, vampires, and more: books2read.com/Artemis-Lupine-1

Turn the page to read Chapter 1 of SONG OF THE MOON.

270

SONG OF THE MOON - CHAPTER ONE

It was our third day away from home. Darren, my father, decided that we needed a vacation away from the drama of our small-town life. I didn't know what drama he was talking about, but it *was* nice to get away. Darren sang along quietly to the song on the radio as we drove towards our third destination: South Lake Tahoe.

The first day, well, technically night, had been Las Vegas with its bright lights and non-stop gambling. I wasn't actually twenty-one, but somehow Darren got fake ID's that allowed both Bret and me to gamble and drink. Vegas had been fun, but the men were very abrasive, throwing offers at me like I was a street walker. Darren had, of course, protected me, but Bret was the one to make them back off. Bret was my best friend of thirteen years and the star quarterback of our high school football team. He just accepted a full ride scholarship to Notre Dame for the upcoming semester. It was the main reason he had come with us, so that we could have one last trip together before he left California for Indiana.

Our second day was spent in Reno, which was a smaller

version of Vegas minus the brightly lit streets. We went to a rodeo, much to Darren's dismay, and then gambled more of Darren's savings away.

That was yesterday though. Tonight, we would get to enjoy Tahoe. Bret silently stared out the back passenger window of Darren's nimbus grey metallic, VTEC Honda Ridgeline. The townspeople made fun of Darren for buying an import truck, but I loved it. What's more reliable than a Honda? I drove a small blue Honda Del Sol. Bret hates my car, often telling me, "It's a death trap waiting to happen." I ignore his domestic car-loving mentality and enjoy driving the small car with my targa top off every summer.

Just as I felt my eyes starting to droop, Darren cleared his throat. "Welcome to South Lake Tahoe."

I turned to the left and stared out at the perfect blue water. The mountains which lined the lake still held on to a thin layer of snow, making the scene twice as lovely. "Wow! It's beautiful."

Bret sat up straight and asked, "Do we get to go swimming?"

Darren laughed. "Of course! I would never bring you to Tahoe and not let you enjoy the lake. That's like taking you to San Diego and making you stay away from the beach."

I started bouncing up and down on the seat. "I can't wait to jump into that lake!"

"You won't be jumping in. You'll be flying in," Bret said as he laughed.

I scoffed. "Like you could catch me!" I knew he could catch me easily, but it was fun to roughhouse with him. We spent a lot of time wrestling and goofing around. He easily outmuscled me, but that's to be expected since I'm a small girl and he's a football player. It just makes me feel better to play tough sometimes.

Darren laughed quietly. "Now, children, remember we are supposed to be acting like adults."

Bret shrugged. "You said we only had to act in our early twenties, and I guarantee any guy in his early twenties would try to throw Artemis in the lake."

I rolled my eyes. *Boys are so weird.*

Darren sighed. "I don't think you two will ever grow up."

Bret and I shrugged in unison and then laughed together.

Darren finally stopped in front of a large hotel. "This is my favorite hotel, so no screwing things up. You can use an underground tunnel to go from this hotel to the one across the street."

"Awesome!" I said

"That means there are twice as many restaurants for us to eat at," Bret said with a smile on his face.

Darren and I groaned at Bret.

"You always think about food," I complained.

"Come on! It's been like four hours since lunch. I know you're hungry, too," Bret said.

I started to deny his statement, but my stomach growled loudly, giving me away. I sighed. "Guess I can't deny it now." I looked down at my stomach and whispered, "Traitor."

Darren shook his head smiling. "Come on. Let's get checked in and put our bags away and then we'll get some food."

Darren pulled into the valet parking line and handed the valet the truck keys. I stepped out of the truck, jogged to the back, and opened the compartment in the bed to get out my duffel bag of clothes. I hated those girls who packed five bags of crap for only being gone three days, so I made sure to pack as light as possible.

I started to sling my bag over my shoulder when Bret took it from me. He slung it over his shoulder with his. I smiled at him as I followed them into the hotel.

Darren checked us in, getting our room keys before guiding us towards the elevators. No one was waiting, so we got the elevator to ourselves. I breathed slowly, trying to fight my paranoia. I kept imagining the elevator reaching the highest floor then plummeting back to the first level, killing us. Bret hugged my shoulders and rubbed my arm to calm me. Darren rolled his eyes at me and pushed the button for the tenth floor.

I groaned. "*Tenth* floor?"

Darren shrugged. "At least it's not the top floor. There are fourteen."

I snarled. "Four more isn't that big of a difference."

Darren smiled sideways. "It is when you are falling to the ground. Four less floors may be the difference between death and being permanently paralyzed."

I started breathing faster and turned my face into Bret's side. Bret shook his head. "Darren, was that necessary?"

Darren scoffed. "She's such a baby about heights. One day she'll have to get over her fears."

I shook my head. "It's not the heights, Dad. It's the elevator. I would more than gladly take the stairs up. I just hate the thought of plummeting to my death in this tin can."

Bret rolled his eyes. "But you drive the Del Sol and feel safe. Isn't that kind of backwards?"

I shook my head. "Nope. *Nikkou* is very safe." *Nikkou* was the Japanese word for "sunshine" and my little car always makes me think of the sun.

Darren rolled his eyes as the elevator door opened.

I ran out from under Bret's arm and sat on the tile of the tenth floor. "Oh, thank God. We made it."

Bret picked me up under the arms and set me on my feet. "Come on scared-y cat. Let's go."

Bret and I followed Darren as he wound the way down the hallways towards our rooms. Darren stopped next to two doors. "That one is your room and this one is mine." He handed Bret a keycard and then walked into his room without another word to us.

Bret turned to our door and opened it with the keycard. I walked in before he could and looked around. It was a large room with two queen sized beds and a gorgeous view of the mountains. I walked into the bathroom and giggled happily. A large jetted tub sat to the side waiting for me to get in. I turned on the bath and then walked out to the bedroom.

Bret flipped through the channels on the television and then groaned. "All that is on is some breaking news story."

I shrugged. "I have a few minutes before my tub is full. Let's watch it."

Darren burst in through the side door that connected our rooms and took the remote from Bret, turning off the television. "No TV! I told you that before we left!" His voice was raised, he was breathing heavily, and his face was flushed.

"Why are you so angry?" I asked.

Bret shrugged. "It's alright. Whatever you want, Darren. I was just curious what the breaking news story was."

Darren shook his head. "You aren't allowed to watch TV. I told you we were getting you both away from the drama and watching TV won't do that. Now dammit, enjoy yourselves without the TV!"

I stared at my dad as he tried to play off his anger and become playful. I wasn't buying it.

"I'm taking a bath." I grabbed my bag and walked into the bathroom. I could hear Darren and Bret talking quietly, but I focused on relaxing. I set my bag down in the area with mirrors, grabbed a towel and set it next to the tub as I turned on the jets, and climbed in. I loved hot baths and any free time I had was spent in the tub. I let my body relax with the gentle humming of the jets. In a matter of minutes, my mind began to wander, and my subconscious took over.

My breath steamed out in front of me as I ran through the thick forest. The other five people around me panted and sucked in air as we fled from our pursuers. The three wolves hunting us yipped in delight, and fear made me trip on a tree root. I dodged around the trees as fast as I could. I knew I only had to run faster than the last three people. I knew I couldn't run my fastest or I would increase my chances of hitting one of the trees and ending up in the claws of those pursuing us. The sounds of the others grew faint as I darted around more trees. Sweat plastered my shirt against my chest. I heard movement beside me, but dodged too late. A large animal slammed into my side, sending me flying sideways. I wrapped my arms around my head to protect it as I slammed into a tree and slid to the ground.

The animal stood over me, snarling and snapping its teeth, but made no move to hurt me. I moved one arm to my stomach and one to my throat to try to protect my most vital parts. I opened my eyes and gasped. A wolf the size of a horse stood over me, snarling. I had never seen such a beautiful animal before. The wolf's jet black fur reflected the moonlight as its muscles flexed. The wolf sat, staring at me with its deep amber eyes. It seemed strange to me for so much hate to be emanating from such a beautiful creature. I reached out and stroked the soft furred neck, and the wolf quieted. I slowed my breathing as I stroked the wolf. I looked down the wolf's body and saw the male sheath and smiled. "Hello, boy. Why don't you change and let me see how beautiful you are in human form?"

The wolf snarled, and I pulled back my hands. The words seemed to come out even though I wasn't sure of their meaning. "I only meant that you are so beautiful in wolf form that I have no doubt that you are gorgeous in your other form as well." The wolf stepped back and stood up on its hind legs. I scooted backwards to get farther away from him and watched in amazement as the wolf's body rippled like water and became human. The man before me smiled and walked forward. I couldn't help but stare at his naked perfection, although I kept my gaze above his belly button so as not to offend him. "What's your name?" I asked.

The man smiled and held his hand out to me. He spoke with a voice like honey and said, "Ares."

The dream ended as quickly as it had started. I sat up and stared at the wall in front of me. I slowed my breathing as I focused on reality, and then sighed heavily. It was the same dream I had been having for the past week. I wished it wouldn't end in the same spot every time. I wanted to know what happened next.

Bret knocked on the bathroom door. "Are you alright, Artemis?"

I inhaled one more long breath then called back, "Yes, I'm fine. Just fell asleep in the tub." I climbed out of the now luke-warm water and dried off quickly.

Bret sighed. "Well, hurry. I'm starving."

My stomach growled in agreement, and I groaned. "Alright. Sorry." I threw on a pair of jeans and a low-cut t-shirt then ran my brush through my shoulder length black hair before throwing it up into a ponytail. I pulled open the door and ran into Bret's chest.

He stumbled backwards and smiled at me. "Shit, you caught me off guard."

I smiled back. "Don't lie. You know I'm just stronger than you."

Bret rolled his eyes. "Yes, you, a five foot two, hundred and ten-pound girl, are stronger than me, a six-foot, hundred and eighty-pound guy. Not likely."

I shrugged. "It's okay that you don't want to admit it. I know the truth."

Bret sighed and motioned towards the door. "Let's go eat." I hurried out into the hall to find Darren, who stood against the opposite wall waiting for us. He acknowledged us with a smile and then started walking down the hall towards the elevators. I tried to listen to the guys' conversation, but all I could think about was the wolf-man of my dream.

Darren interrupted my thoughts by pushing me into the elevator. I frowned at him, but ignored his taunting. *Could the man be real?* I shook my head. *Of course not. There aren't men who can turn into wolves or vice versa. That's all just fantasy. Wait... wouldn't he be a werewolf then?*

Darren cleared his throat making me look up at him. "Are you alright?" he asked.

I nodded. "Sorry. I fell asleep in the tub and I'm still trying to wake up." Wrapping my arms around myself, I kept taking slow, deep breaths to calm my fear of being in the elevator.

Darren rolled his eyes. "I was thinking we would go to a steak house."

I licked my lips. "Steak sounds great!"

Darren frowned at me, and Bret laughed. "I swear if we took red meat away from you, you would end up eating one of us just to get your fill."

I wrinkled my nose in disgust. "I don't think you would taste very good."

Darren rubbed his temples. "Let's not discuss eating each other." He walked out of the elevator as soon as it opened and led us through the now crowded hotel. A line of at least thirty people formed at the steak restaurant, but Darren strolled up to the front and the hostess nodded as he spoke to her. She darted into the restaurant. Bret and I walked up to Darren who stood, looking smug. The hostess came back and waved us in with a smile. Darren followed her and sat down at the largest booth. Two waiters came up and handed us menus and took our drink orders without even asking for ID.

I turned to Darren. "Why are they treating you like royalty?"

"The owner is a longtime friend of mine," he said.

A short, very muscular man with a three-inch-tall, bright green Mohawk walked over to our table. His very nice, very expensive looking suit fit every curve of his body.

Darren smiled wider, but it seemed to almost look like a grimace. "Koda! I didn't think you would be here. I thought you were still in Germany."

Koda smiled wide, flashing perfectly white teeth. I stared at his face and guessed him at about twenty-five, but that made no sense to me since Darren was close to forty. "We came back from Germany a few weeks ago. I'm sure you know why."

Darren smiled slipped down into a frown. "Yes, yes I do." Darren's sudden mood change made me stare at Koda longer. He was very handsome and looked strong. Darren shook his head and smiled again. "Where are my manners? Koda, I'd like you to meet my daughter, Artemis, and her friend Bret."

Koda turned his attention to me, and his brows lifted. His

bright blue eyes pierced through me as he stared into mine. He slowly reached his hand out towards me, and I took it, shaking hands like Darren had taught me. His skin was extremely warm, and I felt a small tingle rush up my arm and to my head. Koda smiled and shook my hand back with an equally firm, yet gentle shake. "It is a pleasure to meet you, Artemis. I have heard so much about you."

I frowned. "Unfortunately, I cannot say the same. But it is nice to finally meet one of Dad's friends."

Koda dropped my hand abruptly, making the tingling disappear, and turned to Darren. "She hasn't heard about me?"

Darren swallowed hard and he couldn't meet Koda's gaze. "I have not told her of my past life."

Koda's lip twitched in a snarl. "That is very interesting indeed." Koda turned to me, smiling again. "If you want some time away from your father and friend please feel free to find me. I am always around this restaurant and, if not, my staff can reach me at any time, day or night." He took my hand again and kissed the back of it. "And I would be more than happy to show you around."

Bret stiffened beside me, and I smiled nicely at Koda. "Thank you, Mister..."

Koda shook his head then winked at me. "Call me Koda."

I smiled wider. "Thank you, Koda, but we are only here for one night and I'm sure the guys have a lot planned."

Bret relaxed back against his seat, and Darren let out the breath he had been holding.

Koda shrugged. "As you wish, but the offer is open any day."

Koda smiled at me then stepped closer to Darren and whispered into his ear. Darren's face fell, and he nodded once, very short and quick, as if he were afraid to make any other movement. Koda walked away without glancing back. The waiters came by and took our orders. Darren smiled again and shook his head. "It has been too long since I've seen him. So, how does gambling for a few hours, then a trip to the hottest dance club in town sound?"

Bret smiled. "Awesome!"

I groaned. "A dance club? Why don't you just stab me in the eye with this fork?"

Bret and Darren talked in about the night to come, but I couldn't listen to them. I stared in the direction Koda had disappeared and wished I could find a way to speak to him further. I remembered the strange tingling and wondered what had caused it. My ruminations ended as our food came and I ate my medium rare steak quickly. I ate the fries and salad as fast as my steak. Then downed my beer. I looked at Darren and Bret. "I need to use the restroom. I'll be right back." I started to get up then realized I had no clue where the bathroom was.

Darren noticed my problem. "Straight back and to the left."

I walked in the direction he had told me and felt butterflies as I realized it was the same way Koda had gone. I turned right down a dark hallway and ran into Koda's wide back. I hadn't seen him in the darkness. He spun around, and his surprised expression turned into a warm smile. "Hello, Artemis. Get tired of your friend so soon?"

I laughed. "Hi, Koda. Sorry. I was just going to the bathroom and wasn't paying attention."

Koda shrugged. "No harm done."

He stepped to the side to allow me to pass him, but I stayed still. "Koda, what did my dad mean about not telling me about his past?"

Koda's eyes squinted in anger. "I'm sorry, Artemis, but it's not my place to discuss your father's past with you. Your father will have to tell you."

I sighed. "Alright."

I continued past Koda and into the restroom. I went pee then washed my hands and walked out of the bathroom. Koda stood in the same spot as before, talking quietly on his cell phone. I hurried to the table where Darren and Bret had already finished their food. "Time to gamble?" I asked.

Bret nodded. "Let's go!"

Darren rolled his eyes. "So eager to waste my money?"

"It was your idea." I lifted a brow at him.

Darren laughed. "True, very true."

We started to walk out of the restaurant when I felt some-one's hand on me. A quick rush of heat raced up my arm, making me gasp. I spun around and stared at Koda. He dropped my arm and the heat stopped. "My apologies, Artemis, I didn't mean to frighten you."

I smiled. "It's alright. No harm done."

His smile widened at my reminder of his comment. He held out a small piece of white paper. "Take this. If you ever need anything feel free to call me."

I slowly took the paper and nodded. "Th-thanks."

He winked at me. "No problem."

I couldn't help but stare at his backside as he walked away. Darren cleared his throat, and I hid the piece of paper in my hand and turned to him.

Darren asked, "What was that about?"

I shrugged. "He was just saying bye."

Darren stared at me for a second then shrugged. "He's a nice guy." We started walking out of the restaurant again, and I put the piece of paper in my pants pocket. There were so many questions about Darren that I wanted answers to. Maybe I would call Koda and see if he could answer them. Darren stopped in the middle of the gambling area and turned to us. He pulled out his wallet and made three piles of bills. He handed one pile to me and one pile to Bret before pocketing the third pile for himself. "Now make this last at least two hours."

"I'm sure I can do that, but Bret will probably spend it in ten minutes," I said with a laugh.

Bret rolled his eyes. "You only spend it slowly because you play slots."

I shrugged. "I think slots are fun."

Darren laughed. "Play nice, kids. I'll meet you back here in two hours." He started towards the blackjack tables.

I turned to Bret and smiled. "See you in two hours."

He rolled his eyes again. "Have fun with the slots."

"I will," I said. I strolled towards the slot machines when the hairs on the back of my neck stood on end. Was someone staring at me? I rubbed the back of my neck and looked around, but couldn't see anyone. I shrugged it off and walked faster towards the five cent slot machines. I felt a warm tingling sensation spread over me and turned to my right.

Koda stood a few feet away, talking to someone whose back was towards me. Koda's eyes widened when he saw me, and he whispered something to the man he was with. I smiled at Koda and waved, starting to walk away when the man turned around. I gasped and stopped moving. The man with Koda smiled politely at me, but I stood dumbfounded. He was the man from my dreams, the werewolf man.

Koda walked quickly to my side and whispered, "Breathe!"

I inhaled a big breath and then stopped breathing again as the man walked towards me. I started to ask his name when

Darren, appearing seemingly out of thin air, grabbed my arm and yanked me behind him. The man snarled softly at Darren, and I gasped at his wolf-like growl. I shook my head, clearing my thoughts. *I'm just projecting what I want to hear.*

The man seemed angry and stood in a loose fighting stance, like he was preparing for an attack. "What are you doing?" His voice was tinted with anger as he glared at Darren.

"Leave my daughter alone," Darren said with menace in his voice as he pushed me farther behind him and away from the man.

The man smiled. "I haven't done anything and you know I would never hurt our kind, especially not one as beautiful as her."

My cheeks instantly flushed. What did he mean by that, though?

Darren's lips twitched up in a snarl. "Are you here for what I think you are here for?"

The man frowned. "Darius sent us here to continue our mission, yes."

Darren sighed then walked backwards and grabbed my arm. "Come on, Artemis. We're leaving."

I shook my head and stared at the gorgeous man in front of us. "I don't want to leave." I could feel the man's dangerous potential and yet I could tell he was good. How did I know this? I had no idea.

Darren looked from me to the man and then back again. He shook his head and dragged me away by the arm. "We are leaving."

I grabbed at my stomach so that I wouldn't reach out towards the man from my dreams like I wanted to. The man blew a kiss at me, and I felt my blush intensify. I forced myself to turn away from him and followed Darren. Darren grabbed Bret, and we hurried to our rooms. We walked in silence until we reached our rooms, and then Darren turned to us suddenly. "I can't explain this, Artemis, but you two need to trust me. We have to leave, now."

I nodded and hurried into the hotel room to pack my bag. Bret grumbled about being on a streak as he packed his bag, too. I turned to walk out of the room and stopped dead. Koda stood at the end of the hallway by the elevators staring at me. I dropped my bag and hurried to him.

He frowned. "I wanted to make sure that you did as your father says and leave. Do not come back."

"Who was that man? I-I've had dreams about him," I said while wringing the bottom of my shirt.

Koda's eyes widened, his jaw dropped, and then he shook his head. "Just leave. If you want to call me later you can, but do not try to call me for at least two days."

I started to ask him why, but the elevator opened and Koda hurried inside, staring at the back of the elevator. The elevator doors closed a few moments before Darren spoke from his room. "Where's your bag?"

I turned around and smiled. "Sorry, I was trying to catch the elevator and dropped it by the door." I rushed back down the hallway and grabbed my bag as Bret followed me out, shutting the door and handing Darren the keycard. Darren watched me curiously, but didn't say anything. We took the elevator down and Darren paid the front desk clerk. I walked quickly towards the doors which led to the valet area, but I felt someone looking at me again and turned around, raising my gaze to the second story of the lobby. The man from my dreams stood on the upper level staring at me. He started to move towards the escalators, but Koda and another man grabbed him and held him back. I hurried out the door and inhaled the cool, refreshing night air. Darren walked out just as the valet brought the truck up.

I threw my bag to Bret and climbed into the truck, slamming my door and putting on my seatbelt. Darren climbed into the truck and started it, sighing as the motor started up. I looked back in the hotel and saw the man and Koda inside the lobby. Koda was holding onto the man's arm and talking sternly to him. The man was yelling at Koda, but he stopped mid-rant and turned to look at me. I stared into his beautiful blue eyes and wanted nothing more than to have him hold me.

Darren yelled, "Artemis!"

I stopped moving and realized that I had unbuckled my seatbelt and was opening my door. I slammed the door and put my belt back on and faced forward. Darren put the truck in gear and raced away from the hotel, leaving Koda and the mystery man behind. We drove in silence for an hour, and then Darren pulled into a small diner. We got out, and I numbly followed them into the diner. Darren ordered a burger for me and shoved a soda under my chin.

I drank as I thought about the mystery man. Who was he? Why did I feel so strange when I was near him? The news chiming on the television brought my attention back. I stared at the news reporter as his sad face told me that it wasn't going to be a happy report. "We know you all have heard of the devastation that is sweeping the Orient. It started in Japan and spread through China at an alarming rate..."

Darren yelled, "Can we change the channel?"

Our waitress came over, smiling politely. "I'm sorry, Sir, but there are more people here that want to watch it than those who don't."

Darren sighed loudly and stood up, dragging me with him. The news reporter continued. "We just learned that Russia has been…"

Darren shoved me out of the diner so hard and fast that I fell on my face on the concrete outside. Bret rushed to my side and picked me up in his arms. Bret growled. "What the hell is wrong with you, Darren?"

Darren shook his head. "Get in the truck!"

Bret set me down in the truck and got in the backseat. I stared at Darren, eyes wide. "What's happening? Why won't you let us watch the news? What's going on?!" I screamed at him, knowing he was up to something.

"Just do what I say." He started the truck and took off out of the parking lot, spraying gravel from his tires as we raced to the highway again.

My anger rose at Darren and my body began to heat up. I turned to yell at him then felt my body starting to twitch. I grunted in frustration as I had a seizure.

Bret screamed, "Darren!"

Darren pulled over and Bret held me down against the seat so I wouldn't thrash around and hit my head. Darren grabbed a cold water bottle, unscrewed the lid and splashed it on my face. I closed my eyes and focused on the cold feeling, willing myself to calm down. My body slowed its convulsions and then stopped altogether.

Bret sighed. "I wish I knew what the hell caused those."

Darren just stared at me with anger and worry filling his eyes as I regained control.

I whispered, "You can let go, Bret. I'm fine now."

Bret sat back in his seat and Darren started driving again. We listened to the radio in silence the rest of the way to town.

We hurried home, and I climbed straight into bed. Bret

followed me in and closed the door behind him. He set our bags down and sat on the bed next to me.

"I'm sorry we had to leave so early," I said to Bret.

Bret shrugged as he settled himself next to me. "It's not your fault, Artemis."

I rolled over and laid my head on his chest. We had been sleeping like this for so long that I barely thought about it. I focused on the beat of his heart and closed my eyes. Bret softly rubbed my back, and I fell asleep.

The rain poured like a giant waterfall down my face as I scanned the forest. I swiped at my face, but nothing helped. I put my hands over my eyes and screamed in frustration. I tensed as a wolf howled nearby, answering my scream. I walked backwards into the cave, pressing my back against the wall. My heart hammered against my chest, threatening to break through as I wiped the water from my eyes, and stared at the black opening of the cave. Lightning flashed, allowing me to see outside, and my entire body stilled. A large black wolf stood in the cavern's mouth, smelling the ground. The wolf turned its head towards me and sniffed three times quickly. I tried to slow my breathing, but my adrenaline was pumping too quickly to allow it. The wolf walked into the cave and whimpered. I shook my head and closed my eyes. The sound of bones snapping and popping echoed in the cave. I hugged myself tighter, fear consuming my rational thought. A familiar male voice whispered, "It's alright. I won't hurt you. I'm Ares."

I sat up in bed and focused on slowing my breathing down. I looked around the room and realized I was in my bedroom, not a forest, and Bret was sleeping soundly beside me. I crawled over the top of him and walked into the bathroom. After I flipped on the light, I stared at the blank wall where a normal household would have a mirror. I opened the wooden medicine cabinet and took out my nighttime contacts. I forgot to put them in, in my hurry to get to sleep. I took out the ones already in and threw them in the garbage. I let my eyes rest for a minute without any contacts in, and then put eye drops in to refresh my eyes. A sigh escaped me as I slowly put in the nighttime contacts.

It took me a while to be able to put contacts in since we didn't have a mirror, but I learned to do a lot of things without mirrors. So much so, that I never even look at one when away from home. Bret thought it was weird that I didn't have a mirror, but to me it was just how I was raised, like the kids who didn't have televisions. I closed the medicine cabinet and walked out into the living room. The TV was turned to the news, but Darren wasn't there. Gunfire in the distance let me know he was out target shooting or coyote hunting. I sat down and turned the news up so I could hear it.

To read more of Song of the Moon (Artemis Lupine #1), order it here: books2read.com/Artemis-Lupine-1

CONNECT WITH CATHERINE BANKS

I really appreciate you reading my book! I hope you enjoyed it.

Please consider leaving a review at your favorite site.

Here are some ways to connect with me:

www.catherinebanks.com

Follow me on BookBub: https://www.bookbub.com/authors/catherine-banks

Join my Patreon: http://www.patreon.com/catherinebanks

Purchase items handmade by Catherine: http://Etsy.com/shop/TurboKittenInd

ABOUT THE AUTHOR

Catherine Banks is a USA Today bestselling fantasy author who writes in several fantasy subgenres and has multiple pseudonyms. She began writing fiction at only four years old and finished her first full-length novel at the age of fifteen. She is married to her soulmate and best friend, Avery, who she has two amazing children with. After her full-time job, she reads books, plays video games, and watches anime shows and movies with her family to relax. Although she has lived in Northern California her entire life, she dreams of traveling around the world. Catherine is also C.E.O. of Turbo Kitten Industries™, a company with many hats including being a book publisher and Etsy store full of nerdy fun.

facebook.com/catherinebanksauthor

twitter.com/catherineebanks

amazon.com/author/catherinebanks

bookbub.com/authors/catherine-banks

MORE FROM CATHERINE BANKS

ADULT PARANORMAL & FANTASY ROMANCE SERIES

Zodiac Shifters Paranormal Romance Series

Centaur's Prize

Tiger Tears

Lion About

Ciara Steele Novella Series

True Faces

Barbaric Tendencies

ADULT REVERSE HAREM PARANORMAL & FANTASY ROMANCE SERIES

Her Royal Harem Series

Royally Entangled

Royally Exposed

Royally Elected

Royally Enraged

Her Royal Harem, The Complete Series

The Demon's Fair

Her Royal Harem, The Coloring Book

Wings of Vengeance Series

Of Dragons and Cruelty

Of Minotaurs and Sacrifice

Wings of Vengeance, The Complete Series

Anderelle: Minloa Trilogy

Queen of the Stars

Empress of the Galaxy

Goddess of the Universe

Anderelle: Minloa, The Complete Series

Bonds of Madness Series
Sealing the Deal
Racing the Clock

Her Super Harem Series
Lucky Strike

Her Hellish Harem Duet
A Demon's Heart
A Demon's Soul*

*Coming Soon

MORE FROM CATHERINE BANKS

Last Ama Princess
Transforming Rose
Alys of Asgard
Phoenix Possessed
Stone Heart

STANDALONE URBAN FANTASY BOOKS
The Pawn

CHILDREN'S BOOKS
Calvin's Alien Adventure

MORE FROM DAISY EMORY

The Boyfriend Deal

Their Purple Girl

ACCIDENTAL MOBSTER SERIES

Accidental Mobster
Unintentional Pirate
Suddenly Baroness*

*Coming Soon